WESTERLEA COVE

THE WESTWIND TRILOGY
BOOK ONE

LYNN BOIRE

enjoy!

Lynn

Cover design by Steven Novak

ISBN eBook: 978-1-7771458-7-3
ISBN Print: 978-1-7771458-6-6

PRAISE FOR LYNN BOIRE

All for Love

"It's what many of us have feared....the time climate change becomes a reality. *All for Love* is about a family enduring all the trials, tribulations, and uncertainty they face, trying to find a new normal in the midst of chaos. Riveting!" ~ *Dave*

"*All for Love* opens a readers' eyes to how easily the idea of security can shift. Prepare yourself for a thought provoking tale." ~ *Suki Lang*

All for Family

"Enjoyed this one tremendously!" ~ *Darlene Y.*

"I really enjoyed the snappy dialogue. Perceptive glimpses into an Intention Living lifestyle opened my thoughts on this way of life." ~ *Karen G.*

All for Peace

"A refreshing novel that shows no one is perfect, but with love and honesty, relationships can work. Loved it." ~ *B Johnson*

"It was hard to put the novel down, the intriguing plot of romance, illusions, and murder kept me engaged until the end." ~ *A. Evans*

Finding Hope

"I was blown away by the very interesting details of the time, place and people's lives of that era. It is obvious that Lynn Boire is very knowledgeable and her research is impeccable. Her ability to do setting is fabulous, almost like a film set. She has done stellar work portraying Canadian Life during the Depression years." ~ *Sarah Stewart*

"I thoroughly enjoyed reading Lynn's book. Her characters were engaging and the historical content well researched. Lynn has set her novel in history without overwhelming the reader with too many facts. I look forward to reading more of her books." ~ *Jenny Geddes*

"I've read and enjoyed Lynn's detail in her story writing in all of her books. *Finding Hope* was by far my favorite! Just when I thought I suspected where the storyline was headed, she fooled me. Great work at keeping me glued to the pages. I didn't want the book to end. Looking forward to your next release." ~ Wanda S.

PROLOGUE

The southwesterly gale was as treacherous as forewarned.

The tide was running high in this stretch of the Russell Channel as Theo struggled to control his vessel, 'The MissB-Haven,' as it shuddered and slammed into another deep trough. Trimming the motor down, he adjusted the stabilizer tabs so his boat could plow into the waves rather than ride the crest. It would cost him time, but it was better than the jarring back pain the trough pounding caused.

Besides, ten minutes wouldn't make a lot of difference now.

Theo heard the rattle of dishes in his tiny galley kitchen, then a crash of what must've been his steel thermos. Theo would have to deal with the mess later. He glanced at his speed, wiped the foggy windshield again, and assessed the situation. Mid-afternoon was the worst part of the day to travel this stretch of the strait in Clayoquot Sound. Garbled chatter from his VHF made it impossible to understand, so Theo turned to channel 83A for the Canadian Coast Guard

Radio. He listened for clear reception, then pressed the call button.

"MissBHaven, MissBHaven requesting assistance to place a collect call. Do you copy?"

"Copy, MissBHaven. CCG Radio, are you in immediate distress?"

"Not me, sir. I have a medical emergency at home. My name is Theo Sorensen. Please place a private collect call to my daughter, Jenna, at 250-555-4232."

"We'll do our best. With this storm, the connections are spotty. Hang on. It may take several attempts."

Theo nervously scratched and rubbed his beard as he listened to the operator trying to place the call with no success. He gripped the receiver so tight that he reminded himself to loosen his hold before cracking the plastic unit. Theo felt his face flush as his heart pounded anxiously. On the fourth try, he heard Jenna's voice answering and accepting the collect call.

"Dad! You're not traveling in this storm, are you?" Jenna's voice trembled with worry. "It's crazy out there!"

"You know me, Jenn. Nothing will stop me from coming home as soon as I can. How's your mom? How are you?"

"Dr. Walker says she's in a coma. Aunt Pat is here with me. She's exhausted, and the doctor suggested I bring her home. We'll have a bite to eat, and then I'm getting ready to return."

"Call Rollie at the Fourth Street Dock and ask him if I can borrow his truck to go to the hospital. It'll be quicker to go from there than from our wharf."

"Ok. I'm worried about you."

"Don't be. I've been through worse. I'm probably a half-hour away from Maurus Channel, where the waters should be calmer. I'll be there soon. I'll head straight to the hospital.

Before leaving Westerlea Cove, I called so the staff knows I'm coming."

"Alright. I'll be there waiting for you. The hospital staff moved Mom to a private room, where Dr. Walker put her on life support. He convinced us to remember her without that image. I argued with him, but it didn't do any good."

"Your mom and I'd discussed end-of-life options a few years ago, so he knows what we both wanted. Neither one of us wanted you to see us in that situation." Theo paused, unsure how his daughter would receive his next request. "Please don't come. Honor your mom's wishes. You've said goodbye, and that's the best way to remember her." A dead silence told him his appeal probably shocked Jenna.

"But I wanted to be there with you, Dad," Jenna whined. "For you, for both of us."

"No. Absolutely not." Theo closed his eyes as he regretted his bossy tone. He lowered his voice, acknowledging her desire to help. "I need time alone with your mom. I'll be ok."

"Please let me come. I'd really like to be with you." Jenna's voice quivered as she struggled with his decision.

"No, Jenna. I need to do what your mom wanted. I'll be home later. You two look after each other."

"We are. Aunt Pat couldn't sit still and asked Uncle Fred to get fresh ingredients for lasagna. She plans to make one for us and bring one home once you return. I might as well help her." Jenna's tone dropped as she accepted her dad's wish.

"That's my girl. Don't worry about me. I'll see you later, sweetie."

"Ok. I love you, Dad. Be careful. I'll call Rollie right now."

"Thanks."

"See you later." When Jenna hung up the phone, Theo signed off with his boat name and call sign as required by the Coast Guard. He turned his attention to the turbulent seas ahead, adjusting the left or right trim tab, depending on the wave direction. Relief coursed through Theo when MissBHaven entered the protected waters between Vargas and Meares. He could see the outline of the Tofino Harbor Authority and pushed the throttle to the max. The screaming pitch of his dual 130 mercs warned him to back off. Recognizing the potential disaster, he reigned in his emotions before blowing an engine he could hardly afford to lose.

Almost an hour later, Theo pulled the controls back to a slow crawl as he entered the marina. Rollie was striding down the dock, waving his arms and pointing to an empty mooring. Theo killed the engines and let the boat glide into the pier. He unzipped the canvas top and threw out his floats just as Rollie threw him a line, pulling him into place.

"I'm sorry to hear about Meg. You go. I'll finish up here." Rollie dug in his pocket, retrieved his truck keys, and tossed them to his friend.

"Thanks." Theo hardly recognized his gruff voice. His lips worked to express gratitude, but he doubted that anything but a grimace came out. It'd always been hard for him to accept people's sympathy or concern.

He grasped Rollie's hand as he dismounted from his boat, nodding his appreciation while avoiding the man's eyes. Theo pulled his woolen cap on to stave off the rain and hurried down the pier.

Theo jumped into his '97 Dodge Ram 4x4, flipped on the heater, and cranked the fan to avoid foggy windows. He crawled to Main Street and turned right, following it to First Street, then turned left to Tofino General Hospital.

CHAPTER 1

Theo strode forcefully down the main hall, approached the reception nurse, and growled. "Where's my wife?"

The nurse's raised eyebrows showed her surprise as the usually gentle person barked at her. She pointed down the main hall. Everybody knew everybody in this small town of fewer than three thousand people, and the Sorensen's were a well-respected family.

"Meg's in the last room on the left, Room 108. I'll page Dr. Walker to meet you there."

Theo raced down the corridor, loosening the tight fists he'd made upon arrival. He gritted his teeth, and his jaw clamped to control the tightness in his throat. Theo would *not* break down now. He saw their physician coming toward him.

"What the hell?" Theo approached their family doctor, going nose to nose with him. "How could you have let this happen?" Theo muttered, his fists bunching again with frustration.

"Calm down, Theo." Dr. Walker put his hand up, then

lowered them, indicating he was disturbing others. "Come with me." Dr. Walker turned and led him to the end of the hall.

Theo grabbed the doctor's shoulder to stop him from going any further. "I want answers, and I don't give a shit if I'm upsetting anyone. Why didn't you have Meg under medication?" Theo growled through clenched jaws, forcing his voice to lower.

Dr. Walker tore himself from Theo's grasp and continued toward the privacy area before addressing him. "Why would I? She told us there wasn't any history of strokes or heart attacks in her family, so we only monitored her blood pressure. Meg always had good readings, so there wasn't any need to go further." He lifted his hands. "I'm sorry."

Theo paced around the seating area and into the hall, throwing his hands up. "Bullshit. She'd been having migraines for the past year. Pat and I saw her suffering with them. Why didn't you do something?"

"I would have, Theo, if she'd told me. I'm guessing she didn't think they were bad enough to bother me." The physician's eyes softened as he acknowledged the surprise and pain his patient was experiencing. "Pat told us about her symptoms today, but there wasn't much we could do by the time she brought Meg here."

Theo's eyes teared, and he blinked rapidly to stop them from spilling over. His eyes darted about the hallway as his shoulders slumped. A low rumble emanated from his chest as exasperation ripped through him.

Dr. Walker tempered his tone compassionately. "I'm sorry, Theo. I wish I'd done more. Technically, she was too young to have experienced this. She was fit and lived a healthy lifestyle. A stroke would've been hard to predict without a family history." He gestured to a pair of chairs at the end of the hall. "Before seeing her, would you like to talk first? I'm sure you have more questions."

Theo followed the doctor before collapsing on the chair, but his voice was still angry. "Couldn't you airlift her to Victoria?"

"It wouldn't have helped. Meg's vital signs were rapidly spiraling downwards. I thought you'd want to see her as soon as possible, so I decided to continue treating her here. I remembered our end-of-life discussion, so this seemed the best scenario."

Theo shook his head slowly from side to side, his explosive reaction dissolving into a slow leak from his soul. "She's forty-eight years old, for chrissakes. How does this happen to someone her age? She eats healthy and is in better physical shape than most women." Theo slapped his hand on the metal armrest as his steamy aggravation dissipated. "I don't get it."

"I know. We think Meg suffered a brain aneurysm. Pat told me that when she visited Meg for tea, your wife complained of another migraine. About a half-hour later, she was shaky and nauseous. Pat called 911 and drove her to save time rather than wait for an ambulance. When Meg arrived, her mouth appeared lopsided, a classic indication of a stroke. Her eyes flickered open and shut as if the light was excruciating." Dr. Walker touched Theo's forearm, hoping to calm him. "Meg kept rubbing her temples and said that her head felt like it was splitting open. We wheeled her into emergency, hooked up the heart monitors and oxygen, then gave her Activase to dissolve the blood clot." Dr. Walker waited until Theo looked at him before continuing. "Shortly after, Meg stopped hurting. Jenna arrived and held her hand, but Meg was in agonal respiration about an hour later."

"I talked to my daughter on the way from the lease, and she sounded terrified." A tremble escaped Theo as he ran his fingers through his hair.

"Of course, she was. After the first hour of tears and shock, Jenna calmed down, relieved that she could sit and talk with her mom. Pat and Jenna stayed until I put her on life support, just like we'd discussed, and then they went home to wait for you. I'm afraid they weren't too happy with my request, but I reminded them it was what she asked for."

Theo put his elbows on his knees and clasped his head in his hands. "That must've been hell for them." He listened as Dr. Walker explained the events that led to this moment.

"Fuck. Fuck." Theo slammed his fist against his thigh again and again. "Kids aren't supposed to see their moms die." Theo rocked back and forth in his chair. "I should've been with her. It should've been me beside my wife."

"You tried. Considering the weather, you got here in record time from the lease. I'm so sorry, Theo." There wasn't anything more he could say or do to comfort him except leave him to grieve and say his goodbye in private. Dr. Walker gazed at the broken man beside him, stood, then touched his shoulder. "Call me if you need me."

Theo nodded and pinched the bridge of his nose to stop the tears. He cleared his throat, coughed, then pounded the tightness in his chest. His breath was shallow and rapid, making him feel dizzy. Theo didn't have enough oxygen to clear his thoughts or move. He swiped his trembling hand across his eyes, took a deep breath from his belly, and exhaled with a whoosh. As Theo forced himself to inhale and exhale to a count of four, his pulse returned to normal.

Theo needed to be strong before going in to see his wife.

He wouldn't fall apart. But how, in God's name, would he handle seeing his wife's beautiful Scottish curls without looking into the bluest eyes he'd ever seen? Theo blinked his eyes rapidly to stop them from spilling over.

This wasn't fair. Why her? Meg was a treasure to everyone who knew her. I don't understand.

Finally, Theo pursed his lips together, pushed his hands on his knees, and propelled himself to the door. He wouldn't forget this number. 108. Theo felt caught in a time warp of slow motion, watching himself approach her room. When his outstretched hand gripped the doorknob of her room, his heart went into overdrive, thudding madly. The sensation traveled up his tension-filled neck, tightening his throat and rushing into his ears.

For God's sake, get it together!

Theo refused to let his final goodbye turn into a pity party. He needed his farewell to be filled with appreciation for their years together. Theo closed his eyes momentarily, searching for the courage to enter.

This room would be the last place he'd touch his wife. The last time that he'd run his fingers through Meg's soft, curly tresses and feel the gentle warmth of her cheeks. There'd be no more teasing about her deep dimples on either side of her full, sensual lips. He'd never hear his darling's spontaneous, vibrant laughter again.

Inching the door open, Theo peeked into a softly lit room towards the still form on the hospital bed. The beeping of the monitors and the sound of the respirator working slammed home the inevitable. Despite the breathing tube, Meg looked peaceful, as if sleeping. Meg's favorite mauve afghan was draped over her, softening her features. Someone had brushed Meg's auburn-brown hair and placed her hands on her quilt. Tiptoeing to her bedside,

Theo slipped his fingers between hers, stroking the back of her hand with his thumb. His eyes closed to enhance the pretense she was still here with him.

But maybe, just maybe, she could hear him.

"Ah, Meg, my love. I'm so sorry I wasn't with you today. I'm glad your sister and Jenna were." Theo whispered gently. He lifted her hand and kissed her fingers. His eyes opened and traveled to his precious wife's face. Knowing it would break his heart that Meg couldn't return his caress, Theo stroked her hand, then traced his fingers up her forearm, over the freckles she'd always complained of, and smiled. She hated the freckles that adorned her nose and appeared across any expanse of skin when exposed to sunshine.

"I love you with all my heart." Theo gently touched her velvety cheek and outlined the dimple that made her smile so contagious. "You know I loved every one of your freckles. A Scot through and through." Theo reached behind the respirator, threaded his fingers through her soft curls, and sighed. "When I look at Jenna, I see you. We made a beautiful daughter together." Theo bent and pressed his face against the crown of her head, feeling the softness of her hair tickle his nose. He traced her broad forehead, outlining her eyebrows, then kissed her smooth, soft cheek.

Theo fought the tears away and then leaned his head on her shoulder. "I remember the night on the beach when I proposed to you. The bonfire burned down to a glowing coal bed, and we were lying on a blanket looking at the stars. I kept clearing my throat and sipping my beer. Finally, you asked me to spit it out—obviously, I had something to say. I looked over, and your eyes were sparkling. Then we both laughed. You knew me so well." Theo's voice trembled as he listened to her faint heartbeat, recognizing it wasn't the loving throb he remembered. "You always could sense when I was bothered, and we'd work it out. Who's going to help me now?"

Theo slowly raised his head with shame. "Sorry, darling. I'll be fine. Jenna and I will look after each other. I wish we could've shared more time. We've known each other almost thirty years, and it still wasn't enough."

Damn! Poor Jenna. He pictured his girls in happy times, and sorrow tore his heart open. Now ripped apart, Jenna would never be the same.

Theo wondered how he'd ever be the parent Meg had been for their daughter. She was mature for seventeen, more than her looks gave her credit for. And now she'd be motherless. They'd been so close, planning her graduation this year and throwing ideas around post-secondary education. None of the usual angst mother and daughters often had. They'd seen challenges together as a family, but they'd been lucky. Theo continued to murmur snippets of precious memories until, hours later, he ran out of words.

Theo felt a serenity flow through him as he realized there was nothing more to say. He hovered over her, tracing her features and memorizing their feel. He kissed her forehead again for the last time, then pressed the call button. It was time to let her be the true angel she was.

IT's strange how time changes pace. It seemed like months had passed since Theo last held his wife. Besides the hectic time preparing for Meg's funeral over a month ago, each hour seemed to drag by until another day passed. Theo barely moved from his worn leather recliner, staring at the family photos on the mantle ahead. Sometimes, he wondered if he'd lost his hearing. People came and went, murmuring their condolences or attempting to coax him outside in the sunshine to go for a walk. He was sure he responded. He knew he nodded often, but to what he later wondered.

"Dad!"

Jenna's strident voice brought him back from the fog. Theo looked up at her and shrugged his shoulders. "Sorry, pumpkin. What were you saying?" Theo slipped into her old nickname from early childhood, something he hadn't done in many years.

"For the third time, dinner's ready. You *have* to come and eat. I've made mom's garlic prawn stir fry that you love." Jenna stood in front of him with her arms crossed. "Please, Dad. I'm worried. I get you're sad. We all are. I miss her, too. But you're losing weight and often still sitting there when I get up at night." Jenna leaned over and smacked both her hands on his knees. "Enough!"

"I'm not trying to annoy you, Jenn. I've lost my appetite, I guess. It's hard to sit down and eat when you aren't hungry." Theo's eyes flitted from Jenna to the kitchen, then back to the family pictures on the mantle.

"Maybe you would be if you got your ass out of that chair. Come and sit at the table and eat something. That's it. Tomorrow, you and I are getting out of the house."

"Alright, alright." Theo heaved himself from his chair and hitched up his jeans, which threatened to slip down. Hmm. He'd have to notch another hole in his belt tomorrow. He'd already done that once a while ago. Last week? Two weeks ago? It didn't matter. Theo straightened and caught Jenna's worried glare. He strode to the table, sat at his usual chair, and glanced at Meg's empty place. No wonder he'd lost his appetite. Glancing at his daughter again, Theo saw her anger simmering to the surface. She was right. He'd been wallowing. If Meg were here, she'd be chewing his ass off.

"Smells great." Theo reached for the platter and spooned a small serving onto his dinner plate. He caught Jenna's slight smile of approval before she scooped a large helping for herself. He ate slowly, surprised to taste the garlic and the tang of sweet Thai chili sauce. Nothing seemed to smell or taste right lately—another reason to skip a meal. For Jenna's sake, he needed to try harder.

"What's the date today, sweetie?" Something significant was happening soon, or maybe he'd already missed it.

"June 8th. If you're wondering about my exams, the finals start next Wednesday."

"I knew it was coming up. When's your graduation ceremony?" Theo took another bite of the stir-fry, acknowledging the hunger beginning to lick at his insides.

"June 25th. I'm not sure I'm ready for that, though. I might skip it."

"I get it, but I think your mom would be disappointed. Maybe it would help if you went to the ceremonies at least. All the shopping the two of you did to find the perfect dress. It seems..."

"I know. Aunt Pat told me the same thing. Carla and Judy have been asking if I'll be there with them. Would you come to the ceremonies?"

Theo's fork paused in mid-air at the thought. "Ohhh...pumpkin..."

"I know. It's too soon."

"It is for me. But I'll think about it. My baby girl will graduate high school, and I should go. That's a pretty big deal." Theo finished another mouthful. He needed to start going out once in a while, get used to seeing people's sympathy, and listen to their condolences. He made a decision.

"Where do you want to go tomorrow?" Theo lifted his eyes to see his daughter's pleased expression.

"Where else? Chesterman Beach?"

"Sure, that would be great." Theo hoped his forced smile was convincing. "We'll pack a cooler and head out."

"That'd be awesome, Dad."

Jenna's wide smile told him how much she needed his attention. It wasn't *all* about him. He promised Meg he'd look after her, and so far, he'd done a piss-poor job. That needed to change.

After dinner, he helped Jenna clean up the kitchen. She kissed him on the way to her bedroom to study. "Thanks, Dad."

"You're welcome. You're right. It's time." Theo watched his daughter skip lightly down the hall and smiled to himself. He reached into the cupboard above the microwave and pulled out a bottle of gin. A shot or two would probably help him sleep tonight.

CHAPTER 2

Saturday dawned in a grey cloak. The ocean fog had moved inland, so there was no point heading to the beach until it began to lift. Jenna finished making her dad's favorite salmon salad sandwiches with lettuce and cucumber and turned her nose up. Whoever heard of cucumber with salmon? Adding a few cans of soda and a coffee thermos, she carried the cooler to the back door.

What else did she need? It felt strange taking her mother's place, ensuring all the necessities were there for a day at the beach. Before, all she worried about was grabbing her Banana Boat sunscreen and towel. Jenna scanned the kitchen for other things that might tempt her dad's appetite and added a few granola bars and a leftover bag of salted pretzels.

Satisfied she had packed enough for the afternoon or longer, Jenna went to her bedroom. She changed into denim shorts and slipped on a pair of navy-blue sweatpants over them. Jenna pulled on the matching sweatshirt over a white tank top. There was no sense in getting surprised. The weather could change quickly on the coast, and she didn't want to cut the day short because it became too hot or a chilly wind blew up.

Always think ahead. Theo drilled that motto into Jenna's head since early childhood. The family often took day hikes, occasionally even backpacking with pup tents to find a remote hideaway overnight. Locals took great care not to leave a trace of their presence when they stole into restricted areas that the park rangers ignored.

Jenna finished loading detergent into the dishwasher and pulled the top tray out to reorganize it. Her dad wasn't great at that, often wasting space. She spied the treasured Norwegian shot glass at the back and sighed. *Again.* That was her grandfather's and was only used on special occasions. Jenna reached up, checked the Tanqueray bottle, and, disappointed, closed her eyes. She realized that the second bottle in the past month was almost gone. She'd seen him have a few shots after the funeral, which was understandable. It seemed evident that he drank at night or when no one was around to escape his pain.

Jenna's escape was running. The slap of her running shoes hitting the pavement kept time with her heartbeat as she exorcised the pain of missing her mom. Focusing on her physical energy shoved her emotions away, giving her a much-needed distraction. She welcomed the sweat that slipped between her breasts as she pushed herself past her limit, feeling triumphant at each new objective she set.

Running daily, sometimes twice, helped Jenna work off the deep sorrow that threatened to engulf her. Stepping on the scales, she was surprised at her weight loss. *Six pounds had disappeared without dieting.* Now, she easily jogged three miles in each workout without stopping halfway. No more speed walking to catch her breath or relieve a stitch in her side. She hoped to convince her dad to join her so the gin wouldn't become a crutch to manage his pain. Her mom would've hated to see him go down this road. But the Sorensen's were stubborn, so it would have to be his idea.

Jenna was excited that they were hitting the beach today. She heard the shed door outside opening and items clattering around. Likely, he was getting the folding beach chairs.

"I thought that's what you were doing. Good idea. I'm ready to go anytime you are. Do you want me to grab your hoodie?"

Theo smiled at her attempts to look after him. "Sure, although I'm used to windy weather. Better safe than sorry, right?"

"Yup. That's what I've been told." Jenna giggled. "The cooler's ready whenever it suits you." She ran back into the house into her parents' bedroom. She wasn't allowed to clean or tidy up there on her dad's directive. As she stepped inside, she noticed that her dad was now sleeping on her mom's side of the bed. Jenna wondered why.

She opened the sliding mirrored doors and hunted through the hangers for his favorite sky-blue hoodie, noting her mom's clothes were still hanging neatly. A faint scent of lilacs from the room freshener her mom kept in the closet triggered a memory of her replacing those twice a year. It was her mom's favorite scent, and despite the heavy feeling in her heart, she took a deep breath and momentarily shut her eyes. Hearing movement outside the house, she returned to the present and hurried outdoors.

"Here you go." Jenna threw the hoodie to him, closed the kitchen door, and stepped toward their truck. She stopped suddenly, aware that her dad hadn't moved an inch. "What's wrong?"

"I'll be right back." Theo bypassed her and sprinted up

the steps and inside the house, returning less than a minute later. He tossed a green hoodie in the truck and motioned for Jenna to join him. "Are you coming?"

Shit. She'd forgotten the blue hoodie was a gift from Mom on his birthday in March. So many triggers. *Damn, it was exhausting trying to avoid them.*

"Ok. Let's hit the road." Jenna slammed the truck door shut, then looked at her father to see him shake his head. He hated when people slammed doors. Jenna took a deep breath and muttered *sorry* under her breath.

The drive to Chesterman Beach on the west coast of Tofino was brief, probably no more than four minutes. They had only to cross the main highway to downtown Tofino at South Chesterman Road to access the parking lot provided for beachgoers. When she was younger, she often walked there with her paddleboard and backpack. Jenna and Carla spent many hours with friends, talking with the crowd of boarders frequenting the beach as soon as the waves were warm enough.

"There, Dad. I think they're leaving."

"Good eye." Theo put his blinkers on and nabbed the spot near the public washroom and outdoor shower. Jenna rolled the cooler behind her while her dad took the beach chairs and oversized beach bag. Glancing back, Jenna saw her dad smiling at the vista before him. Already, the outing seemed to bring her father back to life.

The morning fog slowly dissipated, the last vestiges lifting from the treetops on the small islands ahead of them. The tide was midway out and still receding, so they found a spot close to the shore's edge. Theo made himself comfortable on a chair while Jenna plopped onto the warm beach and shucked her runners and socks. She buried her toes in the damp sand and grinned. "Thanks for coming today. I needed this."

"Me too, pumpkin. I feel better already." Theo searched his daughter's face, mentally comparing his daughter to his wife. Jenna had darker, thicker hair than her mom and no dimples to frame her smile. But her lips and eyes belonged to Meg. His breath hitched as he pictured his wife watching approvingly.

There was no time like now to start the bonding process as he'd promised Meg. "C'mon, Jenn. Let's walk in the surf." Theo cocked his eyebrow and smiled. "Do you know how often you remind me of your mom? I probably hadn't told you how your eyes get as stormy as hers when she was frustrated with me. Like last night when you gave me hell about eating."

Theo raised his eyes to the heavens, searching for the strength to share his feelings. "I'm sorry if I've ignored you, Jenna. Your mom's absence has made me selfish. I sometimes forget how much you must also be missing her." Theo reached for his daughter and embraced her tightly, relishing the hug she returned as they acknowledged their pain.

"I know. But I worry about you, too." Jenna felt her face flush as her voice quivered.

"Don't. I'm an adult, and I know how far I can go. I've had some tough nights, but I'll get through them. Ever since I started sleeping on your mom's side of the bed, it's easier. At least it's not her empty side I'm looking at when I wake up."

"Ooh. Yeah. Now I get it." Jenna bit her lip as she processed her dad's first emotional sharing. "The worst time for me is after dinner when we'd clean up and talk about our days. I miss her laugh. I miss her nosy questions about boys at school. I even miss her getting pissed off when I got behind on my homework."

"I agree. Your mom didn't get upset often, but when she did, watch out." Theo squeezed his daughter's hand. "I'll never be as good as your mom was, but I'll try harder to be part of your life, sweetheart. It's just tougher than I thought it would be."

"I understand. Just don't shut me out. And Dad?"

"Yes?" Theo's eyebrows rose.

"I've noticed you calling me pumpkin a few times. That was okay when I was younger, but I'd rather you didn't use it. I can handle sweetheart, just not the baby nickname." Jenna pleaded.

"I'm sure I'll forget sometimes, but I'll try. You're almost an adult now, and I need to remember that. But never forget who's boss." Theo laughed as Jenna sent him a comedic glare.

Theo challenged her. "Are you ready to race? On your marks, get set—" Theo jumped the gun, running down the packed sand and shallow surf toward Frank Island.

Jenna tore after her dad, quickly surpassing him, to his surprise. She turned back now and then to gauge her father's progress. After collapsing on the warm sand on the Island's shore, she lay back against a driftwood trunk and waited for him to arrive, puffing and wheezing.

"I guess I better start jogging again if I want to beat you." Theo sat with his hands on his knees, catching his breath.

"Anytime you want a partner, I have a three-mile loop that I do every day, sometimes twice if I'm stressed out."

"Ha. I'll tell you when I can manage one mile." Theo walked up to the roped-off area and studied the changes around him. He shrugged his shoulders and returned to collect his daughter.

"Nothing ever stays the same, does it, Dad?"

"Nope. And there's not a damn thing we can do about it." Theo shifted his weight from one foot to the other, glancing around him. "How about I buy you lunch?" Theo's eyebrows raised questioningly.

Jenna grinned. "It's a bit early, don't you think? Besides, I made us lunch." Jenna reminded him.

"I know. I wanted to sit on the patio at Middle Beach Lodge and watch the waves crash in. It's already 11:30. Do you feel up to snacking on nachos?"

"Sure, I'm always up for that." Jenna and her father strolled toward shore, picking up odd shells or chunks of smooth driftwood and sharing their treasures before arriving at Middle Beach Resort. They followed the path to the lodge, then forked off the trail to the patio access. She pulled her fingers through her thick, windblown hair to make herself presentable, then glanced over her shoulder. "Ok, over here?"

"You bet. Wait here. I want to say hi to Ted and make our order."

"Ok." Jenna turned to view the paddle boarders passing the lodge.

Theo caught his daughter's pensive sigh and took a deep breath. They were both caught in precious memories of times gone by. And that was Ok. These would stop hurting one day, and gratitude would take its place, but Theo knew it would be a long wait for both of them. His gaze searched the horizon, wishing things were different, but as he acknowledged earlier, nothing ever stays the same, and they could do nothing about it.

Theo hoped to find the grace Meg talked about, the spiritual connection that sometimes overcame her at the most vulnerable times in her life. He'd never experienced that elusive state, but if Meg believed in it, he'd continue to hope for the possibility of feeling it. Maybe then, he could accept her absence and move on, but he doubted it would happen soon. Theo shook his head and padded across the deck to place an order.

AFTER EXCHANGING A GUARDED GREETING, Theo asked for nachos smothered with cheese, black olives, green onions, and tomatoes. Then he ordered iced tea for Jenna and a gin and tonic for himself. "Ted? While I'm waiting for the drinks, pour me a double shot of Tanqueray, will you?" Theo half-turned and looked outside, avoiding the look of pity so many people offered these days. Give me a break, for chrissake - he'd snap out of it. Meg had barely been gone a month - he didn't need judgment. He only needed a little help to get him through this.

Theo heard his glass placed on the bar and a discreet knuckle tap at its arrival. Waiting a few long seconds, Theo turned and downed the shot in one long gulp, savoring the burn. The bartender was facing away from him while making Theo's mixed drink. He placed it on a round serving tray, then headed for the cooler for the iced tea.

Ted looked into the mirror to address Theo. "Don't bother waiting, buddy. It isn't busy. I'll bring the drinks out in a minute."

"Thanks, Ted." Theo walked out and pasted on a smile when he noticed Jenna watching him. He spotted a surfer dude approaching his daughter from a nearby table. As he leaned over the table, Jenna's smile drooped into an ill-concealed frown as the young man spoke to her.

Theo cleared his throat and pulled a chair out to seat himself. "Drinks will be here in a minute."

The young man turned to extend his hand to Theo. "You probably don't remember me—I'm Vaughan." At Theo's puzzlement, he explained. "Carla's brother. I used to cut your grass when I was younger."

"Of course. I didn't recognize you. Another foot taller and thirty pounds heavier makes a difference. How are you?" Theo shook his hand and was about to offer him a seat when he noticed a slight shake of his daughter's head.

"Great. I'm bartending at the new Black Fin Pub on Main Street. If things go well, I'll be part of that business before you know it."

"Good for you. Please excuse us, but our lunch should be here any minute."

"Oh sure, no problem. I only wanted to extend my condolences to Jenna—and you."

"Thanks." Theo pulled his chair closer to the table, relieved the young man had taken the hint and moved away.

Jenna leaned forward and lowered her voice. "I'm glad you didn't ask him to sit, Dad. He thinks he's a hotshot, and he's not."

"The look on your face told me he wasn't welcome. I wish people would be kind enough not to bother us. A simple nod would be enough."

"Most people are. But Vaughan can be intrusive by being too friendly. Carla's so embarrassed when he sees us together. He always makes a point of coming over and putting his arms around us. Vaughan loves to make a scene and draw attention to himself."

"But Vaughan's harmless, isn't he?"

"He's ok. He's a dreamer but doesn't cause any real trouble."

"If you ever have a problem—" Theo let the offer hang there.

"I know, but you don't need to worry about Vaughan. Carla keeps him in line."

A waitress appeared with their drinks and nachos, and the subject changed to watching people enjoying the water in various ways. A pair of kayakers went by, prompting Jenna to share a memory about her mom. Theo listened to the loving way his daughter spoke of Meg and noticed her eyes water.

"We're lucky to have so many good memories. It's okay to miss Mom." Theo placed his hand on hers and patted it. He reached for another nacho smothered in cheese and popped it in his mouth. "You better grab the last handful before I polish those off. They're addictive."

"I know." Jenna pulled apart a section and bit into the salty concoction. "It's weird, but sometimes I smile at the memories of us, and other times, the oddest detail will make me cry. I'm thankful that we paddle-boarded around here a lot. We often veered into this place, where we'd sit on the outdoor patio, just like you and I are doing now. And we'd be so hungry that we'd pig right out. I'll never forget those days." A tear threatened to escape Jenn's eyes as she absorbed the treasured memories. She picked up a napkin to wipe her sniffly nose and regain her emotions.

"I hear you. I have a hard time, too. Everyone keeps telling me that time will heal my heartache, but sometimes it feels like that will never happen. It hurts too much to imagine that will go away." Theo looked away to the shore and cleared his throat.

Jenna nodded. "Me too. Let's head back, Dad."

"Yes. Let's go before we become sad. It's a beautiful day.

Let's enjoy it. If your mom could see us now, that's what she'd want to see."

Theo scraped the chair back and went inside to look after the tab. He felt lighter today, more hopeful. Theo's heart warmed, thinking of the emotions he and Jenna shared today. Maybe being the only parent wouldn't be as hard as he'd worried. As Jenna skipped down the stairs to the beach, Theo soon caught up with her, and they began an old tradition of searching for sea shells on their return to Chesterman Beach.

Fortified, the afternoon passed smoothly. The powder blue sky and light westerly wind made for rolling three-foot waves that surfers tried to catch. Jenna caught up with a few school friends, and he waved her on to join them. Watching his daughter laugh with them eased his mind.

Youth! So quick to adapt. Theo knew Jenna would have her days when coping would be difficult, but he could see how much her girlfriends supported her. Thank God. He hoped his daughter would manage well because, honestly, he wasn't sure he could. For all his bravado, he knew the truth. The black dog was threatening to come home.

HAVING Jenna's friends join them for a late afternoon lunch was the perfect end to the afternoon. Their boisterous spirits brought the sparkle back in Jenna's eyes, and Theo was sure he hadn't laughed so much in an hour than in the whole last month.

In deference to Meg's death, Jenna's dear friends encouraged her to attend the graduation service. They would receive their diplomas and congratulate those who earned bursaries for further education. Then, they'd skip the dance to spend the night at Judy's place on Chesterman Beach. A small group would continue a toned-down celebration around a bonfire, toast their futures, and remember their past.

Listening to their chatter and seeing the light of mischief and adventure in the young girls' eyes was both a curse and a lift to Theo's spirits. Would he ever be that joyous and carefree again? He doubted it. But maybe he could learn to live his life without his soulmate. Theo began to fidget, catching Jenna's attention.

"Guess we should head out, hey Dad?" Jenna leaned over and touched his knee, checking his expression.

"It's almost time for me. Why don't you stay with your friends? They can give you a ride home."

"Nope. I go home with the guy I came with." Jenna turned to the girls and made arrangements to meet the following afternoon.

"Don't be silly. Stay with your friends." Theo pleaded. "I could use some quiet time, and you'd bounce off the walls. Stay and enjoy yourself. I'll take the cooler with me. Do you want me to leave the chairs behind?"

Jenna glanced at her friends and grinned. "Ok. You're right. I wouldn't be able to sit still. Take the chairs with you, and I'll see you later."

"That's my girl. Have fun." Theo collapsed the beach chairs, and Jenna picked up the cooler.

"I'll bring this for you." They trudged single file through the loose sand back to the trail that led to the parking lot. Together, they put their gear in the back of the truck. Then suddenly, Jenna wrapped her arms around her dad and hugged him tightly. "Thanks, Dad. I had a great day with you." Jenna looked up at her dad's face, then pressed her face to his chest. "We'll get through this."

"I had a wonderful day, too. And yes, days like this give me hope."

"Yup. Love you." Jenna gave him another quick hug and then quickly walked away.

Theo didn't miss the quiver in his daughter's voice. The quick about-turn was another sign that her emotions were running high. She was as private with her feelings as he was, so today's conversation was a good sign. Maybe talking about their sadness wouldn't be as bad as he feared.

Waiting for the cross traffic to pass, Theo thought about home. It had been an enjoyable day, filled with distractions, and he dreaded going home to sit in front of the TV. Theo knew the temptation to soothe himself with a few gins and tonics would probably get out of hand.

Way, way back before he married Meg, he'd lived in Vancouver, working construction labor for old-school friends of his dad's. Theo let liquor become part of his after-work routine. Following a hot afternoon of heavy labor, nothing tasted better than an icy beer or two with his team. The trouble was, sometimes, that Theo didn't know when to stop. Then he became argumentative, and after a few street brawls, his bosses warned him.

Shape up or ship out. After witnessing Theo's grandfather's abusive language toward his family and his swift decline into dementia, his bosses wanted no part of a Sorensen out of control. Theo was stunned and ashamed. Losing his boss's respect sent him down a rabbit hole of self-doubt. Would he end up just like his grandfather, as they warned? Would his family also turn against him?

That was the first time the black dog bit him, lasting an entire week. After that, Theo returned to work and vowed to confine and limit his drinking to the weekend. He remembered the talk he'd had as a teenager after listening to his mom's telephone conversation.

"Hey, Mom? Who does that black dog that comes around and bites Grandpa belong to? Has he ever bitten Grandma? Why haven't they reported him to the SPCA?

"Well, son, it's not a black dog. It's what the old-timers used to call the "blues." Nowadays, we call it depression. Some people who are prone to the blues often avoid the warning signals until their symptoms explode. Then they retreat into themselves or push their family and friends away." His mother opened the cookie jar and offered it to him before continuing. "Grandma told me there were times when your grandpa didn't speak to anyone for two weeks. Or he'd say mean things to her and their sons, so she always walked on eggshells when the blues hit."

Theo's mother sympathized, "Your grandma had it rough, but she seldom complained. It was part of the life they shared. Those dark moods usually came after something unpleasant at work, but sometimes, there'd be no reason. Fine one day and so miserable the next that it might last a week." His mother shrugged her shoulders. "I could always tell by the worried look on your dad's face if he called there, and your grandma would say, "Sorry, son – the black dog came around, and your dad's sick."

"But why wouldn't Grandma just say he had the blues?" Theo asked as he leaned against the kitchen counter with a perplexed look.

"It wasn't acceptable back then to be depressed. People would talk about you and wonder what was wrong with you – as if it was something catchy or something to be ashamed of. So, it was a kind of code within the family. If someone said the black dog was around, you stayed your distance. And if the black dog bit, you waited until Grandpa called you for something. That meant he was ready to move on. Living with Grandpa must've been hell for Grandma. I know your dad doesn't like to talk about it." His mother went to the fridge, poured Theo a tall glass of milk, and offered the cookie jar again. Second offerings were seldom, so Theo quickly snagged two more chocolate chip cookies before she changed her mind.

"Did the black dog ever bite Dad? Will it bite me?"

"Fortunately, your father and his brothers were careful. It's too bad you never got to meet your uncles. I think you would've liked them. The Second World War took a lot of brave young men." His mom had paused, a soft smile on her face. Turning to face Theo again, she asked him. "Have you ever seen your dad drink more than a drink or two on a special occasion or at Christmas?"

"Uhh. I guess not. I didn't think about it. Dad always says he doesn't need liquor to have fun."

"That's true. But another part of your dad's decision was that he was scared of liquor, losing control, and ending up like his father. Your dad occasionally struggles with the blues, but we know how to handle it now. If your dad starts giving me the silent treatment, he's worried about something. So, we figure it out together. I doubt you'll ever have trouble with it, Theo, but you should know the signs."

"That won't happen to me, Mom."

"Probably not – you don't have a mean bone in your body. Don't worry about it. You'll be fine." Theo's mom kissed him on the forehead, ruffled his hair, and sent him off to do his homework.

A CAR HORN beeped and startled Theo from his reverie. Nope, he wasn't going to end up like his grandpa. He switched his right blinker on and pulled onto the highway. He'd have coffee and a visit with Pat and Fred. They had two grandsons they often babysat, which kept their lives busy and full of the mischievous joy that only little ones can bring. He could use more distractions today.

CHAPTER 3

J enna blew the steam from her skinny vanilla latte while she thought of the degree she'd recently completed at the University of Victoria. She missed her friends who had made the time fly by. The Bamfield Marine Station scooped up Lisa, which was no surprise considering her excellent grades and cheerful personality. Sara still had another year of school to reach her teaching degree, and Tracy had abandoned university life and gone to work at Munroe's bookstore in downtown Victoria. They kept in touch by text and Facetime, but it wasn't the same as sharing the ups and downs of university life. A handwave in front of her brought her daydreaming to an end as Alicia's petulant voice grabbed her attention.

"Earth to Jenna... what's with you today? You're way in left field. I asked if you're attending the webinar Jackie Hildering is hosting next Friday. You've always gone on and on about her. I'd have thought you'd have jumped all over that meeting. What's going on?"

"Sorry...just a lot on my mind. I didn't sleep well last night, and I'm feeling dozy. But yes, I've registered for the

Zoom event. I wouldn't miss it for the world." Jenna shook her head and took a deep breath to center herself.

Ali enthusiastically continued, "She's showing clips of her underwater photography they used in Animal Planet's "Wild Obsession series." That woman is famous. Did you know she won the Ecostar Award for educational leadership? I can't wait to meet her, even if it's in a Zoom presentation."

"All her years of dedication have paid off, that's for sure. I met her once while working for the summer at the Deep Bay Marine Field Station. They don't call her 'The Marine Detective' for nothing. She really knows how to grab your attention with her presentations." Jenna took a sip of the hot, rich brew before continuing. "At the time, I wondered if I'd bit off more than I could chew by enrolling in the two-year Aqua Tech program. I almost gave up on it because I was worried about my dad handling everything back home. And I wasn't fond of all the lab and classroom time. Meeting her inspired me."

"Your dad's okay now, isn't he? I only met him once when he came to help you move in. Quiet guy. Seemed like the serious kind."

"Dad's always been a bit of a loner, which suits him well on the oyster lease. He keeps more to himself than ever before. I *think* he's back on his feet, although I'm not sure," Jenna's forehead creased with worry. "My dad doesn't talk to me much anymore—or anyone else. My aunt keeps an eye on her brother, and she's promised to let me know if there are any problems, but I've got a sneaky suspicion that I'm not hearing everything."

"Maybe your aunt wants to save you from worrying about him and the family business."

"That's true. Maybe one day, we'll work together on the

lease, and I can suggest some changes that might help our bottom line."

Ali glanced at Jenna and chuckled. "You'll probably have difficulty getting your dad to listen, but who knows? He might be inclined to listen once he realizes you know what you're talking about."

Jenna shrugged her shoulders. "That's probably a long time away."

"Well, you accomplished getting your certificate, and even though I know you were disappointed not to get hired in the Bamfield station, you're getting good experience here in Nanaimo. Have you decided to take more online courses to strengthen your resume?"

"Not yet. Other than registering to re-certify my PADI license and marine safety, I'm still enjoying the freedom to have a life after quitting time. I've studied enough both day and night for a while. Where did you do your summer practicum?"

"At the Marine Tech Centre in Sidney. That was pretty cool. And it attracted so many cute guys coming and going on different assignments." Ali's eyebrows shot up suggestively.

"I'll bet your sassy mouth attracted their attention." Jenna teasingly bumped her shoulder into her friend's. "Those two years were tough, but they flew by. Never any time to get bored, that's for sure."

"Definitely. What's university life for if you don't get to work off the stress with some quality partying?" Ali glanced at her watch and reluctantly pushed away from the table. "C'mon Jenna, time to head back for the afternoon."

"Don't you wish we could just skip out of Friday afternoons like we did at school?"

"Yup, but we're *grown-ups* now. We have responsibilities.

Besides, I need every dollar I can earn on a paycheck. Rent's not cheap here, and paying back the student loan doesn't leave much leftover for party time." Ali gathered the mugs and utensils and brought them to the counter. "Have you got plans for the weekend?"

Jenna reached the door first and held it open for her co-worker. "Sara's coming over tonight and staying until Sunday. She's meeting up with an old friend, Neil, who lives in Nanaimo. I think something's brewing between those two. Lisa-I mean, Lee might be joining us too."

"Learning to call your friend Lee must be tricky."

"It is. It's not automatic yet, so sometimes I forget." Jenna grimaced.

"I'm sure Lee understands. Do you think Sara will try setting you up again with a date?"

"Probably not. Sara knows I've been seeing Drew, so she's backed off. I told her I'd asked him to join us so Sara and Neil would get to know him. Lee might be joining us too, so it'll be like a reunion."

"Are you and Drew officially dating now?"

"Yes, I guess you could say that. I like him a lot. We have fun together."

"Yay! You two look good together and certainly seem happier. I guess sex might have something to do with that." Ali giggled.

Jenna elbowed Ali and grinned. "Quit fishing for info. I'm not discussing my personal life. I'm glad he's around, though, that much I'll admit to. Move on."

"Okey-dokey." Ali's rueful smile tugged at her lips. "Is Sara still living on Shelbourne? Does she have new room-mates now that L-Lee and Tracy are gone?" Ali rolled her eyes as she almost made the same mistake with Jenna's friend's name.

"A girl named Tamara, who's working on a first-year para-legal course, and someone named Jonathan, who's in his second year at UVic and, believe it or not, is in first-year medical. He begged to join them by offering to cook dinners at least two nights each week." Jenna smirked as she considered the drama that might create. "I wonder how living with a guy around will last? I'll bet any money there's no more walking around nude in that apartment." Jenna giggled as she remembered the casual abandonment that the three girls shared.

"Probably not. Might be worth it if he's a good cook." Ali shrugged. "I guess we all have to grow up sometime." Ali checked her watch and picked up the pace. "Better hurry. Mr. Dylan always has one eye on the clock. He hates tardiness."

Grumbling at the interminable afternoon ahead, the two girls zipped between slow-walking pedestrians until they reached the steep incline of Hammond Bay Road that brought them to the Pacific Marine Station. The weekend couldn't come fast enough.

JUGGLING A BAG OF GROCERIES, a boxed pizza, and a case of beer up the stairs to her second-floor apartment, Jenna grinned, anticipating the fun night ahead. She'd pop the pre-made pizza from Quality Foods into the oven when Sara and Neil arrived, and they'd catch up with each other's lives before heading out to Sara's family restaurant and bar. Always a busy destination on Friday nights, it was a perfect way to relax and reconnect with old friends. The small dance floor would be jumping by midnight, releasing tension and inhibitions, as usual.

Jenna was happy with the last-minute text she had received at work from Lee. Sara had also begged her former roommate to join them for the weekend. Luckily, Lee had managed to rearrange his weekend to spend with his pals. Jenna checked the time as she put the groceries away, calculating the approximate time of Lee's arrival. It was a two-and-a-half-hour drive from Bamfield to Nanaimo, so assuming he would quickly toss essentials in an overnight bag and come directly there, his arrival time should be around 9:00 p.m. An hour to catch up here, and they'd be at the Carvery between 10 and 11:00. Perfect.

Hustling into a hot shower, Jenna let her mind wander. The last time she'd visited Tofino to see her family and her childhood friend, Carla, was almost six months ago. She'd slept at Carla's house, ensuring freedom to celebrate the long May Day weekend. They'd had a great time, enjoying the surf at Chesterman Beach, then hitting the pub where her brother, Vaughan, worked. It felt good to talk with old friends and immerse herself in small-town life again, where everybody thought they knew everything about everybody. In a town of three thousand people, it was hard to hide.

Jenna lathered her legs with Shea body wash and lifted her right leg, shaving it carefully as she reflected on small-time life. She didn't miss listening to the town's opinions, narrow as they could occasionally be, though she had to admit that giving up the cozy feeling of living there was sometimes a high price. Definitely, it was a far cry from the isolation of living in a city of seventy thousand people, where neighbors barely took the time to do more than nod and smile in your direction.

Trading one thing for another, mused Jenna. Independence could be lonely, but the claustrophobia she sometimes felt when pressured in her hometown was much worse. Jenna rinsed, then turned the water down to cool off before leaving the shower.

With her thick hair toweled above her head, Jenna wiped the steamy mirror and noted the mischievous glint in her eyes. That May weekend was the last time she'd also seen Lee. The night felt like a blast from the past. There was such a difference in seeing his personality change from the center attraction on the dance floor to the mellow and confident man he was. At university, Jenna had initially felt uncomfortable with the touchy, feely relationship that Lisa, Sara, and Tracy shared. But Jenna took Sara and Tracy's explanations to heart and accepted the behavior for what it was. Lisa/Lee was a happy, generous soul whose sexual inclinations were their business. After a solitary, brief flirtation, her friend recognized that Jenna didn't swing that way, and their friendship became solid. Now that Lee openly identified as male and dressed appropriately, he'd matured and needed much less limelight than when they attended university. It made his life less complicated.

Jenna blow-dried her hair and took the curling iron to the sides, dragging out a soft wave. She hoped Sara and Neil would like her date. Drew worked as an environmental tech at the same marine field office she worked at. They'd shared several lunches while attending seminars. Tall, with dark hair and golden-brown eyes, his physique was something most of the women had noticed and pined over. Drew's dedication to the research facility and eagerness to move up the ladder took precedence over his appearance, and to date, Jenna hadn't seen a smidge of vanity. He delivered his reports directly to Jenna, who typed the requisite forms and forwarded them to their supervisors. That connection slowly led to a lighthearted relationship outside the workplace.

Spraying a mist of Red Door cologne on her wrists, Jenna rubbed them together, inhaling the sexy scent. She applied charcoal liner to her eyes and then swiped tinted gloss to her lips, making them look plump and inviting. A smile played on her face as she imagined the evening ahead. Jenna slipped on a sky-blue long-sleeved sweater with a pair of skinny black jeans and pirouetted in front of the mirror before a loud knock followed by double doorbell rings startled her.

"Hey, guys." Opening the door, Jenna leaned forward and snagged the bottle of wine that threatened to drop through Sara's grasp. With the wine safe, she hugged Sara, then stood back, assessing Neil's presence. She'd met him a few years ago at Sara's family barbecue at Comox Lake. His looks had matured, and his scrawny frame had filled out nicely. Obviously, construction work agreed with him.

Neil held up the overnight bag, "Hi, Jenna. Where do you want me to put this?"

"Down the hallway and on your left. Sara's sleeping with me this weekend. I hope she's not a bed hog." Jenna teased.

"Bed hog, no. But I hope you have earplugs. After a night out, she can get pretty noisy." Neil winked. "You can always send her my way if it's too much for you."

"Ha. You can only hope. Last time, you and Sara stayed at the Bastion Hotel for a romantic weekend. This weekend's our time to catch up with all the gossip." Jenna turned to Sara. "I told you that Lee was joining us, didn't I?"

"Yes. This weekend will be so much fun. It's been too long since we got together. Where's he sleeping?"

"He gets the living room futon. The last one here has to make do. But knowing him, once he crashes, he won't even notice if it's lumpy. That guy can sleep anywhere." Jenna slipped into the kitchen and put the pinot grigio in the fridge. "Anybody hungry?"

"Starving is more like it. Got any cold beer to go with it?" Sara followed Jenna into the kitchen, putting her hand on Jenna's shoulder and peering into the fridge.

"You bet. Let me get our dinner in the oven. Stella or Coors Light?" Jenna gave her a choice.

"Let's start with Stella."

Jenna leaned forward, grabbed three bottles, and turned to offer Sara one. A glint sparkled from her hand, causing Jenna to gasp. "Oh my God—is that what I think it is? Sara!"

Sara wiggled the fingers on her left hand and giggled. "It is. I'm so excited." Sara's eyes twinkled as they flitted from Jenna to Neil. "He proposed last Sunday, and it was the hardest secret to keep. I wanted to wait until I saw you and Lee in person before telling our news."

"Congratulations to both of you. When's the date? Have you decided?"

"My parents want to plan the wedding at their place on Comox Lake next summer. So, it'll probably be the long weekend in July or August. I'll be on a partial summer vacation from teaching, so I'll be able to help a lot." Sara grabbed Jenna's arms and swung her around, giggling. Unable to contain her emotions, Sara jumped for joy, hugging Jenna tightly, then lunged into Neil's arms.

Neil chuckled, his brown eyes crinkling at his fiancée's reaction. "She's been waiting all week for this. Time for a toast." He opened the bottles of Stella, passed them out, and then held one up. "To our new life together and the future that I'd always hoped Sara would be part of." Neil clinked his bottle to Sara's and then to Jenna's. "I feel so lucky to have this woman in my life." Neil winked before continuing. "And she tells me she feels the same way. To us!"

Jenna noted a tear in Sara's eyes and knew their long friendship had turned into true love that would stand the test of time. "Cheers, guys. You two were made for each other. I'm so happy for both of you." Jenna joined them for the toast, then kissed them on the cheek. "Tell me all about it, cuz. Did he get on bended knee? I want all the details."

Watching the shared glance between Neil and Sara, Jenna retreated. "Never mind, I'll hear all the details later. What did your parents think?"

Sara cocked an eyebrow at Neil. "They asked me what took so long." Sara shrugged as she thought about their long courtship. "We've been together off and on for over four years—ever since my brother brought him to visit us on Comox Lake. There's been a lot to work through. I wasn't sure why we gravitated together, but I wanted to be certain it wasn't just because of Dan and what happened."

"And your parents? Are they coping better? I know how worried you were about your mom. It was tough on all of you after the boating accident. Do you ever hear from Danny?"

"No, the little shit hasn't shown his face, and that's fine with me." Sara shrugged. "Mom and Dad are closer than ever, which is great. There are still some issues that must be dealt with, but my parents have told me not to worry about it." Sara leaned against Neil, who wrapped his arm around her protectively.

Neil shrugged. "I don't blame her for procrastinating. It was tough back then, and it's still a time neither of us likes to dwell on. We both needed to find ourselves and know we weren't together to help us get through that terrible summer. Shared experiences aren't enough reason to base a relationship on, especially one like that."

Glancing back and forth between the two of them, Jenna

nodded. "I get it. It's totally understandable and very wise. Almost everybody has baggage, but it's not something you want to carry into a new relationship until it's sorted and dealt with." Jenna tilted her beer toward them and toasted them again. "Congratulations, my friends. Now go get comfortable while I stick the pizza in the oven." Jenna turned the oven on, popped the pizza on the middle rack, then joined them on the futon.

HOURS LATER, encircling her arms around Drew's neck, she kissed him gently before looking into his soft brown eyes. "I need some time. This decision isn't something I can just jump into."

"I know, but this transfer isn't an opportunity to pass up, at least for me. It's a plum opportunity. Meeting Dr. Milligan at the UBC Marine Science seminars prompted him to recommend me when this transfer came up. A case of being in the right place at the right time." Drew tilted his head to the side, probably looking for her understanding.

"I hear you. Let's talk more after my company leaves. How about dinner Tuesday night?"

"Sure. Where?" Drew pulled back and scanned Jenna's face.

Jenna recognized her boyfriend's relief as the tension eased from his body. She hoped she wasn't leading him on. "How about I'll text you or catch you at work?" Jenna slid her gaze away as the hopeful tinge in his voice gave away his excitement.

"Perfect." Drew bent and touched his forehead to hers. "I can't wait." He kissed her lips softly, then released her. He waved to the group in the living room and grinned before slipping around Jenna. "See you guys again soon, I hope. This evening was fun."

Closing the door, Jenna leaned against it momentarily, expelling a long-held breath. "Whew. What a night. You guys get engaged, I get offered a relationship in Haida Gwaii, and Lee meets a cute chick." Jenna held her hands in front of her. "What more could you want?"

"Love is in the air, alright." Sara quipped. "You don't look too excited, though." Sara checked with Lee for confirmation.

"I'd say Jenna's got a lot to consider. Drew's a great guy, a little too serious for my taste, but I can see the attraction." Lee's eyebrows snaggled up and down suggestively.

Neil jumped to defend his new friend. "What's wrong with being serious or planning a career future? It sounds like he's rock solid, and there's no doubt that he's nuts about Jenna. I think it's great that he wants Jenna to join him. Shows a lot of commitment to his personal and career life."

Jenna agreed, "True. Although, I'm not sure I'm ready for that kind of relationship. Like, I enjoy being around Drew. We have a lot in common. I'm just not sure it's strong enough to leave Vancouver Island and be isolated in a small town again. It'd be worse than living in Tofino. At least there, within a couple of hours and a full gas tank, I can be anywhere on the Island."

Jenna retreated into the kitchen and grabbed a fresh bottle of wine. "Who's ready for a nightcap?"

Sara and Neil declined and opted to end the evening with a walk outdoors. Jenna grabbed two wine glasses and joined Lee on the lumpy futon. After toasting each other, the room fell silent.

"No comments?" Lee asked. "I'm not sure that isolation is the only reason you're holding back from Drew's plan."

Lee crossed his legs, leaned back, and settled into the throw cushion, ready for a heart-to-heart. 'C'mon, 'fess up." Lee grabbed the bowl of tortilla chips from the table and began to nibble.

"You always could see right through me. What is it with you?" Jenna deflected the question.

Lee gave her friend a lopsided smile. "It's not hard. You wear your emotions on your sleeve. I just call you on it."

"No pretense on anything with you, is there?" Jenna shook her head sheepishly. "And you're one to talk. I always know when you're interested in someone. You glow."

"Then I guess I glow all the time," teased Lee. "Seriously, say the first thing that comes to your mind when you think of Drew."

"He's a really nice guy." Jenna tilted her head from side to side. "He's hard-working, thoughtful, and I can always depend on him to be there when he says he will be."

"Okay. Not exactly the answer I was looking for. And probably not what Drew would want to hear. Would you miss him if he took the transfer and you stayed here?"

"Of course, I would. Drew's a great friend." Jenna's voice softened as she contemplated that scenario.

"Aha. Now we're getting somewhere. But would you be brokenhearted? Would you regret not going?" Lee paused. "Or would he just be another memory of a good friend with benefits?"

Lee waited expectantly for Jenna's answer, then leaned over and patted her forearm. "Something to think about before you see him next. I guess I'm saying I don't see an over-the-moon look on your face when you're together. That has to be there to make a serious relationship work."

"You mean like the look on your face when you met Lauren?" Jenna shot back. "Sparks were flying from both of you. Let's talk about that for a change. When are *you* going to get serious with someone?" Jenna leaned over and gave Lee a light jab on his shoulder.

"Touche. Let's leave our love life alone and enjoy the wine." Lee capitulated.

Both friends knew the answers were more complicated than they would deal with tonight.

CHAPTER 4

Theo checked the calendar beside the fridge and flipped the page. Another month had gone by. His supplies were low, along with the gin, so it was time to head into town and restock. Theo stretched his visits to Tofino as far apart as possible. With Jenna now living in Nanaimo after finishing university in Victoria, there wasn't much pulling him there anymore. His sister, Pat, had taken over Meg's nursery business once Jenna left. Meg wanted her to have it free and clear, but Pat refused. Theo sold it to her for the nominal fee of five hundred dollars per month, payable to Jenna, for as long as she was in university. Then, it was hers to do with as she pleased. This arrangement seemed like a good compromise, and now, five years later, there were still no regrets.

God knew Theo wanted nothing to do with it.

Glancing about the one-bedroom float house, Theo eyed the mess, deciding whether to clean it. If he chose to stay a few nights in town, he'd better do the dishes and a light clean-up to avoid attracting mice. Theo started the generator to heat the hot water, then stripped the sheets off his bed, stuffed them in the overflowing wash basket, and put the dirty laundry into the back of his boat. Theo also added two large recycling bags of garbage from the outdoor storage shed to dispose of in town.

When the dishes were washed and put away, Theo had enough hot water left for a quick, lukewarm shower. He put a kettle of water on the wood stove for shaving. Theo gathered his ledger and last month's unopened mail and popped them into a plastic tote, safe from prying eyes and shredding mice. He'd need to pick up another one to bring back. One day, he'd get organized again.

Maybe.

Staring at his reflection, he felt a stab of guilt. Meg wouldn't be pleased—Theo's appearance had aged far more than the five years since she'd passed. He'd lost weight, and his eyes carried puffy bags beneath them. He threw his shoulders back and pulled out his shaving supplies. Eyeing his new salt and pepper facial hair, Theo sighed, then trimmed his beard to an inch in length. He carefully shaved a clean line from his cheeks to his sideburns, then a sharp edge to border his neck. Much better. Theo silently apologized to his late wife and vowed to quit procrastinating and be the man he used to be. It'd been a few months since his last haircut, so it was time to get that tamed down. Public opinion mattered in town. Theo still had some pride left, and it was time to show it. Wiping away the remnants of shaving cream, he drained the sink and brushed his teeth.

Theo would pick up the crab and prawn traps on his way to Tofino for his regular customers who bought the fresh seafood, which helped subsidize him. Lord knew the oysters weren't enough to sustain him anymore, but he didn't need much, as the income from his home rental covered most of his expenses.

After Jenna left, he rented his house for fifteen hundred per month, freeing him from maintenance obligations. It also helped not to be reminded of the life and happiness he enjoyed when Meg was alive. Thank God his wife had a modest life insurance coverage, which looked after Jenna's university education and gave him a cushion while he got back on his feet.

Theo started the engines, and as they idled, he glanced over to his oyster lease and frowned. A few blue barrels were floating low in the water, and the mainlines were drooping in places. Globs of green algae covering the anchor lines to the rockface were a testament to his inattention. He needed to get his act together before losing the whole damn shebang, and his savings and investment were gone.

Too daunting to even think of an immediate solution, he turned to his float house. The aluminum siding showed neglect as rusty streaks from the leaky downpipes scarred the once sparkling white structure. The two-by-twelve deck planking exhibited signs of rot here and there. For the past three summers, he hadn't bothered to scrub the mossy areas off the planks, and now it was apparent how much that had affected his deck surface.

His eyes narrowed as he checked out the front left corner of his float and groaned. He'd probably lost a flotation device in the last winter storm that hit his lease. *Why did Meg's death turn me into a procrastinator?* There was a time when Theo would be out checking his floats and lease immediately after a storm, securing and fixing whatever damage the lease had sustained. He had a lot of work to bring this place back into shape.

Theo hung his head in shame.

Without Meg to inspire him, he'd lost his ambition and drive. There was a time when this five-acre lease meant the world to him and his family. He was proud of being an oyster farmer. *Now? I just don't care.* Meg was gone, and Jenna worked at the Pacific Biological Station in Nanaimo. It didn't surprise him she'd chosen that field of work. Her love of the ocean made it a foregone conclusion. She was making a life for herself, and he was happy for her. Theo ran his hand across the back of his neck, searching for a reason to live. His life felt so unimportant. It seemed his existence was mired in a haze he couldn't clear—or didn't want to clear.

What the hell's the matter with me? As the years dragged by, Theo felt his integrity gradually slip away as he withdrew from his old life, lost in the welcome fog of indifference that his friendship with Tanqueray encouraged. If he ever hoped to regain his health, pride, and livelihood, Theo needed to get a grip on his liquor consumption. He was a *Sorensen*, for chrissakes. *Man up!*

Two brief horn blasts startled Theo from his introspection. He saw Wayne approaching from his oyster lease on the south side of Flores Island.

"Mornin', Theo. It looks like you're headin' out. Goin' to town?"

"Yes. Time to pick up supplies. Do you need anything?" Theo and his neighbors often picked things up for each other. Last time, Wayne brought in Theo's fifty-pound propane tank for refilling. Cooperation made life a lot easier here.

Wayne pulled a bumper out on the side of his skiff and moved in closer to Theo's dock. He tied off on a cleat and then ambled over to visit.

"I was headin' out to catch a few cod, and I thought ya might like to join me. But, seein' as yer goin' into town, can ya pick up a couple of dozen eggs and a bag of potatoes? I called on yer VHF, but ya didn't pick up."

"Sorry, I shut it off in the house and haven't turned it on in the boat yet. I might stay in town for a few nights, but I'll let you know when I get back with your groceries. Anything else?"

"Might as well tack on a case of beer and a carton of Players Light. I'll call an order into the Co-op with my credit card, so they'll have it ready."

"Sounds good."

"How's the back these days—gettin' any better?" Wayne lit a smoke, then puffed as he leaned against 'MissBHaven's windshield.

"Can't lift a damn thing over thirty or forty pounds, or I'm flat on my back. As long as I'm careful, I can manage. Thank God for dollys." Theo lied as he rubbed his lower back.

"Did ya go to the chiropractor like I told ya?"

"No, they creep me out, all that cracking stuff." Theo wasn't about to go down that road when he didn't need to.

"Well, if ya need a hand, I've got two guys coming to help me harvest a few lines. I can send them over when they're finished with my job if they aren't booked anywhere else."

"Thanks. I'll probably wait until I can do more work myself, but I'll let you know." Theo looked at his wristwatch, and Wayne took the hint.

"Ok, I'm off. See ya when ya get back. Safe travels." Wayne gave a two-finger salute, untied his skiff from the dock, and puttered out of Westerlea Cove.

"You bet." Theo waved, untied his boat from the cleats, and climbed inside. He pushed away from the pier, slipped the throttle in gear, and gently edged from the oyster lease slow zone.

September and October in Clayoquot Sound were Theo's favorite months. Most tourists were gone along with the foggy mornings of August—often called *"F'August'*. The seas were usually calm with a gentle swell, and the days bright and clear. Fall gave a brief respite before the changing weather patterns would bring the winter storms. It gave him time to relax and enjoy this piece of paradise he called home.

At low tide like today, the tall evergreens that grew close to the waterline looked like they'd been professionally trimmed, their branches parallel to sea level several feet below. Seals and sea lions were abundant near the mouth of creeks and rivers, gorging themselves on returning salmon stocks. Eagles perched high above, their sharp eyes eager to swoop down and clutch onto any leftovers.

Peaceful synchronicity seeped through Theo as he breathed in the salty, cool air. He took several long breaths, concentrating on nothing but the view ahead of him, and felt better than in months. He stole a look at his watch. One more hour and it would be three days without a drink. Maybe this time, Theo would be strong enough to resist temptation. A hopeful smile passed his lips as he crossed his fingers.

He spotted the red floats a half-mile ahead, where he'd dropped his traps at dawn. Baiting them, each with two fish heads, he knew they'd attract the rock crabs and prawns he needed to sell in Tofino. Fall was an excellent season for harvesting, so he hoped no one raided his traps. That was sometimes a problem in the summertime unless you went at daybreak to harvest. He pulled back on the throttle to neutral, then moved all his laundry and garbage bags to the front of the boat so that he could haul and empty his traps.

Theo slipped on his rain gear and pulled on a pair of oyster gloves. He used his six-foot pike pole, hooked the float, and dragged it to his boat. Dropping the aluminum hooked gaff to the floor between the seats, Theo began pulling up the rope, hand over hand, counting the pulls. The shellfish liked to congregate in depressions on a sandy ocean floor, and this eighty-foot hole was perfect. Not too deep that it was exhausting to haul the traps in, but deep enough that they could scavenge whatever floated down to it.

His father taught him the secret to hauling in the traps was the rhythm to the pulls that weekend warriors were unaware of. Within five minutes, Theo saw the crab trap come to the surface and gave a final tug to bring the round net against his boat. Several crabs with seven to eight-inch bodies were scrambling to escape. Theo unclipped the center entry and dumped the contents into a giant rubber tub on the deck. He quickly slapped a plywood lid on top and anchored it with two ten-pound lead weights. After emptying both traps, it looked like he'd scored fifteen to twenty, which should earn him around fifteen dollars each.

Dumping the empty bait traps into the water one by one, Theo planned the following setting. Leaving them bare guaranteed no crabs would climb inside and attack each other if he wasn't there within eight hours. Never one to waste resources, Theo would set the gear up again on his way home. If Theo couldn't snag a few fish heads at the docks, he had tins of cat food on hand that he could puncture the tops and use for bait. Then, he could return to harvest later after high tide. The yield wouldn't be as great, but Theo only needed enough for himself—any extra he'd share with Wayne.

Easing the throttle forward, Theo moved to the next hole, where his prawn traps were waiting. The same procedure ensued, and he filled another tub of shellfish, each prawn about the size of his thumb. Theo figured he'd harvested close to sixty pounds between the two collections. He should yield over five hundred dollars between the crabs and the prawns—enough to fill his gas tanks and pay for groceries. After dumping the empty traps back into the sea, Theo removed his rain gear and hung them to dry. He sat and rested with a cup of coffee, planning the rest of the day. He turned his VHF on and called Pat at work, where marine traffic was part of the background noise in her nursery.

"'MissBHaven', 'MissBHaven', calling Pat or Fred MacKenzie." Theo released the button to listen for a response, then called again.

"Fred here. How are you, Theo? Are you coming into town today?"

Theo heard the anticipation in his voice and considered himself blessed to have them. "Yes, I'm on my way now. Are you ready for a feed of prawns tonight?"

"Always. I hope you'll be staying a few days with us. You know your bed is always here waiting for you."

"Thanks, I'll take you up on that. I have a few deliveries to make but should be at your place by 6:00. See you then."

"You bet. Travel safe, my friend." Fred signed off, and Theo smiled. After Meg died, they'd become a safe harbor for him, always available to lend an ear or a hand without judgment. He'd be lost without them. Although he thought of Jenna often, Theo avoided Jenna's attempts to coordinate extended weekend visits as much as possible. Like her mom, she would see right through his façade, and he didn't want her worrying about him and returning home or having to justify himself. Isolation suited him.

Theo continued his route at moderate speed, choosing the inside passage to conserve fuel. He grabbed his Helly Hansen windbreaker to ward off the chill of a westerly breeze picking up strength. This was another reminder that the fall and cooler days had arrived. He piloted his craft into his annual berth and walked to the storage shed, where he would use the hefty wheelbarrows to unload and load return supplies. Theo greeted Rollie, but he was busy signing in a berth rental and only waved instead of joining him for their usual gossip session. Theo would catch him on the way back to the lease.

It took three trips from his boat to his truck to unload his catch and bring his gear up. Theo greeted a few resident fishers who lived on their boats in the harbor and exchanged a handshake and a few words. His heart warmed at their welcome. He reminded himself that his loneliness was self-imposed. Any one of these fellows would enjoy spending a day with him, shooting the breeze. Theo had known most of the marine folk since he was young, and they shared a long history.

Disposing his garbage in the recycle bins took longer than he'd thought. He glanced at his watch and gave himself a push. He was hungry enough to eat a bear, but if he wanted to sell all his products, he needed to hit his buyers by early afternoon to feature it on their menus that night. He kept a gallon pail of prawns and a sizeable Dungeness crab to bring to Pat and Fred's. Theo sold the last shellfish a few hours later, so he grabbed his overnight bag and hurried toward the Schooner Steakhouse with a growling stomach. Theo loved his seafood, although today, his mouth was salivating thinking about a thick, juicy rib steak with all the trimmings.

"Theo. Nice to see you, stranger. How long are you in for?"

"A few days. I need the biggest steak you've got."

"You got it. Baked potato, mushrooms, and a Caesar salad, right?"

"You bet."

"Can't go wrong with rib-eye steaks. What will you have to drink? Beer, wine?"

"Coors would hit the spot. I'm going to clean up and be right back."

It was mid-afternoon, and not many people were in yet. Theo went to the washroom and checked to make sure it was empty. He peeled off his shirt and washed his face and hands. He brushed his hair and beard, dressed in a fresh shirt, and felt human again.

An empty frosted glass, now beading with condensation, sat waiting for him to fill. Theo cracked open the bottle and poured it in more slowly than he wanted to. The icy crisp brew slid down his parched throat, and Theo continued to drink until he quenched the dryness. Half the glass was already gone. *Beer was never a problem.*

"Noah, you better bring me another one."

"Coming right up."

The bartender understood how thirsty fishers were when they came home. It was the first place those without family went after being out for so long—a place to socialize and get comfortable again after a stint of solitary living. Noah returned with another icy beer, a crisp Caesar salad topped with fresh shaved Italian asiago, and crunchy, home-made croutons.

Theo launched into his appetizer, enjoying the creamy garlic sauce with the spicy bite of Worcestershire and lemons. The fireplace was crackling and lending warmth while the moderately loud music reminded him of Saturday nights out with Meg and friends over the years.

He must be getting better, Theo mused. It didn't cripple him with pain anymore when he thought of his wife. Time was doing its magic, thank God.

The sizzling aroma of steak came from behind him, and he pushed his beer aside to concentrate on his meal. *Damn, that looked good.* He wished he had someone to share it with, though. He seldom socialized for over a year after Meg died except at Pat and Fred's. However, the summer before Jenna left for university, they'd started to enjoy lunch or dinner out now and then. Theo wanted his daughter to remember good times together before she went away, to believe he was on the mend. He didn't want her to feel guilty, and watching her relax as they dined out seemed to ease her anxiety.

"Anything else, Theo?" Noah appeared soon after Theo pushed his plate away.

"No, thanks. That was fantastic, as always."

"Great." Noah gathered his utensils and balanced them on his tray. "How's Jenna, by the way? I miss seeing her around. She was part of our kayaking group expeditions. We all miss her competitive streak and snappy jokes."

"I'll be calling her tomorrow from her Aunt Pat's. They say no news is good news, so I'll find out soon. She enjoys her work and seems to be happy. Shall I pass on a message?"

"Just a hello and the club misses her." Noah nodded as Theo reassured him that he'd pass the message on.

Theo paid his bill and left a generous tip. Living on the lease made him appreciate the friendly service, and he tipped more generously now than ever. As he descended the stairs to the street, he absently palmed his beard. Clean, a full stomach, shellfish treats for the family, and a bottle of gin would round off the night nicely. He couldn't go there empty-handed, and enjoying a few drinks with them shouldn't be a problem.

THE COMPANIONABLE EVENING STARTED WELL, with steamed prawns, crab, salty garlic butter, and Pat's large shellfish bibs. Theo ate a lot of seafood at his lease, but it tasted so much better when he had someone to share it with, to laugh with. The cold beer went down well during the meal.

Fred talked about Theo's home and the family who now occupied it. He'd gone to install a new gutter that ripped off after a nasty squall last month, causing a mess on the back porch. He checked the house and yard and was satisfied with the tenant's property care.

"Thanks again. Don't forget to send me a bill. All of that is tax-deductible, you know."

"Sure will. But now that you mention it, I sent you a bill two months ago when I replaced the front door lock. Did you get it?"

"Ah, shit. I did see it, but I must've forgotten. I'm sorry, I'll send you a cheque for both. You're getting my monthly auto-deposit for general maintenance, aren't you?"

"Regular as clockwork. That two hundred dollars goes into our trip account, which we appreciate."

"Well worth it. Thanks to Pat and you, I don't have to worry about anything with my place."

After he and Fred cleaned up the mess, Pat took out the old Rummoli board and poker chips. That game was probably as old as Jenna, and the families enjoyed many evenings trying to win the table. He remembered those great nights of family fun as they settled down to play the familiar game.

Theo pretended not to see Pat and Fred's concerned glance when he retrieved his overnight bag and pulled out a bottle of gin. Having a few drinks with his family reminded him of playing this game years ago. And sharing a festive evening was different from drinking alone, Theo reasoned.

Fred shrugged and brought glasses, ice, and tonic before the game started.

"I'm done. You boys are full of the devil tonight and twice as noisy—you've given me a headache." Pat sighed, threw the last of her chips into the center pot, and pulled away from the table. "See you guys in the morning. First one up puts the coffee on."

"Sure will, doll. We won't be long. We'll play a poker pot at midnight and call it quits." Fred blew his wife a kiss, then began shuffling the deck. After another couple of hands of rummoli, he and Theo pushed all their chips to the center and played a five-card stud to determine the winner.

"Fred, you lucky old bugger—a full house? That's the last time you get to deal poker."

"Helps when you can read your opponent. I knew you had diddly squat, and I could afford to take a chance on another card." Fred slapped the table, laughing at Theo's frowning expression. "Pass me the tray to put the chips back in."

Theo reached for the side counter and returned the plastic container, knocking over his gin and tonic. "Oh, shit. Sorry, Fred." Theo scraped his chair back and wobbled to the kitchen for a tea towel.

"It's ok, Theo. I'll get it. Why don't you head to bed, and I'll finish putting this away."

Theo nodded, then swiped his hands over his beard, giving them a tug. A few highballs turned into an evening of drinking. There was a time when Theo seldom consumed more than three drinks, but the self-control that stopped him at his usual limit had disappeared. Ashamed, Theo shifted his gaze away and left the kitchen.

THEO GROANED as he awoke in the downstairs bedroom, sprawled across the bed with a sour taste in his mouth. He closed his eyes and pinched the bridge of his nose as he often did when he needed to focus. Theo breathed slowly and deeply several times before carefully checking for dizziness. Last summer, he'd stood up too quickly after a bender, became dizzy, and collapsed, cracking a rib when he fell against the dresser. Theo squeezed his eyes shut and rubbed his temples as he struggled to recall the end of last evening. How he got down the steps was beyond him. Maybe Fred helped him. Theo hoped not. They'd had fun last night, and he was sure he hadn't done anything embarrassing. Nevertheless, Theo had lost control. And he'd been so sure of himself.

Bloody hell.

Kicking the gin habit would be more challenging than he thought, although he'd have nothing but time to conquer it. He wouldn't bring any back to his lease and wouldn't come home until he was absolutely sure it would never pass his lips again. Theo crossed his fingers and kissed them, hoping that this attempt would be the one that worked.

CHAPTER 5

"Ali, this is Jenna. I've left a key to my place under my mat. My dad's had a bad accident, and I'm heading home." Jenna took a quick breath to steady her trembling voice before continuing. "I don't know how long I'll be. Text me when you get this." Jenna threw clothing and essentials into two suitcases and thought of her trusty co-worker, Alicia. She could depend on her to empty the fridge, collect the mail, and keep an eye on her place. Jenna couldn't think past that.

Thank God she had her boss's personal and business email stored on her cell. Jenna left another voice message explaining her father's accident and that she'd likely need an extended leave of absence. If Mr. Dylan refused her request, she'd quit her job. Jenna enjoyed working in Nanaimo for Fisheries and Oceans Canada but was still on the lowest tier, doing the grunt work. It would take years before she'd be the one gathering data on marine pollution and its effects. Jenna had hoped to be hired at the Bamfield Marine Center, where Lee worked, but she'd need more qualifications than she had to get such a top-notch job.

Truthfully, Jenna didn't want to return to university. She'd work hard, move up the hard way, and earn a transfer there.

Maybe.

After leaving her hometown almost four years ago, it now looked like she'd be returning to her roots, at least temporarily. Jenna's mind flitted from one subject to another as she raced along Highway 4 to Tofino.

"*You bloody IDIOT.*" Jenna slammed her brakes on and veered onto the right-hand access lane, allowing an aggressive and impatient driver to pass on a double solid line. That was the trouble with this two-lane highway between Port Alberni and Tofino. Because of the high mountain passes, there were limited areas where drivers could pass the slower traffic. Jenna stopped in a pull-off place where snow still snugged the far edges and turned her hazard lights on. Her palms were sweaty, and her heart beat so hard that Jenna could feel the pulse in her ears.

Jenna compared her reaction to what her dad must've experienced as he navigated a new highway section under construction around Kennedy Lake. Highway 4 was long overdue to be straightened and expanded, yet it still presented problems for drivers two years later, especially in heavy rain. Rock cliffs turned into waterfalls, overfilling the catch basins and flooding the makeshift road. From what Aunt Pat relayed, her father wisely chose the rock face rather than plunging a hundred or more feet into Kennedy Lake. Jenna's traffic diversion today was tame compared to the deadly split-second response her father had to make. She couldn't imagine the fear he must've felt.

Jenna laid her head against the steering wheel, her breath still short and panicked. Her fingers trembled as she straightened in her seat and began deep breathing exercises. Jenna rubbed the center of her forehead up and down to calm her emotions, then reached for her water bottle. People who would risk lives to arrive at their destination ten minutes before others were beyond her comprehension. After several sips of water, Jenna felt her heartbeat slow and return to normal. She held her hand before her, relieved that the shakes had subsided. She waited another few minutes, then pulled back onto the highway and resumed the journey to Tofino General Hospital.

Jenna pulled into the parking lot an hour later and put on her mask before approaching the automatic doors. Hospitals petrified her, and she avoided them like the plague. Jenna stood in line on the recommended circles six feet apart and waited her turn. Although the Covid pandemic restrictions were relaxed, no one seemed ready to take a chance. Certainly not in a setting like this. Once she received her dad's room number, she walked down the hall to the semi-private room he occupied.

As Jenna pushed open the door, the first person she saw was her Aunt Pat, who came right over and pulled her into a hug.

"Don't be too alarmed. It looks worse than it is. No internal damage, thank God. Dislocated shoulder, spiral right fibula and tibia fractures, and bruises all over."

"Oh my God, look at him." Jenna approached the bed, running her fingers atop the blanket. Jenna turned to her aunt, looking for answers. "Dad's a local. He knows better than to travel in the heavy spring rains right now. What was he thinking?"

"I've no idea, Jenna." Aunt Pat glanced at Theo when she heard moans from the bed.

Jenna quickly returned to her father's left side and squeezed his hand gently. "Dad, I'm here now. That's a tough way to take time off of work. Why didn't you call me and tell me you needed a holiday?"

Theo struggled to open his eyes. His gaze squinted upwards, and a sheepish grin crossed his face. "That would make better sense, alright. You didn't have to come right away, pumpkin." Theo licked his chapped lips as he struggled to speak. "Your presence won't make me heal any faster, you know. You could've waited."

Jenna ignored her old nickname, giving him leeway. She poured him ice water from a jug and popped in a straw. She leaned toward him and offered him a sip. "I know. Why the hell were you on the road last night in that rainstorm?"

Theo sipped carefully and moaned his appreciation. "Stupid, I guess." Theo's voice was scratchy. Sheepishly, he looked away from Jenna. "I'd put off picking up a shipment of rope that was delivered to the Port Authority for me two weeks ago." Theo winced as he tried to change position before continuing. "I received a text message telling me they wouldn't hold them anymore and they'd send it back at my expense in the morning."

"And you couldn't have waited until dawn to go and get them? Since when have you become so impatient? They know you over there. I'm sure Drake would've held it one more day if you'd ask."

"Well, I didn't, and the rest is history. Drake's probably sent them back by now." Her father's brusque reply surprised Jenna. She frowned at his tone.

That wasn't like him.

"I'll call them and check. I can always rent a truck and get the supplies myself. I might as well be doing something."

"Go ahead, but it'll be a waste of time. I'm sure the shipment's been returned." Theo turned his head and closed his eyes, dismissing Jenna's comments.

Jenna stole a look at her aunt, who shrugged her shoulders. She pointed to herself and the door, and Jenna nodded. She'd join her aunt as soon as possible. "Give me an hour, and I'll head to your place. Dad should probably be resting."

Pat agreed. "That's what Dr. Walker says. The physical therapists will probably come by to check on him and set up a rehab schedule. Your dad's lucky to be alive. They say he should expect to be here for a week at least. Then it's a matter of healing and physical therapy when the cast comes off." Pat approached Theo and patted his left knee. "I'll come by tomorrow after work for a visit. Do you want me to bring you anything?"

"I guess I'll need my brush, toothpaste, and personal things like that, please."

"I'll get that for you, Dad, and bring them back tonight."

"OK. Thanks." Theo paused as his eyes flickered closed. "The painkillers the surgeon gave me are great. I don't feel anything but can hardly keep my eyes open. It seems all I do is sleep."

"Then go ahead and rest. I'll stay a little while with you, then unpack my things at Aunt Pat's. If you're sleeping when I leave, I'll be back around 7:30. Is that okay with you?" Jenna leaned over, brushed his wavy hair away from his forehead, and kissed his stubbled cheek. "You had me worried, mister."

"Sorry, Jenna. I'll be good as new before you know it, and you can go back to work." Theo's eyes drooped as they fought to remain open while his voice deepened and slowed.

"No worries, Dad. I'm here for as long as you need me." She felt his fingers slacken as her father slipped into a heavy sleep. Jenna removed her jacket, hung it on a hook near the bedside table, and sat beside him. She wished she could take her mask off and be more comfortable. Jenna sat back in her chair and eyed her dad.

It had been almost four months since she'd seen him last, and he'd lost weight again. After her mom died five years ago this month, she'd seen him like this, then he rallied and started looking after himself, gaining the weight, muscle, and energy he used to have. However, since she went to UVic, she'd noticed a change in him. If her mom could see him now, she'd be so disappointed. He used to be a go-getter, always looking forward, and an eternal optimist.

Jenna relaxed and closed her eyes, remembering the good times she'd shared with her parents. It seemed so long ago. Her dad and mom were happiest when they'd spend a weekend exploring. They found joy being together as they hiked the many trails on the Esowista Peninsula or kayaked and overnighted in isolated coves throughout Clayoquot Sound. Her dad usually worked the oyster lease alone unless it was harvesting time. Then he hired help to handle the strenuous job of pulling lines and clipping off oyster clusters weighing two to three hundred pounds each. Her mom started a small nursery to keep her busy, hiring her aunt to help her as the business grew.

Jenna loved going to McKenna Island every summer with her family. They'd spend a week or two seeding lines. Then, they enjoyed the rest of their time reconnecting with nature. That's probably where her curiosity became an obsession, as she learned all she could from her father. Her father seemed to know its story no matter what she pointed out.

Theo knew precisely where to drop shellfish traps, the best place to find sea cucumbers or dig for geoduck clams.

He was a fountain of information about the natural world he lived in.

Where did that man disappear to?

Her mom must've been his driving force during their marriage. Jenna often wondered if her dad only pretended he was healing so she would leave for university. Probably.

"Jenna?" Dr. Walker's soft voice shook her out of her daydream. "Theo will be sleeping a lot in the next few days. Maybe we could go for a coffee in the cafeteria if you have a few minutes. I want to speak with you."

Jenna looked at her father and saw he was still sleeping deeply. "Sure. I could use a cup of tea and maybe a snack." Her stomach growled as if verifying her hunger.

"Tea's probably a better choice. The coffee here's usually bitter. We won't be gone for long. Your dad probably won't even notice you're away." Dr. Walker held the door open and guided her down the hall.

After retrieving a tray in the cafeteria, Jenna filled a large teapot with steaming water and popped in two bags of Tetley. Dr. Walker took two mugs and lifted an eyebrow at the cream and sugar.

"No thanks, I like it black. That carrot cake looks yummy and will hold me until I have dinner with Aunt Pat. Do you want one?"

"I'm a sucker for lemon meringue pie. Grab me a slice of that, will you?" Dr. Walker insisted on paying for their snack and motioned her to the far corner of the cafeteria.

Jenna poured the tea for both of them and then tasted her cake. The cream cheese icing was light and fluffy, the cake's cinnamon and nutmeg a perfect blend, causing her to moan in appreciation. Fortified, she steeled herself and fixed her eyes on Dr. Walker.

"So, what's going on? Aunt Pat told me the surgeon

reported the injuries were consistent with the accident's severity, but Dad would heal as strong as ever within a year. Is there anything else wrong?"

"Yes. I wanted to be the first to tell you. The RCMP will charge your dad with impaired driving. His blood-alcohol content registered 1.2, which is well above the legal limit."

"*My dad? Impaired driving?*" Jenna slammed her fork onto the table as her mouth hung open. She shook her head from side to side. "My dad never, ever drove when he drank. He walked or called for a ride. That's been drilled into me since I was a teenager. Don't ride with anyone who'd been drinking or *ever* fool myself that I'm ok to drive." Jenna's forehead scrunched, and her eyes narrowed as she searched Dr. Walker's face. "Are you sure? They couldn't have mixed up his sample with someone else?"

"No, I'm sorry, Jenna. The tests were administered immediately after he arrived at the hospital. And our staff continued to monitor it until it subsided enough to put him under general anesthetic to repair and set his injuries. There's no doubt."

"My God." Jenna closed her eyes momentarily, trying to grasp its significance. "I hope no one else was hurt." She raised her eyes to their family doctor, questioning her assumption.

"No one else was involved, thank goodness. But I doubt the insurance will cover the truck's damages. It would've probably been a write-off, but Theo won't get financial help to replace it because he was impaired."

"Oh, great." Jenna suspected money was tight lately because of the tension in her dad's voice when they discussed his problem with supplies. "Well, he'll have to pick up a second-hand one that keeps him going."

"He could, but he'll probably have his license suspended

for six months, maybe even a year, so there's time to figure that challenge out later."

"Shoot, I hadn't thought about that. Asking for help will be hard for Dad—he's always been a proud man."

"I know. Theo will need to get back and forth for therapy. I'm not sure of his living situation when he's in town because I know your dad rented your house a few years ago. Theo definitely can't operate a boat, let alone go to his lease and do any work there."

"Can this get any worse?" Jenna's lips quivered as she thought ahead. Her fingers drummed the tabletop as she wondered what she could do. She looked down, grabbed a napkin, and dabbed her eyes to ward away tears.

"Yes, it can." Dr. Walker looked away and refilled his tea before slowly stirring in some cream. He lifted his gaze to hers and cleared his throat. "I think your dad's developed alcoholism. The blood tests we've also run show biomarkers for possible liver disease. All the signs are there —the weight loss, the depression, and his self-imposed isolation. He was born here and has many childhood friends and working associates. They're worried about him. Your uncle Fred tells me your dad doesn't always return their calls, and if his friends see him downtown, he cuts their conversation short as if he has nothing to say. Hadn't you noticed that?"

Jenna moved her head slowly from side to side, denying the doctor's observations. "No. Aunt Pat would've said something. Even though I've only come home a few weeks in the summer and a week at Christmas, I'm sure I would've noticed something wasn't right." Jenna heaved a deep breath and sighed. Her shoulders slumped as her worst fears materialized. "Since I left UVic and started working in Nanaimo, I've tried to get him to visit me, but there's always an excuse.

In over four years of being away, he's only come to see me twice."

Jenna paused as she remembered her suspicions after her mom died. "I knew he often had a few shots when he had trouble sleeping after Mom passed, but I thought that cleared up." Jenna reached over, took another napkin from its holder, and blotted her eyes. "Damn it. I should've paid more attention."

"You're an adult, Jenna. You've your life to lead, and it's not to be a babysitter for your dad." Dr. Walker's tone was brusque as he shook off Jenna's guilt. "He's quite capable of getting help if he wants. It was his choice to follow that road. However, I think this may be a great time to help him along to a healthier and brighter future. When he's more mobile, I suggest he go for counseling."

"Ha. Good luck. My dad doesn't share his emotions. Maybe with Mom, he did, but very seldom with me or anyone else I know." Jenna pushed her chair aside. "I need to get outside and walk this off. I feel like I'm going to explode."

"Good idea. Call my office when you're ready to discuss your dad more. Maybe I can offer a few suggestions." Dr. Walker reached over and put his hand on her forearm. "Don't take this all on yourself. You can't save or make him do anything he doesn't want to."

Dr. Walker saw Jenna's misting eyes darting around the room, looking for an escape. "Look at me, Jenna." When Jenna turned to him, he lowered his voice and offered thoughtful advice. "What you *can* do is look after yourself so you can help him recuperate physically. His mental state is *his* responsibility, not yours."

"Thanks for your time, Dr. Walker. I'm not sure what the hell I'll do, but if I need help, I'll come and see you." A shaky smile was the best she could give him as she absorbed his advice.

"Smart girl. Give him some tough love that will make him open his eyes. Your mom was good at dishing that out when times got stressful. It isn't a bad trait to have."

"Yes, I can remember getting an odd lecture now and then. I hated to see my mom upset with me, so it usually set me straight."

"Don't underestimate the challenge not to disappoint someone you love." Dr. Walker tipped his hand goodbye as Jenna left the table. "Take care, Jenna."

AFTER LISTENING to the care her father would need in the foreseeable future, Jenna made a trip to Port Alberni and traded her car for an older Dodge van. It was good that she'd inherited the Sorensen's frugal ways and could pay the difference from her savings account because, as confirmed with ICBC, no settlement would be forthcoming.

It took a week before Jenna faced reality. It didn't take a genius to realize she couldn't manage her father's care long distance. She needed to quit her job and give notice for her apartment. Thank God for good friends. She'd enlist the help of both Ali and Sara to pack up her things and put them in storage. When things calmed down, she'd have to call Drew in Daajing Giids, formerly Queen Charlotte City, and bring him up to date. Thank God she hadn't followed Drew to Haida Gwaii. As much as she missed him, she was glad she didn't need to choose between the two men who meant so much to her. *Was this why she held back on the transfer?* Stop it, she told herself. You couldn't have known the future.

News of Theo's accident traveled quickly. It was no surprise when Theo rejected his sister's offer to stay with them. After brainstorming with her friend Carla and her parents, Jenna gratefully accepted their offer to rent their summer cottage. Jenna's aunt and uncle brought Theo's extra clothes that he kept at their place, along with homey afghans for sitting by the fire or enjoying the outdoors. Lee came to help organize their things in the cottage and make it easier for her dad to get around. They'd have a place to call home for a year while her dad recuperated, and paying the nominal rent while keeping their own tenants would help with other living expenses.

Besides, rehab was only part of the problem. If the situation was as dire as Dr. Walker hinted, it wasn't only his physical needs but the consequences of his drinking that needed addressing. The mounting stress led to several sleepless nights as Jenna wrestled with the right approach for her father.

Jenna's secondary focus would be checking out her dad's financial situation and the condition of their oyster lease. If her dad's responses were as hostile as her suggestion for them to live together while he recuperated, that would be another battle.

Her dad wasn't going to like it, *but too damn bad*.

A week later, Jenna wheeled her dad from the hospital and then helped him into the van's passenger seat. She loaded the crutches, collapsed the wheelchair, and slid them into the carry compartment. Jenna shut the van's loading door and then checked on her dad. She pulled the seatbelt across his chest and buckled him in.

"I'm not crippled, Jenna. I could've done that."

"Probably, but with your sling, it might've been difficult. I was only helping." Jenna glanced at her father, sitting morosely in the passenger seat, avoiding eye contact. She closed the passenger door, walked around the van to the driver's side, and took a deep breath. She chastised herself for her impatience. Jenna needed to be more understanding, but darn it, anyway. *He could at least be thankful.*

"I picked up groceries yesterday. Aunt Pat came by with both your clothes and my suitcases. We're all set." Jenna started the ignition, put the car in reverse, and then pulled out of the parking lot. She headed for the Walsh's residence on Arnet Lane, where they'd be leasing their one-bedroom and loft cottage.

"Have you ever been to their place, Dad?"

"Not except for dropping off or picking you up to see Carla at the main house."

"You'll like it, I think. The Walshs built it about fifteen years ago for Carla's grandma. It's an open-concept plan, wheelchair accessible. You'll love the wall-to-wall folding glass doors that open onto a covered veranda. A few evergreens in front of the cottage help to break the wind, but there's still a beautiful ocean view. I'm sure we'll use the oceanfront gazebo in both winter and summer."

"I doubt I'll be going there for a while," Theo grumbled.

"That's true, but it'll be an incentive when you can start moving around on your own." Jenna stole a quick look at her father and shrugged. She may as well add this to the list of changes that needed tackling.

"It may be a good idea to move your boat to the First Street Dock so it'll be easier for me to take a quick run and check the oyster lease."

"Who asked *you* to go check my lease? I'll get Wayne to watch over it until I get better."

"I'm sure that's a good short-term solution, Dad. But Dr. Walker warned us it could be a year before you can work there again." Jenna saw the scowl cross her father's face and gentled her voice. "You can't expect Wayne to watch over it for months on end. He has his own lease to take care of."

Jenna leaned sideways and placed a hand on her father's forearm. "I'm here, and I want to help. Why can't I do it? I know the way there like the back of my hand. I can operate the Furuno navigation if it's foggy or stormy. You know I can do this, Dad." Jenna glanced toward him, noticing his sullen expression, and pleaded her case again. "Why would you want to pay Wayne for maintenance when I can do it for free?"

"It's too much for a girl," Theo growled. "Besides, Wayne knows the process better than you do. I'd trust him to look after it for me for a percentage of sales."

Jenna's eyes widened in surprise. Her dad wasn't sexist. He'd always preached women could do things as well as men and probably better because they needed to work smarter. Theo had become a father she didn't recognize anymore. She paused, wondering the best way to approach this. She lowered and softened her voice.

"Nobody will look after it better than I will. You know that, Dad. You always said that yourself. Owners who live onsite are vested in keeping it in top shape. I think Wayne has enough to look after on his own property."

"Don't argue with me. I'll look after it from here." The low thrum in Theo's voice and adverted eye contact indicated there'd be no further conversation.

Hmm. That didn't work.

Jenna sighed deeply and bit her tongue from mounting another argument. She switched on her turn signal for Arnet Road, then glanced at her dad. His right arm, supported by a sling, now had his left arm crossed over it, proof that she wouldn't budge his stubborn stance on the matter—at least not right now. Jenna sucked in a breath and counted to ten. Baby steps. Their journey could only be successfully traveled with small incremental changes. She'd make her point gently but resort to tough love if that failed.

Whether he acknowledged it or not, he needed her. And equally as important, she needed to help him. Edging gently onto the grassy slope toward the cottage, Jenna discarded her worries. Only here and now mattered. The rest could wait.

Jenna parked beside the broad cement sidewalk thoughtfully built for Grandma Walsh. She opened the sliding van door and transported the accessories that the Tofino Red Cross Cupboard lent them. There were long-handled grips to reach items from a shelf, an adjustable rolling tray for eating meals, and a shower bench. When her dad became more mobile, they'd return them and probably exchange them for a walker to help make him more independent.

She opened the passenger door as wide as possible and brought the wheelchair nearby. Noticing he'd removed his seat belt, she gently repositioned his legs outside the van, then held her arm out for balance. Her father grasped her forearm and let his left leg descend slowly to the payment. Standing on one foot, he gave a little hop to turn himself, then let go of Jenna, grasped the arm of the wheelchair, and lowered himself in it, as practiced so often at the hospital. His barely audible hiss didn't go unnoticed, but Jenna didn't comment as she noted the beads of sweat on his brow.

Jenna positioned the instep for her father to place his feet on, then released the brake and began moving him to the access ramp for the verandah. "Dr. Walker warned us to take things easy. Do you want to go inside, or would you like to stay on the verandah?"

"I've been cooped up too damned long. I'd rather stay out here."

"Ok." Jenna pulled the chair close to a coffee table and put the brake on. "I'll join you in a few minutes. Would you like anything to snack on while you're out here?"

Theo drank in the fragrant evergreens and the warm smell of low tide baking in the afternoon sun. "I don't care, whatever you want." His eyes searched the parameters of his new domain before returning to his daughter's face. "Thanks, Jenna. I already feel ten times better than in the hospital."

Jenna's eyes moistened at her father's sincerity. "I'll bet. Are you warm enough?"

"I am right now, but I might need something later. Can you bring me a blanket, please?"

"Of course. Aunt Pat brought a few small afghans for us." Jenna hurried to fetch a couple. She placed one on his lap, then draped another beside him. "There you go, for whenever you need it. I'll be back soon."

Jenna went to the kitchen, pulled out her dad's favorite Balderson cheese, and cut several slices alongside crackers, arranging them on a plate. Carving up a crispy gala apple, she placed them alternately with red globe grapes, another favorite of his. Jenna grabbed several napkins, brought them outside, and put them on the table between her and her dad. She returned to fetch a pitcher of iced tea she'd made earlier and two glasses.

"Here you go, Dad. We have to keep you hydrated, like the doc says." She held up her glass and tilted it towards her father. "Cheers—to a speedy recovery."

"To a speedy recovery." Her father clinked his glass with hers and drank several gulps. "I guess I was thirstier than I realized." He paused, still reveling in the vista before him.

"Thanks for being here with me. I know I'm not easy to live with. You've bitten off a lot, giving up your job and coming here."

"I'm glad you let me. I wouldn't want it any other way." Jenna patted his hand before offering him the snack platter.

"Hmph. As if I had a choice," Theo chuckled. "You might be even more stubborn than your mom was." He chose a sample on his napkin and then nibbled on a slice of Balderson atop a cracker.

"True. I know I can lose my temper quicker, that's for sure." Jenna picked at the offerings and then settled the platter between them.

"Yes. Sometimes I need that. But don't get any ideas that you can boss me around whenever you want." Theo raised his eyebrows at her as if challenging her.

"Never. Only when you need it. Deal?" Jenna picked up her glass of iced tea and tilted it toward her father.

"Deal." Theo tapped his glass against hers. "Somehow, I feel that may happen more often than I want."

"Maybe not. It depends on you. Mom told me she had to light a fire under your ass when the blues hit you."

"She did?"

"Yup. What do you think girls talk about? Usually, the guys in their lives. And since you were hers..." Jenna's tone teased a smile from her father.

"Got it. But you didn't have anyone steady to talk about. You were too busy hanging out with your girlfriends or working at the nursery."

"Yeah, well, what can I say?" Jenna took a slice of apple and bit in, relishing the apple's crunchy, cold sweetness.

CHAPTER 6

Jenna swore that April was the unluckiest month for her. It was supposed to signify spring and the rebirth in nature and their relationships. Instead, two of the most horrific events in her life occurred then. The death of her mom, then her dad's almost fatal accident. Now, three months later, she knew better.

Crap can happen at any time.

As 'MissBHaven' approached Westerlea Cove, the reality of her dad's past hit home. One corner of the cabin deck was barely visible. The structure itself looked abandoned and mistreated, probably for years. Many double-blue barrels that kept the main lines afloat were partially submerged. Jenna pulled the throttle back to idle as she toured the lease and checked for more damage.

Today's low tide of 1.4 feet showed the extent of her father's negligence. Starfish clung to the rocky shoreline, and sludge hung from the anchor lines holding the lease in place to McKenna Island. *Good Lord, what a total shit show.* How could she even start to repair this?

"What the hell?" Jenna yelled out in frustration. "Dad,

what the hell happened?" Jenna's eyes darted around the cove, noticing the rampant deterioration on their oyster lease.

"You beggar. You gave up. No wonder you didn't want me to come here!" Jenna's yelling echoed in the silence. Westerlea Cove had been in the family for sixty years, each generation enlarging and improving it. No wonder he strenuously fought her when she'd bring the subject up. He didn't want her to see what his drinking had done—or not done. From its appearance, it was hard to believe that barely five years had passed since her mom died and her dad stopped caring. It looked like the lease was neglected far longer than that. Her shoulders slumped as tears threatened to fall.

Jenna maneuvered the 'MissBHaven' into place on the dock and threw the buoys out to protect it. Turning off the ignition, she hopped out of the boat and cinched the rope onto the cleats. The silence was overwhelming, almost accusatory. The loss of its beauty and usefulness was shameful.

"What the hell, Dad? What the hell?" Jenna angrily paced up and down the deck. She sobbed with frustration, her voice booming louder and louder as she tried to exorcise her anger. Her voice was hoarse, and her nose runny before she finally collapsed on a weathered Adirondack. With her elbows on her knees, Jenna placed her head in her hands and closed her eyes to hide from the neglect. Letting the August sunshine warm her chilled bones, Jenna concentrated on deep, even breaths and kept her mind blank, hoping she'd see this more objectively.

With her emotions under control, Jenna pushed herself forward and approached the door. It was scary to even think of the condition inside. All her and her mom's efforts to make the cabin cozy and comfortable would probably be ruined. Jenna pushed the key in the doorknob and wiggled it one way and then the other, trying to get the mechanism to unlock. She slammed the door with all her might and tried again, this time with success. Jenna flung the door open, then stood back.

Warm, stale air blasted from inside, scented with rotten garbage and mildew. Jenna believed her dad when he said he'd contacted Wayne and asked him to empty the place of anything that could go bad. Either he lied, or Wayne didn't bother. Jenna retreated to the boat galley, tied a tea towel around her nostrils, and entered, heading straight to the windows. She opened the curtains and the sliding glass panels for air circulation. Jenna surveyed the disaster with hands on her hips and a growl in her throat.

"Oh. My. God." Jenna surveyed the chaotic clutter in front of her. "I don't freaking believe this. What the hell?" Jenna seldom swore like she had today, but she'd never seen a mess like this, especially a fiasco made by her fastidious father. Jenna ran outside, tore the towel from her face, and bent forward from the waist. With her hands on her knees, Jenna steadied her breath and resisted the urge to puke.

Disgusting. Simply disgusting.

Jenna remembered how often her father spoke about commitment and integrity. Her father's words always portrayed a simple truth. Everything is linked, so take care of each link and forge a strong unit—whether it was family, friendship, or the environment, they were all connected. Break those links, and things will fall apart.

How could he have abandoned his core beliefs? Everywhere she looked, that's all she saw—broken links.

Jenna straightened and began pacing the dock, her eyes darting from one decrepit or broken link to another, each stabbing her heart. The Sorensen name had been tarnished by her father, by his alcohol consumption and depression.

Screw it.

Jenna wouldn't succumb to her father's disappointing mistakes. Jenna tied the towel around her head again and went inside, searching for garbage bags. Picking up empty bottles strewn throughout the living room and kitchen, she filled two bags quickly and took them outside. Opening the fridge that had run out of propane, the sight and smell made her gag. This time, nothing stopped her from running out and retching into the chuck.

To be fair, her father obviously expected to return quickly, but leaving a messy cabin cooped up for over three months at this time of year meant disaster. Once Jenna regained control of her nausea, she installed a new forty-pound propane tank, connected it, and lit the hot water tank. She emptied the fridge into a garbage bag and brought it to the shed. After washing the appliance interior and counters with hot soap and water, Jenna poured a half-empty bleach container into a five-gallon pail. She sterilized every nook and cranny in the kitchen before taking a break.

Exhausted, Jenna went to the boat, washed up in the galley, and changed clothes. As the smell in her nostrils diminished, she realized her hunger. Not surprising as breakfast was over eight hours prior. Jenna brewed a small pot of coffee and then rummaged through the cooler. She took a ham roll, rye bread, and fresh tomatoes and quickly made two sandwiches.

Jenna took her coffee and dinner to the back of the boat and propped herself against the cushioned bench. She forced herself to eat slowly and drink the potent brew. Thank God Jenna thought to bring a sleeping bag and her pillow. She'd probably sleep on the boat for the foreseeable future. Once she established a clean cabin, she could make a list of priorities and tackle the next project.

I can do this. I will do this. Jenna opened and closed her fists as she fought to stay strong. *Come hell or high water, I'll get Westerlea Cove back in shape.* Damn rights, she would. No matter what her dad had to say about it.

Stretching onto the bench, Jenna closed her eyes and relaxed. The boat's gentle rocking, full stomach, and warm sun lulled her into sleep. A sharp blast from a boat's horn catapulted her from her nap.

"Ahoy, MissBHaven. Is that you, Theo?"

Jenna recognized Wayne's voice and leaned over the port side, "Nope, you won't be seeing him for a long time."

"Jenna, is that you?" Wayne's hand was shielding his eyes as he approached.

"It sure is. Come in and tie up if you've got time."

"Of course. I haven't seen ya here since before yer mom passed away."

"I know. I went to UVic the year after my mom died. Then, I got a job at Fisheries and Oceans in Nanaimo. You've heard about my dad's accident, I guess?"

"Yea. Damn shame." Wayne threw a rope over to Jenna as he edged closer to the dock. He jumped out as Jenna pulled the line tight while Wayne tied up his skiff.

"Come aboard, Wayne. I'll make more coffee. It's not fit to be inside the cabin right now."

"I'll bet. Yer dad didn't trust anyone with a key, so I couldn't go in and check things out. I've tried to reach him many times since the accident, but he hasn't called me back. Yer Aunt Pat said yer looking after him." Wayne sat on the rear deck, shaking his head. "Damn shame the way yer dad went. We tried to stay in touch with him, but he made it clear he didn't want any company."

"Hmm." Jenna emptied the cold coffee, prepped a new pot, and set it on the stove to boil. "Once I arrived, I wondered about that. He told me he'd arranged for you to look after things. Then, when he became stronger, and I felt I could leave him, I began asking his permission to come and check this place. He'd get so angry whenever I wanted to go. Dad told me he had you covering for him, and it wasn't a place for a woman. I should have suspected..."

"I'm sorry, Jenna. Yer old man took yer mom's death hard. He couldn't accept it, and I think he started drinking to ease the pain and loneliness. He probably couldn't face having ya see how he'd let this place go." Wayne's sad brown eyes showed his compassion.

"I can see that now. I can't believe how much it's deteriorated. Haven't the authorities raised a fuss with this?" Jenna returned to the stove and lowered the heat for a slow perk.

"Oh, I'm sure they have. I've seen the Aquaculture officers around here plenty, taking pictures. Before the accident, I'd call him now and then on the VHF just to make sure he hadn't croaked. He'd answer the call, then tell me he hurt his back and couldn't do the work he used to. I offered to come or send my crew for big jobs, but he refused." Wayne raised his hands in a what-can-you-do motion.

"Not much else you can do. And for the record, Dad hasn't ever suffered from a bad back. The Sorensen's are known to be a healthy but stubborn lot, extremely independent." Jenna's voice held a hint of frustration.

"That's true. My dad told stories of yer great-grandpa starting this place in the early '60s. If he could do it himself and save a quarter, he would."

"I've heard tales of him, too." Jenna sat across from Wayne while waiting for the coffee to perk. "Do you know when he started drinking? I knew my dad had a problem when mom died, but he looked almost like his old self when I left for UVic." Jenna shrugged her shoulders. "I guess I was too naive to suspect anything. Dad kept reminding me that Mom would've wanted me to continue my education, and I thought he was coping okay." Jenna was gesturing with her hands, emphasizing her observations. "He seemed to be doing well, often coming here for a week or two. That made me feel less guilty about leaving him."

"I don't know for sure, but I don't think he held back any on the drinking when he came here. He was always doing something around the lease whenever I went by, but not so much lately. And once in a blue moon, we'd go fishing together. When he pulled a good setting, he always brought me an ice cream pail of prawns. But after yer mom died, he had one excuse after another, and I soon figured he didn't want my company." Wayne accepted the proffered coffee and blew the steam from the top.

"That's what I remember of our summers spent here. You'd pop over for a coffee or a short visit. It made Mom and I feel better that you two watched out for one another, especially in stormy weather." Jenna shook her head at the difference between her father then and the one who'd appeared after her mom's death. "I can't believe how much he's changed. But it wasn't just you that he retreated from. It was everyone." Jenna sipped her coffee, hoping to tame the emotional tightening in her throat. She was *not* going to cry.

"Yea. It's tough to watch someone go through shit like that, and there's nothin' ya can do. Over the years, we've helped each other save the day many times. We used to have a reasonably good relationship. Not too friendly," Wayne held his hand out and tilted it from side to side. "But when one of us needed a hand, the other was there."

Wayne paused, his eyes darting around the float. He

cleared his throat before continuing. "Then, after yer mom passed, we'd see the boat here, but we hardly ever saw him outside working. It surprises me that he also lied to his baby girl. It's a crying shame that his suffering turned him inside out."

"I should've seen the depression progressing, but I was too busy with my own life." Jenna shrugged her shoulders and lowered her gaze to the deck.

"That's not yer fault. Theo knew many people who would've helped if he'd asked. He didn't want it."

"Water under the bridge. I'm here now. Tomorrow, I'm tackling the inside of our cabin. My mom would have a fit if she saw it now."

"Is there anything I can do to help? Oyster life is tough work for a woman."

Jenna pursed her lips—she didn't want to hear another misogynistic comment. "Not right now, thanks. I'm not even sure if this place is salvageable. I'm going to try, though." Jenna watched him stroll silently around the float, checking things out before returning.

"Ya know what? I'll bring my power washer and generator here tomorrow and work on the siding and the deck. It's the least I can do."

"I don't want to put you out." Jenna's knee started bouncing a mile a minute as she debated swallowing her pride. It didn't take long. "Alright, thanks, Wayne. As long as you're ok with it, I won't refuse. Don't bring lunch. I'll feed the both of us."

"OK, I'll see you around 8:00 a.m. if that's ok?"

"Yes, that's fine." Jenna put their coffee mugs in the galley sink, then returned to shake his hand and untie his lines before watching him putter away. Returning inside, Jenna perused the various boxes and clear totes of paper and gritted her teeth. She might as well start organizing this disaster. Sifting through one container at a time, Jenna sorted paperwork, kept what looked important, and tossed the rest.

THAT WEEK WAS an exhausting blur of activity. Wayne came with a hired hand named Terry, who was currently reseeding new stringers on his lease. Terry knew Theo years ago and volunteered to help clean up the float. He soon re-attached loose gutters and screwed down errant deck boards that popped up during winter storms. By the third morning, Jenna issued a request.

"Alright, you two. Today's your last day. We'll quit by 6:00 at the latest, and then we'll barbecue the salmon you brought. Otherwise, I'll have to start paying you or refusing your help. You've been more than kind, but I can't accept anymore. It's probably time to get back to your own work. July is a busy month."

"Ah. The Sorensen pride's kicking in, is it?" Wayne winked at Jenna.

"Yes, it is. Besides, this place looks great. I can't believe Terry remembered the styrofoam block that washed ashore on Flores Island and picked it up. He's darn good at working those awkward things into place. I wasn't much help at all."

Terry blushed as he downplayed his contribution. "I've had lots of practice, Jenna. Besides, I only needed an extra set of hands with a pike pole. You handled yourself well. You're strong for a woman."

"I think I am. I've been physically active all my life. I jog, kayak, scuba dive, and even work out at a fitness center. I'll have you know I can press sixty pounds." Jenna stuck her arm out, showed off her bicep, and then pranced in a circle.

"Ooh. Remind me not to start a fight with you," Terry quipped. "Anything special you want us to tackle today?"

Jenna hesitated. "Maybe you can check all our anchor lines and whatever else seems important? And maybe one of you can make sure the HIAB is greased, oiled, and working properly?" Jenna bit her lip as she wondered if she could operate it. "And maybe I can hire one of you to come back one day to teach me how to operate it? It's been quite a few years since I watched my dad handling the HIAB, and even then, he only explained what he was doing. I was too young to do anything more. Now, I'll need to learn how to run it properly so I can pick up the mainlines and clean them."

Wayne nodded. "Sounds like a good plan. For today, I'll check the float and mainline anchors and do whatever else around them that needs doing. I'm the one that looks after the machinery, but Terry can come back to help when yer ready and make sure yer operating it safely. I have no idea when Theo used the HIAB last, so I'll also check the chains and hooks. That'll probably take up most of tomorrow, maybe even the next day. Are ya ok with that?"

"I have to be. Besides, without your help so far, I probably would've given up. You've saved me a lot of time, money, and mental stress. I can pay for this. What's your rate?"

Wayne and Terry exchanged glances. "We'll give you the friends and family rate. I'll charge ya $50.00 per hour to repair the HIAB, and Terry's time will be twenty-five. But for today, I'll do a general check over everything like ya asked me and fix what's necessary."

Jenna did the calculations in her head. Probably ten

hours at fifty per would be five hundred, plus another 16 hours at twenty-five per hour. "Around a thousand dollars then. I can do that. I'll get you cash next time I go to town. And Wayne, please add their cost if you need to use any of your supplies. Promise?"

"Sure, kid. Yer right. If yer going to get this place going, ya have to put money into it. Ya might as well get used to it. But working that machine isn't a one-person job. Ya better make sure ya have someone helping ya. There's too much to watch out for only one person."

"I know. I'm not going to hoist the clusters. I only want to hike the main line near the surface to check and clean the stringers and barrels."

"Ya probably need to replace or pump the water from the sinking barrels. Another job for at least two people. Are ya sure yer able to tackle this project?"

"I'll do what I can with the money I have. Good thing I don't have to pay myself." Jenna's lopsided smile belied her worries. "Don't worry. I'll be careful."

"Ya can always call us on the VHF if ya run into trouble." Wayne tipped his cap to her, then jumped into his skiff and headed toward the work float with the HIAB.

"Any other priorities?" Terry asked.

"Can you check the wood stove and chimney? Dad used to keep a supply of firewood on shore for us to bring up when it got cool. I haven't been there yet, either. Can you handle that for me and see if there's any firewood still left onshore?"

"You got it."

"Maybe I'll go with you. The kayaks should be in the storage shed, and I'll need one to paddle around here."

Terry nodded, went to the outdoor shed, retrieved a metal pail and small shovel, then headed inside.

Jenna followed him indoors, noting the lingering odor. She'd made a bleach, soap, and water solution to wash down the walls and floors to remove the mildew that had already started growing in the confined, warm cabin. Terry helped her move the futon and bed mattress outdoors to air out, where Jenna had sponged another bleach solution on them to arrest the mildew. Once completely dry in three or four days, she'd probably be able to sleep inside.

Jenna stripped the window curtains, placed them with all the linens and towels in garbage bags, and brought them to her boat to bring home and launder. She'd make do with the meager linen supply in the boat. The fridge was sparkling clean, and Jenna scrubbed the stove as clean as possible. On the next trip, she'd bring more rubber gloves and an Oven-Off to remove the deeper layers of grime.

She heard Terry cleaning and emptying the dirty grate into a bucket, then checking the draft. These two guys had been a godsend. She'd wondered what her reception would be and couldn't have been happier. Even though her dad alienated his old friends, they understood his reasons and were now helping his daughter with generous hearts and hands.

"Jenna?" Terry called her. "It looks like an obstruction up higher in the chimney. A nest, probably. I'll have to go on the roof, take the cap off, and see if I can get it out."

"Do you need me up there?" Jenna offered.

"No, but you can pass me stuff when I yell for it. I'll need a long pike pole and maybe a length of rope. I'll holler when I need it."

"Ok. While up there, you might as well check the propane vent. I'd rather do that now than wait until a cold, rainy night in November."

"Already on my list. Although, I'm surprised that you're

aware of things like that. Not many women understand all the maintenance that goes into isolated living."

"My dad was always teaching Mom and me things like that. It's second nature for us to plan about things that could cause us problems." Jenna spread her hands out in front of her and twirled around slowly. "That's why this has been such a surprise for me. I'd never have believed my dad would've let this place go like this."

"I'm sorry, Jenna." Terry's gentle hazel eyes reflected his concern. "I've always liked your dad. It was hard for us to watch this place go down. I've heard his license will be revoked if he doesn't bring it to minimum standards."

"Oh, no. Shit." Jenna closed her eyes for a moment and cleared her throat. "There's a lot of unopened mail in the plastic tote there. I guess I better look at that and see if there's a deadline."

Jenna stamped her foot and threw her hands in the air. "I can't flipping believe this," Jenna growled as she began pacing the floor. "Wait until I get home and confront him. I'm done with his lying and feeling sorry for himself." Jenna glanced over at Terry, standing still, his mouth agape.

Embarrassed, Jenna turned, walked to the now sparkling-clean front windows, and stared outside at their cove, her hands on her hips. Her face felt hot, so she concentrated on breathing through her nose to slow her racing heart and cool her temper.

"I'll do everything possible to get this place back in shape." Jenna's voice was barely more than a whispered promise, then she turned and faced Terry. "Honestly, I doubt Dad can carry on alone when he recuperates, but maybe we'll manage between us. I guess you know he started drinking."

"I hate to say it, but even though he probably thought no

one knew, the word got around." Terry's sympathetic features stabbed Jenna with their authenticity.

"Since I came home after the accident, we've been renting a cottage from the Walsh's. I know he hasn't had a drink after the accident." Jenna's chin tilted up defiantly. "God help him if he screws up behind my back. Aunt Pat and Carla will check on him, bring him to therapy appointments, or pick up groceries when I'm here. They know not to bring any liquor home. He's lost his driver's license for a year, so I hope Dad's learned his lesson. I *think* he's changed —at least he's making an effort. I guess we'll see."

"I hope it stays that way." Terry nodded hopefully. "If you ever need to talk, give me a shout. The days are long now, so coming over after work is easy."

"Thanks, Terry. I might do that. Are you ready for a hand now?"

"Give me another twenty minutes to get this cleaned up. Then I'll get the ladder and head up there."

"Sounds good." Jenna retreated outside.

The rest of the day passed in a daze. When Terry and Jenna finished the chimney and venting task, they unlocked the chained fourteen-foot aluminum boat from the deck storage unit and slipped into the water. They paddled to shore, quietly reflecting on the work ahead.

"Where do I start?" moaned Jenna as they pulled the boat ashore. "When I arrived on low tide a few days ago, I was shocked at the number of starfish around here. I know that oyster leases are supposed to harvest and dry them out to save the shellfish—that was a job my mom and I often did in the summer. But it looks like that was another job my dad ignored." Jenna shoved her hands in the pocket of her jeans and scuffed at the pebbles on the beach.

"Not a good sign, that's for sure. Those suckers travel

quickly and have probably done a lot of damage here. I don't want to keep saying I'm sorry, but" Terry shrugged his shoulder compassionately.

"I know. Sorry doesn't help anyway." Jenna puffed a sigh of frustration. "Have you got any ideas?"

"Depends on how much money you have. You might try hiring students for a month. Minimum wage, room and board, and exploring this area have a certain appeal to struggling students looking for something different to make money. A lot cheaper than hiring me to help you."

"Good idea. I'll think about that. Even if I only have two kids for a few weeks, that would equal a month's work for me alone. It might be worth it."

Terry walked towards the shingled work shop that blended into the forest. A lean-to on the south side was empty of firewood. "There's your answer on the firewood. You must have a chainsaw here, don't you?"

"Probably in the shed." Jenna unlocked it and jiggled open the wide double doors. "What do you know, we have some good news. The kayaks, paddles, and life jackets are still here." She walked to the north wall where her dad had built shelves for miscellaneous tools, oil, and extra gas tanks. A nine-horsepower outboard for the aluminum boat was clamped on a four-by-four post. "And the motor and chainsaw haven't been stolen." Jenna shook each of the half-dozen five-gallon gas cans and then grimaced. "I guess Dad put the motor away once the gas was gone. He must've figured he wasn't working with it anyway, so why bother buying fuel." Jenna's shoulders slumped.

"I'm going back to Tofino in a few days. We have an order of seed to pick up. How about I fill these gas cans for you? If you call in an order at the Co-op for groceries, I'll bring that too." Terry spread his hands out and shrugged as he noticed her frown. "What the hell? It isn't out of my way. That's what neighbors do, help each other out."

Terry looked on the shelves and found three boxes of spark plugs and a tin of defogging spray. "When I return, I'll check your motor out and make sure it's running okay. Let's hope your dad prepped the engine when he put it away. Maybe you'll be good to go if I can lubricate and change the spark plug."

"You know you can't keep coming to my rescue, right?" Jenna groaned as she battled her pride. She paced around the shed with her hands on her hips and eyed the area. Sighing deeply, Jenna capitulated. "Ok, but I have to pay you if I agree. We'll keep track of your hours, and when I run out of money, you run out of extra work. No more freebies, ok?" Jenna knew she probably looked worried, but she didn't want him to feel sorry for her. She needed to swallow her ego until she got on her feet, even though it rubbed her the wrong way.

"Alright, no more freebies. When you figure things out, think about giving me a budget you can afford each month, and I'll do what I can. Does that work for you?" Terry's eyes sparkled.

Jenna folded her arms in front of her chest, tilting her head at an angle as she tried to figure him out. "You better not be laughing at my independence, buddy. I can, and I *will* get this place back on track."

"I'm not laughing. I'm impressed. Most people would grab my free offers and ask for more, but you're pushing me away."

Terry's gentle voice brought tears to her eyes. "I'm trying to hold onto my pride," Jenna turned away from him as she struggled for an explanation, then threw her hands up. What the hell—she might as well add another request. Her towels, linens, and work clothes were mounting, and he could save her a trip to town. "If you've got room, can I send my laundry and garbage with you? Aunt Pat has offered to do it for me."

"Sure, not a problem. Anything else?"

Jenna worried her lip a moment before blurting out her next need. "I want to watch you service the motor. If I see what you're doing, I'll remember and can do it myself next time. I've got so much to learn, and I need to be as self-reliant as possible." Jenna lifted her eyebrows as she made her conditions, ensuring he understood her needs, reasons, and deep appreciation.

"I get it. No freebies, no big favors." Terry punched her lightly on the shoulder. "How about a beer and a barbecue now and then?"

Jenna relaxed and nodded. "Of course. You bring the catch, and I'll cook it." She stuck out her hand. "Deal?" As they shook hands, Jenna added, "I'll never forget this, Terry. You've been a real friend."

"Good. Then this works for both of us." Terry pointed to one end of the kayak. "Grab your end. We'll bring it to the water. You can paddle it back to the float."

EVERY EVENING AFTER DINNER, Jenna would pull out another tote of paperwork and organize them by date, then again by the sender. She found a tablet of lined paper and started opening and making notes on the paperwork and the writing pad. Under the Department of Fisheries and Oceans, she divided the mail into bills, shellfish advisories, and general notices.

Several warnings were self-explanatory and expired or

of no immediate consequence, but many letters grew more threatening. Then there were the overdue bills from suppliers who finally gave up and put them with a collection agency. The first notification broke Jenna's heart, and she cried like a baby, mourning the man her father used to be. By the end of the third evening, she had no more tears, only a burning ambition to turn things around.

Exhausted, Jenna set the paperwork aside, grabbed a cold beer, and went outside to sit on the Adirondack. Her mind almost felt like mush. It was nearly too much to handle. She sat transfixed, staring into the night sky as the clouds flitted by, playing peek-a-boo with the stars.

Jenna felt the waves slapping gently against the dock, easing her tension. It seemed like a lifetime ago that Drew had asked her to move to Haida Gwaii, but it'd only been six months. His promise of living a stress-free lifestyle was almost enough for her to join him, but in good conscience, she couldn't do it. Jenna wasn't ready to settle down yet, and now, with her dad's accident and the oyster lease troubles, Jenna was glad she'd resisted. How would she have managed this crisis long distance? Caught in a maelstrom of problems, Jenna wondered if there was any hope she could ever fix them. As the breeze turned chilly, Jenna returned inside and collapsed onto her bed, fully clothed, thankful for the nothingness that overcame her.

The following week, Terry returned with full propane tanks, clean laundry, groceries, and two university students. When Jenna asked Aunt Pat to watch for a couple of students who'd want to help her, Pat didn't take long to find the right couple, energetic and adventurous. Pat offered them the minimum wage they would've earned with her at Westerlea Nursery and threw in free room and board.

They'd looked at each other and jumped at the chance to have the 'experience of a lifetime.'

Stacy and Liam were entering their second year of university at Simon Fraser in Burnaby. Excited to be working and experiencing the Clayoquot Sound, they brought laughter into Jenna's life. After watching the pair kayak and run about in the aluminum boat, Jenna felt satisfied that she could trust their abilities to handle working on the water with her.

"Have you ever used a chainsaw, Liam?" Jenna enjoyed the second evening with them, sitting outside on the deck and watching the stars.

"You bet I have. My parents live on a dairy farm near Quesnel. Every year since I turned fifteen, part of my summer job was cutting at least four cords of wood." Liam lifted his arms and showed off his muscles. "You don't get these without hard work. I didn't need to join a gym, that's for sure. How much wood do you need?"

"Terry fell three good-sized trees a few weeks ago. They must be limbed and cut at sixteen inches to fit my woodstove. That'll give me two, maybe three cords, which should be enough. If I run short, I have a propane furnace to supplement it."

"Not much time to dry it out for the winter, but better than nothing. I'll make sure to leave circulating airspace between the rows. I guess you've got axes and such?"

"You'll find the power saw and axes in the work shed. I doubt they've been used for a few years, so they may need sharpening. I hope you know how to do that; otherwise, I'll contact Wayne to see if he'll sharpen them. It sounds like you've got the experience to handle things."

"No problem with sharpening the tools. Getting your firewood cut and split can be my first job. If you want, I'll stack some firewood on the float behind the storage shed." Liam grinned at the challenge. "Shall I start tomorrow?"

"Perfect." Jenna fingered her lip as she wondered about jobs Stacy could do while her boyfriend was busy with that. She snapped her fingers as an idea came to her. "Stacy, how do you feel about picking starfish?"

"Why? What do you do with them?"

"They're predators, and there are too many in our cove. Starfish is an oyster farmer's nightmare. You wouldn't believe how fast they travel or how many oysters they can eat."

"I've never seen one move, so I always thought starfish stayed in one place for a long time. How fast do they go?"

"When the tide comes in, they can travel between six and twelve inches within a minute. You usually notice them only when the sea levels drop, and they're attached to a rock or something. But when the tide comes in, they start searching for dinner. They usually feed every second night, but when they glom onto our oyster clusters, their suction cups can pry open an oyster and absorb it quickly." Jenna shuddered at how many empty oyster shells she'd probably find on the clusters. "They can eat between ten and thirty oysters per week. And considering oysters take three years to reach their harvest time, they can't mature unless we control the predators."

"Whoa. That's wild. How do you get rid of the problem?" Stacy's eyes widened at the destruction the colorful and deceptively dainty starfish could create.

"Starfish usually need to be pried from a surface on low tide, then dumped in a bucket. There's an easy trail up to a rock ledge about a quarter-mile from shore. You'll need to place them upside down on the ledge so they dry out. Then we bury them later."

"Sounds mean in a way, but I didn't realize their impact. If it's a choice between dead oysters or dead starfish, it's a simple answer. No problem."

"True. Few companies in the Pacific Northwest buy starfish, but oysters are a billion-dollar annual business in BC—and growing. Starfish reproduce like rabbits and live for ten to thirty years, depending on the species. My father was sick for a few years and neglected this cove. I need to save it, so they gotta go."

"I get it. Starfish are attractive with their shape and colors, but they're predators—end of the story for me. I can do that while Liam looks after the wood. Terry said he didn't know how long you'd need us. We can give you two weeks if that helps, maybe a few days extra."

"That would be great, and besides, I probably couldn't afford much more. You guys can take off and explore during your free time after dinner. I've got a map on the wall inside, and I can show you a few places you might like."

"Perfect."

Jenna grinned at the exuberant smiles the couple shared. "You guys can have the bedroom. I'll sleep on the futon in the living room or on my boat. Is that a deal?"

"Of course. Liam's a great cook, too. We'll do our share of cooking and clean-up duties."

"Thank you so much. You don't know how much time and work you'll save me."

"Our pleasure." Stacy giggled. "Shall we bring our bags in the bedroom?"

"Give me half an hour to get my stuff out, and then you can move in."

"Ok. By the way, do you have a casting rod? Can we cast off the dock?" Liam asked.

"Yes, and yes. I can't guarantee what you'll catch but

have fun trying. I like bringing a rod when I kayak, so I'll give you my spare, and you can look through the tackle box."

Two extra pairs of hands were a godsend and worth emptying her bank account. The first week, they looked after the wood and the starfish jobs before constructing a canopy on the work float to shelter them. Between the water glare and the hot sun, Jenna suffered a nasty sunburn on her fair skin and now needed to cover up completely. A hat and sunscreen weren't enough. Lesson learned.

The second week, Wayne spent a day training the three of them on the safety and operation of the HIAB. Liam and Stacy worked alongside Jenna, cleaning the lines and barrels of sludge, the occasional cluster of wild scallops, and errant starfish attached to the barrels. Liam excelled at pumping the water from sinking barrels, sealing and freeing them to bob as they should on top of the water. The stinky smell it produced wasn't fun to deal with, but with a bit of humor, they soon got used to it.

Liam, Stacy, and Jenna were able to pull the work float along the lines with pike poles and took turns using the hydraulic lift to raise the mainlines. Those that looked healthy and worth saving warranted a scrubbing with a stiff, long-handled brush. Jenna noted the stringers that surfaced with shells that looked empty. She'd have to get Terry to come with his skiff, cut them off, and dispose of them into the strait—too much dead weight. At least two mainlines each day was their goal, and it wasn't too hard to manage with the fourteen hours of daylight. They'd stop for lunch around 1:00 p.m., then swim and siesta until the day's heat passed. Then they'd attack the remainder of the line.

Jenna had thirty existing mainlines to clean, and so far, it looked like only a third would be salvageable. Mentally computing seventeen feet per string to start new clusters, multiplied by thirty strings for each mainline, caused Jenna's throat to tighten. Her head swam with the concept of needing five hundred and ten feet of rope for each mainline. With twenty mainlines to re-seed, it was a staggering amount of rope to order. Overwhelmed, Jenna closed her eyes at the thought of ten thousand feet of rope. *Good Lord.* And then there was the labor and the seed also to buy.

She'd need a miracle to pull it off.

~

Six weeks later

WAKING up to a crashing sound of something knocked over, Jenna sprung to her feet, slipped on a housecoat, and ran down the stairs. The angry mumblings had ceased, and now there was absolute silence.

Now what?

Jenna scanned through the shadowy darkness. "Dad? Are you ok?" She kept her voice low, in case it was only the mischievous house cat chasing moonbeams during the night. Penelope liked to prowl, occasionally knocking cups or ornaments off surfaces before. But then again, it could be her dad. He didn't always sleep well and would wander outside to the verandah and 'meditate.'

The trouble was that her dad still needed to use a walker, and sometimes, he didn't turn the lights on in his attempts not to wake her. Then he'd bump into a coffee table, knock it over, occasionally lose his balance, and fall. When Jenna was at the lease, he left the lights turned on both day and night, thank God. Apparently, he didn't have accidents when he was on his own. She wasn't sure if that was the truth or an attempt to make her feel better about leaving him.

"Jenna, go back to bed."

Jenna identified his deep voice coming from the armchair near the window. The nights were getting colder and windy, as usual in mid-October. "Glad to see you're staying inside now. I've told you over and over to keep the light on. Honestly, it wouldn't bother my sleep at all. It would probably make for a more restful night—you wouldn't wake me when you wander about." Jenna teasingly elbowed her dad's shoulder.

"Sorry. I'm just so restless. It's hard for me to stay in bed after three or four hours of sleep." Jenna heard his frustration seeping through.

"What's going on, Dad? Is it pain that bothers you, or are you worried?" Jenna sat on the sofa beside him and put her hand on his.

"Not anything more than usual." Theo massaged his scruff thoughtfully. "I like your friend, Lisa. I'm glad she came and spent a weekend with us. I've heard a lot about her over the years, but this was the first time I'd spent time with her. She's quite the character."

"I agree. But remember when I told you Lisa was changing his name to Lee? Please try getting used to saying he and him. Lee has also applied to have his gender identity changed before going through surgery."

Theo frowned as he shook his head. "Why go through all that? Surgery is a huge commitment, and what if she changes her mind? Can't she be satisfied with being gay?"

"Because she's not 'gay'. She's not a woman who likes women. Lee is transgender." Seeing her father's confused look, she propped herself in the corner of the sofa, prepared to share some insight. "OK, so how about you look at this another way? Every decision Lee makes is made from an instinctive male point of view, not from a woman's perspective, so he wants to see his body in the mirror in sync with that."

"You can't be born in the wrong body, sweetie. Impossible. Whomever she sees in that mirror is who she is."

Jenna jumped up, "Not necessarily. That's up for debate now. How about something to drink, Dad? We're wide awake now, and I sure could use one."

"There's an open bottle of Cabernet in the pantry that your friend left behind. I'd enjoy a glass of ginger ale, too." Theo shifted uncomfortably on the sofa, his uneasiness evident.

Jenna returned with their drinks a minute later and tipped her glass to his. The full-bodied wine mellowed her taste buds, and she leaned back, watching her dad become comfortable again. She grabbed a pillow and hugged it to her chest.

"That's the point, Dad. Lisa—I mean *Lee-* explained the scientific studies performed since MRIs existed[1]. It's not just her—*his* physical look that makes him cringe. He's looked into this identity thing. Research on human sexuality is conducted throughout the world. I can think of three studies that Lee told me about regarding MRI resonance and responses to gender identity. There was a standard theory that when doctors asked certain questions, men and women generally responded to the body they were in. But looking at *brain* patterns with MRIs, some people's answers didn't line up with their birth identity. They identified differently, which implied a transgender personality."

Jenna cocked her head to one side, assessing her father's interest. "Pretty technical stuff, and there's still lots to be studied, but it's opened a whole new dialogue."

"Sorry, you'll need to explain that better." Theo tucked his chin down, lifting his eyebrows slightly.

"Parts of the brain are smaller or larger depending on the sex of a person. The University of Liege exposed voluntary participants to smells called pheromones that produce female or male activity in the brain. The responses on the MRI scans showed how the brain responded."

"Can they do things like that?" Theo's face reflected even more confusion, and his voice echoed hints of skepticism.

"Yes. It's amazing how far science has come in understanding the body and mind." When Jenna saw her dad's eyes cloud with confusion, she simplified further. "Instinctual responses light up different brain parts. When a guy answers a question that lights up the traditionally larger prefrontal cortex usually associated with girls, for example —or vice-versa—there's a chance that they are transgender. There are more categories than that, but that's the one I remember discussing the most with Lee."

"Well, I'll be damned." Theo rubbed his scruff again as his mind tried to wrap around this concept. "So, people like your friend—they don't choose to be transgender? They just are?"

"Depends on who you talk to. For some, the transgender identity starts at an early age, and other people's are triggered at puberty. Of course, there's another school of thought that argues that social interactions, upbringing, and behavioral choices form sexual preference, not brain function."

Jenna sighed. "Lee has struggled since pre-school with his identity and has sought counseling. He recently decided to undergo some surgical treatment and take testosterone."

"Wow. That's a huge step. What do her...*his* parents think of it?"

"They weren't happy at first. They kept hoping that this was just a phase." Jenna said.

"Good God. I hope they're going for counseling, too. This situation must be terrible to deal with for both sides."

"There were a few tough years for sure, but they've come to accept his decision. It's a work in progress." Jenna leaned back and smiled. "And I'm very thankful to be one of his friends. Lee's a great guy."

"Wow." Theo leaned back and ran his fingers through his hair. "Your friend has quite the background. I'd never guessed that she'd been through so much. I mean *he*." Theo rolled his eyes. "This is going to take a while to get used to."

"Yes, but it's worth it." Jenna leaned over and patted her dad's knee. "There's so much more, Dad, although the most important thing to remember is that we love who my friend is, no matter which body he has or whom he chooses to love. Acceptance and respect. That's all that Lee needs."

"It's all everyone needs. It must take a tremendous amount of courage to go through this. Will you tell h-him that I know? And tell him that I may forget, but I'll work on getting it right?"

"I will. I know Lee will appreciate your efforts."

Theo shook his head. "I never knew. Stuff like this isn't common knowledge." He paused a moment. "Thanks for sharing your friend's story."

"You're welcome." Jenna tilted her head to the side and smiled. "It feels like we're becoming more than daughter/father. We're becoming friends. That's the silver lining on this accident—we're getting to know each other as adults."

Jenna paused, looking into her dad's pensive eyes. "I need another glass of wine. I've talked myself dry. Anything else for you, Dad?" Jenna headed to the kitchen.

"I'll take another ginger ale, thanks." Theo switched the

subject. "Lee's endorsement of our application for the Recovery Fund should make a difference."

Jenna nodded. "Our family business has been on the West Coast for a long time, which counts for something. We've always had a good reputation despite a few bad years. When Lee spent a week with me in September, we worked mornings and kayaked afternoons. He loves it there and wants to help any way he can."

Theo cleared his throat. "I'm sorry, Jenna. You've had so much going on in your life, and I didn't even notice. I want to change that." Theo accepted the beverage and continued. "I've sat here thinking I've never acknowledged how proud I am of you for giving up your life to fix my mistakes. I let you down, as well as our family reputation."

"Everyone goes through tough times now and then, Dad. It's not as if there wasn't a cause." Jenna clinked her wine glass to her father's soda. "And look at us. We're making up for lost time, talking for hours. You're still taking your anti-depressants, aren't you?"

"Much as I hate to admit that I need them, yes. It took a few weeks, but it lifted my spirits a lot. Thanks for giving me the push. Dr. Walker's been great, too."

"Push? I had to drag Dr. Walker here for a home visit, so you'd talk to him about it. Best thing I've done since I've been here."

"Maybe. When's Lee coming next? I hadn't seen you laugh like that in months. It felt good to see you so carefree. You two are good for each other."

"Next time I come out from the lease, I'll probably go there. I haven't seen his new condo yet. I can't believe Lee didn't buy something in Bamfield, but it's probably for the best. Bamfield is too small for him to have any privacy. He's renting a basement suite from a co-worker during the week and staying at his condo in Ucluelet on weekends."

"That makes sense. I'm glad you're going to see Lee. You've been working too much. You need to make time for your friends and have fun." Theo put his beverage on the coffee table, eyeing his daughter, a small smile tugging at his lips. "Your aunt told me a young man was in your life before the accident. What happened?"

"Bad timing. Drew and I worked together and started seeing each other. We had a lot in common and enjoyed each other's company. Then, he had an opportunity to accept a transfer to Haida Gwaii, which he accepted. He wanted me to go with him, but I couldn't." Jenna paused. "Although I cared for him a lot, I wasn't ready for a commitment like that. We still keep in touch now and then." Jenna shrugged as if uncertain about the situation.

Jenna got up, poked the glowing embers in the fireplace, and added another log. When she looked at her dad, he seemed sad. "You switched the subject when I asked you what was wrong, why you weren't sleeping. We got sidetracked talking about Lee and Drew, but you're not getting away from my question. Spit it out. What else is bugging you?"

"Gee, I wonder." Her dad's voice was thick with suppressed emotion as he darted his gaze around the room, refusing to make eye contact. "All I can think about is you, working your ass off and the risks involved—it's killing me. I've listened to all your arguments about your capability and strength. Frankly, I'm not convinced. The work you're doing is too dangerous. I should know."

"Look at me, Dad." Jenna's patience and firm tone waited until he turned and faced her. "I'm careful. You've taught me that. If I'm uncomfortable with anything, I call Terry to come and help. Every week I'm there makes me more confident that I can help you return the lease to normal operation."

"Your positive thinking isn't the reality. But with your determination to fix things, you may be even more stubborn than me." Theo puffed a deep sigh, and his shoulders slumped. "Part of this insomnia is guilt for letting things go downhill. If I'd stopped feeling sorry for myself or asked for help instead of hiding my drinking problem, that place wouldn't be in danger. Not only that, but I wouldn't have had the accident that left me like this. Useless." Theo looked away from his daughter and focused on the dark shadows outside.

"You're *not* useless. You're incapacitated." Jenna soothed. "I bet you'll be there too by next spring or summer, directing and helping me restore the lease the way it used to be."

"You're fooling yourself, Jenna. I'll walk again, but probably with a limp. My arm is healing well now, but it'll never be as strong as it was. It drives me crazy that you're handling this instead of living the life you deserve."

"Get over it, Dad. I love being here to help you and working on our lease." Jenna tilted her head to one side and gave him a smirk as she tried to bolster his outlook. "I'm not saying it's a forever job for me, but if we don't clean it up and bring it up to the Pacific Aquaculture standards, we'll lose our oyster license and can't sell it. I'm the third generation of Westerlea Cove, and I'll be damned if we lose it."

"If we lose it, it won't be your fault. This disaster is all on me. I deserve to lose it." Theo's voice was barely audible as he lowered his eyes to the floor.

"Enough, Dad." Jenna's calm and confident voice brought his eyes back to her. "Contact your friends in

DFO and send them a detailed plan of how we'll re-establish it. The lease is still in your name, so I can't do that for you."

Jenna patted his forearm. "I've worked with them, and Lee knows influential people and says that's our best bet. He'll use his persuasion whenever possible. If we can show them how we intend to accomplish it within two years, Lee's sure we'll get it."

Jenna paused as she took in her father's gloomy appearance. His eyes darted away from her to the windy weather outside. "Don't give up. You can do this—you know this business inside and out. Submit a detailed proposal, and with Lee's recommendations, I'm sure we'll get the grant. Let your past mistakes go, Dad. Believe in us, be positive, and let's move forward."

Theo straightened and furthered his argument, raising his voice to stress his point. "But, that's just it. We have to be realistic. What if we don't get the Recovery Fund grant? What if Lee can't convince them we're worth it? We've very little cash to invest. Rope, barrels, seeded shells, and labor costs for the first year alone could run thirty thousand, more or less." Theo paused, and his gaze held a hint of a challenge as he lifted an upward hand toward her. "And then there are the living expenses and unexpected emergencies. Where are we going to get that kind of money?"

"Our home. It's almost mortgage-free."

"Nope, absolutely not." Theo pounded the armrest. "I'm not going to risk losing that *and* the lease."

"Then talk to Aunt Pat. They'd help us out. It would only be temporary."

"Jesus, Jenna! You want me to beg my sister for money? I promised her she'd only have to make monthly payments until you finished university, and she's fulfilled that agreement. The rest is a gift from Meg. What would happen if we couldn't repay them? NO."

Jenna heard the tremble of humiliation in her dad's voice. "Ok, Dad. Let me think of something. I'll figure out a plan." Jenna grabbed her pen and added ideas to explore on the list of supplies they'd need to obtain. She counseled herself not to let her dad's mood swings get her down. After all he'd gone through, it was normal. All Jenna needed to do was give him hope that they'd find a way somehow.

"We need at least thirty, preferably forty thousand dollars, to rebuild Westerlea Cove and save the Sorensen name." Jenna tore the list from her notebook and gave it to her dad. "I'm willing to work my ass off and contact each supplier we've ever used to give us a break. And I want you to consider applying for a temporary line of credit –*not* a mortgage. And I'll see what I can get through my contacts. It's worth a shot. Don't you want to hold your head high again?"

"Yes. Although, I'm not sure I'll ever be able to do that. Right now, that's only wishful thinking." Theo's cheeks reddened as he bared his fears.

"If you keep believing that, it will be. I'm returning to Westerlea Cove in a few days, and I'll be back in two weeks. I gave you my notes, and I want to see a working plan by then." Jenna couldn't help the pleading in her voice, and when she looked into her father's eyes, she saw a smidge of hope and determination. "Please don't give up, Dad. Together, we can do this."

"We'll see. I promise to work on your figures and get up-to-date estimates on our supplies. I'll have it ready for you. Now, go to bed. You've got a long day ahead of you."

"Thanks, Dad. You're probably exhausted, too. We tackled a lot of issues tonight." Jenna leaned over and kissed his cheek, then ruffled his hair. "And don't argue with me. Leave the light on." She giggled at his surprised look, then headed toward the stairs and back to bed, although she doubted either would drift off to sleep quickly. They had discussed so many topics tonight that Jenna questioned whether either could shut their brains off for a while. But by morning, a warm bed and a little rest could inspire them. She already felt more optimistic than when she first came home from the lease.

---

1. The European Society of Endocrinology, March 2018
   The American National Institute of Health, 2008
   The University of Liege, Belgium, 2018

CHAPTER 7

Jenna reviewed her conversation with her best friend, Carla. They enjoyed dinner and drinks together the night before her return to Westerlea Cove. Catching up with Carla's wedding plans kept the conversation light, a welcome diversion for Jenna. She noticed Carla's enquiring gaze and knew the conversation would turn serious.

"Your dad seems to be recuperating well. His attitude has certainly improved." Carla chuckled. "He used to bark at me whenever I visited or checked on him. Now, he's cordial —he must be lonely." Carla's eyes held concern for Jenna.

"I'm glad. He's taking less medication since his pain level has subsided, and he's more clear-headed. Aunt Pat says their visits with him have also been more positive." Jenna grimaced as she acknowledged her father's fight with depression. "Dad's still fighting the black dog, but I see the improvement. He's talking more and less sullen than before."

"Your father still believes you're crazy to try and save the lease. I can't say I disagree. And now we're getting into winter, and the trips back and forth will be dangerous."

Carla sipped on her spicy Caesar, watching for her friend's reaction. "Why are you doing this, Jenna?"

Jenna sighed as she defended her position once again. "Because I can. I want to restore it and the family's reputation." Jenna shrugged her shoulders. "I don't expect you to understand. It might seem ridiculous to you, but it's important to me. We might sell it once we've reached our goal because Dad could be right. His long working days are probably gone, but this represents his pension years. Either Dad will sub-lease or sell it to rebuild his retirement income. Either way, he'll benefit."

"And what about you? And Drew—is he staying in touch? I know you thought he was pretty special."

"I did. I do." Jenna struggled to explain. "Drew knows the situation. I haven't kept in touch as much as I should, but Lee's keeping him in the loop, and they understand. They know how busy I am and the pressures I'm under." Jenna took a long sip of her Crown Royal and soda, stirring the ice cubes before continuing. "I don't have time to think about a relationship. I'm maxed out as it is."

"I know, that's what I'm worried about. You're my forever friend, and I have to say I've never seen you so obsessed with a project." Carla's voice gentled. "I'd hate to see you sacrifice everything that makes you happy, then find out all your efforts to save the lease were wasted." Carla paused. "What's *your* future going to look like?"

"I'm not focusing on that. I can't." Jenna cleared her throat, which had threatened to close up on her. "I'm focussing on a plan to finance Westerlea Cove so that the lease is viable again. Even better would be to restore the Sorensen name." Jenna paused, then shrugged her shoulders. "Maybe I should take the easy way out that Wayne has offered. He'd buy us out at rock-bottom prices, which is about all it's worth now." Jenna shook her head slowly from side to side. "I just can't do it."

Jenna brushed away a tear that threatened to escape, then took a deep breath. "Lee advised me to bring the lease up to minimum standard as quickly as possible, or our license won't be renewed. If we had thirty thousand dollars, we'd have a good chance of that happening. Then Dad's future would look more promising, and I'd have more options."

"Good luck with that. Especially since your dad is against using your home as collateral. By the way, I enjoyed dinner with you and Lee last weekend. He's fun. I'm almost jealous—you two really hit it off. I could see his presence cheered you up."

"We had great times at university with his cousin Sara, and I won't forget them. Being an only child, I'd never experienced the closeness they shared. The whole scene – studying, partying, sharing our ups and downs."

"You had Judy and me beside you since kindergarten," Carla protested.

"I know. I won't forget that either." Jenna quirked her head to the side and patted her friend's hand. "You should know that. You're my rock when I'm home. With Judy married and being a mom, things are different with her. We don't have much in common anymore."

"Is that what will happen when I get married next summer?"

"Of course not. Daryl's a great guy, not like Judy's husband, who won't let her go out anywhere. The last time we went for coffee there, he made me feel uncomfortable— like we were imposing ourselves into their busy schedule."

"He was rude to you a few times, too. I wasn't happy about that, and I don't think Judy was either, but she didn't say anything. I don't understand why Judy doesn't mind that he's jealous of her friends." Carla shrugged. "Maybe she doesn't see it. Her two-year-old son keeps her busy. Being a wife and mother is her priority. When I see her, she apologizes for not staying in touch."

Carla looked up as she felt a hand on her shoulder. "Vaughan, I didn't see you here earlier. I thought you were off on Thursday nights."

"I usually am. The boss called me in to close out. He and his wife are flying to Vancouver for a few days R&R. Mind if I join you two?"

"Pull up a chair. We're talking about Westerlea Cove." Jenna gestured to the spot next to her.

"I've heard you've made quite a difference already. You're crazy for doing it, but I admire your commitment." Vaughan grabbed Jenna's hand and smoothed his thumb over her calloused palm. "The work's too hard for me to bother with —not enough return on the dollar for the labor involved."

Jenna snatched her hand away. "That doesn't surprise me. You like the social life, the easy life. Not me."

"True. But my job's not an easy life either. It might not be physically hard like oyster farming, but it's stressful. Always a smile on your face, even when dealing with an asshole."

"Each to their own, I suppose." Jenna sipped at her Crown Royal and soda.

"I hear you need to raise a lot of money to fix the mess your dad made." Vaughan leaned back in his chair and lifted an eyebrow. "Had any luck?"

"I've applied to the BC Oyster Recovery Fund. I'll get it."

"Maybe. I've heard those grant applications are tough. You must almost not need the money to qualify for them." Vaughan's raised eyebrows challenged Jenna.

"I have friends looking into it," Jenna replied coolly.

"Let me know if you need any help. I have investor friends who could be interested." Vaughan slapped the table lightly with his fingertips. "Ok, ladies, I gotta go. Things to do and people to see." He stood up and scanned the bar, then nodded to a customer as he crossed the room.

"I can't believe you told your brother of my predicament. He's such a blabbermouth. The gossip's probably all over town."

Carla's eyes narrowed at Jenna's accusation. "I didn't say a word. Maybe it's *already* all over town, Jenna. You know nothing stays hidden here for long."

Jenna's eyes dropped to the table, ashamed of her outburst. "I'm sorry, Carla. It's humiliating, that's all."

"You shouldn't be embarrassed. The locals love your family and are rooting for you to succeed." Carla reached over and squeezed her friend's hand tightly. "Shit happens to everybody. We're all proud of you for returning home and helping your dad recuperate."

Mortified by Vaughan's comments, Jenna lost her enthusiasm to extend the evening. She begged off and called a cab to bring her home. Once home, she sat outside on the verandah, her knee nervously bouncing as she grappled with her financial problems. Jenna hugged her coat close to her in an attempt to stay warm.

Jenna had contacted Lee again, letting him know that her dad had agreed to build a proposal and look into other options for them. If anyone could sway the board's decision, it would be Lee. The only problem was that the BC Oyster Recovery Fund was extremely slow at analyzing the applications and issuing the grant. It may not come in time for the spring season, which was crucial for her. Last month, she'd used her Visa to purchase two thousand feet of three-strand stringer rope, but she couldn't afford to do that often.

The cord now came from Texas, and the cost doubled from five years ago with COVID-19 labor shortages and an added tariff.

Never mind. One step at a time. Jenna straightened her shoulders and took a deep breath. She needed to head back to the lease and start prepping some lines.

JENNA DONNED leather gloves and measured and cut the ropes seventeen and a half feet long on the deck. When she'd cut fifty strands, she started weaving a loop at one end for the HIAB to hook onto when harvesting the clusters. After threading the skeins into one another, she carefully burned the ends to seal them from unraveling.

Afterward, Jenna transported them to the beach and hung them on parallel poles between trees to avoid entanglement, as her dad taught her. If the financing came through by spring, she'd hire a crew to help plant each line with seeded oyster shells spaced three feet apart. It shocked her that local oyster wholesalers who usually supplied them with the seeded product could no longer keep up with demand. Now, most oyster leases needed to arrange a sale from Washington State within a twenty-four-hour turnaround time or the seeded shells could die.

Another cost. There seemed to be so much more regulation, documentation, and extra fees to pay than when her dad first acquired the lease from his father. Even the Department of Transport now required an exact map of their oyster lines to ensure the lease didn't interfere with marine traffic. It was not an issue in their isolated areas but another bureaucratic, time-consuming task. Liability insurance on the work float and oyster skiff increased by two thousand dollars annually. No wonder her father felt overwhelmed when he was at his lowest. It was daunting and not surprising that her father wondered why he should even bother.

Preparing the stringers for spring seeding was a defiant act of hope that kept Jenna optimistic. Idle hands would only encourage a negative attitude, so after finishing one job, she found another chore to occupy her mind and muscles.

Jenna returned from shore, tied up the aluminum boat, and showered inside. The hot water streaming over her aching body soothed her, even if it stung her hands. She shampooed her hair, the apple scent reminding her of her mom. Jenna knew her mom would be proud of her effort in the family lease, even though it meant disrupting her personal life. She stood under the cooling spray, rinsing it, and promised her mom it wouldn't be forever. Her dad was getting stronger every month, and she believed he'd take it back one day. Jenna looked at her hands and sighed. Calloused and rough, they could've belonged to a man. No wonder her dad worried.

Jenna heard the crackling of the VHF, calling Westerlea Cove, and quickly shut off the water, grabbed a towel, and ran to answer.

"Westerlea Cove, Jenna speaking."

"Hey, Jenna. How're things over there?"

"Who's speaking?" Jenna couldn't identify the voice.

"Vaughan. The weather looks promising this coming weekend, and I've friends here who want to tour Clayoquot Sound. Would you be interested in making five hundred bucks? We want to moor at your dock for a few nights."

"Five hundred bucks? For two nights? That's a hefty price to pay."

"It might be three nights. These guys are loaded. They don't even blink at spending that kind of money. I could've asked a few other places, but I figured you could use the cash. What do you think?"

"Hmm. I could use the money, but I feel uncomfortable about strangers here. Would your friends expect me to cook for them? What about partying? You know I'm not a fan of drunken idiots."

"They have a forty-foot Boston Whaler. All they need is onboard. They won't have to bother you for anything except dock space."

"I don't know, Vaughan, although I have to admit that it's tempting. How many people?"

"Two guys and me. No pressure, Jenna. Let me know tomorrow so I can check around if you aren't interested."

Jenna knew other people would be listening to this conversation, and it wouldn't surprise her if they would contact Vaughan if she didn't jump on it. "OK, Vaughan. If you vouch for them, I'm sure it'll be fine. When will you arrive?"

"Thursday, probably around 4:00 p.m. Do you need us to bring you anything?"

"If I have company, I better get a few extras. I'll put an order in at the Co-op if you don't mind."

"No problem. I'm glad you're taking this. This rental could end up being a cash cow in the summertime."

"I don't think so. That's a crazy time for me. It's quiet now, and I can use the money, so thanks for thinking of me, Vaughan. I'll see you soon."

Jenna signed off, then moved to the bedroom to put her housecoat on. She brushed her hair and returned to the living room, still thinking about Vaughan's offer. She added another piece of firewood to the wood stove, then sat in front of it, slowly running her fingers through her hair and stretching it out to dry.

Perfect timing.

She'd apply the cash to her Visa when she returned home next week. Maybe Jenna could get a few more bookings like that through Vaughan. So far, all she'd done was shell out money, and nothing had come in except the income from their home rental. And half of that went to paying expenses on the cottage. Because she was looking after her dad, she could collect an EI government benefit for six months, which also helped. Always frugal, Jenna racked her brain to think of possible ways to cut financial corners.

Maybe this was a sign that things were going to change.

Jenna slipped an old Natalie Cole disc into the battery-operated CD player. She was one of her dad's favorite singers when he wanted easy-listening music. Her voice was so relaxing and soothing. It seemed perfect for this evening. A memory of her and Drew's slow dancing popped into her mind before she could stop it. *Not now*, she chastised herself. Jenna went to the fridge, cracked open a Kokanee, and curled up on the futon. Dare she hope?

THURSDAY MORNING DAWNED CLEAR, with only a light breeze creating a chop on the water. Jenna took her tin boat to the outside line to harvest the wild scallops, then headed to gather her prawn trap. She'd offer Vaughan and his friends some fresh seafood for their first night when they arrived, a sign of hospitality.

She checked her dad's map of his best prawning grounds and set a trap yesterday. The yield was only about twenty pounds but more than enough for one or two nights. Jenna put the scallops and prawns on ice in a cooler for later and grabbed a Kokanee to enjoy while waiting for the company to arrive. Vaughan would bring her grocery order, including fresh garlic, butter, lemons, and two French bread baguettes. Simple and delicious. Her mouth watered at the treat. Jenna was sure they'd be out fishing while exploring the Sound, and they'd probably enjoy halibut or salmon for dinner on other nights.

The deck and cabin sparkled in the bright sunshine, filling Jenna's heart with pride. It was such a change in only three months. She sat on a deck chair and breathed in the salty, cool breeze, appreciating the beauty as she sipped her beer. Things were slowly improving, and she cherished every step toward recovery.

Terry often appeared after dinner with a couple of beers to share. After an embarrassing romantic advance, Terry accepted their relationship to be of friends only. *Thank God.* Jenna valued his friendship and likened it to what she imagined was a big brother relationship. Caring, light, and always supportive. He'd be joining them tomorrow night to meet Vaughan and his friends.

It was essential for Jenna that his friends knew she wasn't alone at Westerlea Cove. Jenna didn't feel isolated at her lease. Between chats on the VHF, Terry or Wayne's visits, and the odd passerby, she felt connected, as if her presence was noticed. With the built-in GPS, Jenna was confident with her abilities to navigate 'MissBHaven' in storms or fog. She was the fourth generation Sorensen, able to operate this lease for as long as possible, even if she was a woman.

The days of physical exhaustion and waking up with sore, aching body parts were over. The muscles Jenna developed also made her more self-confident. Jenna wouldn't be looked at as a weak female, easily intimidated. Her biceps were more pronounced, as were her forceps, back, and leg muscles. Even Lee noticed and approved of the difference.

Of course, she'd also learned to work smarter, making the tasks more manageable. She felt as powerful and self-assured as any of her neighboring leaseholders. Barring her financial status, of course. But that would come. The recognition and growing respect for her dedication to re-establishing Westerlea Cove was widespread and deeply appreciated by her father, their long-time friends, and fellow associates.

Bundled in a windproof jacket, Jenna dozed off in the warm sunshine with an afghan stretched across her knees. In her dreams, her mom was paddling the canoe toward her. Still a distance away, she paused and waved to Jenna before pointing to the eagle swooping down to pluck a fish from the water. Her laughter floated over the water. Jenna slowly awoke as the drone of a boat approaching eased into her consciousness. She smiled at the memory of the vivid interlude with her mom and gave thanks for the visit. It seemed to happen more often now that Jenna had things under control and could find time to relax and enjoy the family legacy.

A rumbling sound caught Jenna's attention. She stood with her hand framing her eyebrows, watching the approaching white Boston Whaler with a command bridge. She sighed. *Holy shit, they must be loaded.*

Two short toots greeted her four hundred yards out. Vaughan was throwing fenders over to protect the hull from the deck. Jenna smiled and waved high above her head. She neared the deck edge, preparing to receive a spring line for mooring. Wow, this cruiser looked huge.

"Welcome to Westerlea Cove," Jenna shouted as the

captain killed the triple three hundred horse-powered engines.

Vaughan jumped from the boat and ran to hug her. "Thanks, Jenna. Let me handle this. I'll introduce you to Clint and Murray in a minute." Vaughan took the line and sprinted to the front cleat, allowing enough angle before quickly hitching the knot. Another man pulled the stern line tight and knotted it to the rear cleat when Vaughan finished securing the front one. He strolled toward Jenna, extending his hand.

"You must be Jenna. I'm Murray. Thank you for allowing us to park at your home." His deeply tanned skin contrasted with his sun-bleached, curly hair, making him look like a Greek God.

Jenna looked up at the towering, confident male as he gripped her hand. *Wow.*

"You're welcome." Jenna nervously scanned his face. "Are you new to the area? I haven't seen you around Tofino before."

"In the past two or three years, my partner and I've traveled this area several times from Seattle, Washington. It's a beautiful place to relax and escape the rat race. I doubt that we've crossed paths. We usually moor in Bamfield and Ucluelet, then head north along the coast toward Port Hardy and Haida Gwaii. Sometimes, we return to the eastern side of Vancouver Island before heading home."

"Wow. I hope you'll be comfortable at my humble dock. If you'd like to know anything about the area, I have maps inside with my dad's favorite places."

"Ah...insider knowledge." Murray smiled, the creases by his startling blue eyes crinkling. "Nothing like knowing the hidden corners to get the real feel of a place."

"True. I'm sure Vaughan has shown you a few places on

your way here." Jenna threw the comment over for her friend to join in.

"I sure have. Yesterday, we explored Lemmens Inlet on Meares Island. There's a large oyster lease up there, too." Vaughan puffed his chest in self-importance.

"I know. My dad knew the Arnet family, who started it decades ago. The grandson owns it now. Best nutrient-rich waters around for oyster growing. We wait three years to harvest ours, but they can shave six months off their growing season."

"This looks pristine here, too," Murray commented.

"It is, but we don't get the same currents." Jenna glanced beyond Murray and watched his partner approach. She sent Vaughan a questioning look.

Vaughan turned as he heard footsteps approaching. "Jenna, I'd like you to meet Clint. He's the owner of the *Vagabond*."

"Hello, Clint." Jenna extended her hand

Clint looked around twenty years older than Murray, maybe in his early fifties, with gray tickling the temples of dark chestnut hair. Sunglasses shaded his eyes, and his thin lips were somber.

"Hello. I understand you're a friend of Vaughan and his family." Clint clasped her hand briefly, then stuffed it in his jacket's pocket.

"Yes, I am. I've known the Walsh family since I started kindergarten. My dad and I rent his parent's cottage for a year."

"Hmm. There must be a story behind that." Clint raised his eyebrows and smiled, inviting more information.

"My dad was in a bad accident, and he's recuperating. I returned home to help."

"Nice to have family and friends you can count on."

Clint half turned, eyeing the lease and the cabin. "So, how long have you worked at this place?"

"It's been in our family for almost sixty years. It's a long story, but I'm working on bringing it back to its former glory." Jenna pointed toward the equipment and shed on the shore. "It's a lot of work, but I'll get there."

"I'm sure you will, young lady." Clint nodded his head and then strolled down the dock. Relieved, Jenna blew out a breath she'd held. She noted his eyes were thankfully on the scenery, not her weathered dock. Jenna didn't need to explain herself or her situation to anyone, especially rich know-it-alls. Murray seemed approachable, but Clint seemed aloof and made her feel uncomfortable.

"Have you toured a facility like this before?" Jenna asked Murray.

"No, all I understand is that it's very labor-intensive and risky."

"That it is. But look where you get to live." Jenna lifted her hand and swung it around her. "This is mighty hard to beat."

"Will you show me your place? I feel like stretching out."

"Sure. Do you want to have anything to eat or drink first?" Jenna was pleased with the interest Murray took. At least he didn't ooze entitlement as his partner did.

"No, we're good. We ate a late brunch. I'm ready if you're ready," Murray lifted his eyebrows and tilted his head, smiling.

"Alright, then. Give me a minute, and we'll hop in the tin boat and go to shore."

"In that?" Murray frowned at the fourteen-foot aluminum boat, barely two feet above the waterline.

"Of course! Don't worry. It's safe within the cove in almost any weather. Grab a lifejacket, and let's go."

After teasing Murray about his nervous entry, Jenna untied the craft and sat at the stern, her arm reaching back to steer the nine-horsepower engine. She decided to show him the mainlines, pointing below the surface to the stringers below. "We seed our stringer lines with oyster shells three feet apart. Each shell is professionally prepped to guarantee around a dozen oysters per shell. As the oysters grow, they form the huge clusters you see. The blue barrels keep the lines floating and off the bottom to help avoid predators."

"Vaughan told me about your dad's accident and that you've been doing most of the work here. That's damn hard work."

"It is. See that machine on the work float over there?" Jenna pointed to the right. "It makes my life much easier. It's called a HIAB, and I use it to hook the lines and lift them so I can clean them off or harvest them. I can't do it all by myself as the work's too dangerous when you're lifting two or three hundred pounds of clusters, but we don't harvest every month." Jenna grinned at Murray's surprised expression that she would tackle that herself. "Don't worry. We hire a two-person crew for three or four days to help us. They cut the clusters and drop them in 4x4 square braillers that they haul in our skiff to the wholesalers. With that cycle, we can turn over our stock and always have annual sales ready for harvest."

"And you seed all these lines yourself?" Murray looked at her with a worried expression.

"My dad did. And his father before him. It's never done all at once. It's cyclical. I'm not sure I'll be able to do as much as they did; I'll probably need to hire someone to help me. But once this lease is fully viable again, I think I might figure out a routine that allows me to do it. Dad should've recuperated by then, so we should be fine."

Jenna gunned the engine as they headed to a sandy section onshore, driving the tin boat four feet up onto the sand. She laughed at the surprised look on Murray's face. "You can't be shy about things here—you have to attack situations."

"I see that." Murray wobbled side to side, his hand clutching the heavy aluminum boat as he exited. Jenna followed him, and together, they pulled the boat farther up.

"The sun's gone down a bit, but you'll see our storage shed through the shade beyond those trees. I keep our kayaks, power saw, and miscellaneous equipment in there. I even store the engine inside when I go into town for any length of time—no sense in tempting thieves." Jenna paused as she looked around, pointing to areas and explaining her operation to Murray. "There's a lean-to on the side for firewood to use in my woodstove during the winter. And when I make up the stringers for seeding, I hang them on a pole onshore so they don't become a bird's nest in the spring."

"Wow." Murray looked at Jenna with added respect. "You certainly have a system here. You must work dawn to dusk."

"Kind of. Most of our work schedules follow the tides. When the cove is shallow, we get rid of starfish who love to eat our oysters and clean any mussels or sludge that accumulate anywhere. It's an ongoing patrol to save our harvest. And, it's easier to harvest oysters on high rather than low tides, so we plan our work week on the lunar calendar."

Jenna pointed to the trail ahead. "Want to go on a short hike?"

"Sure, that'd be great. I love boating, but I need to stretch my legs whenever I can, or I get antsy."

"We're going to a stream that empties into a deep pool

on top of the first ridge. We have a waterline from there to the float. It's a great place for summer skinny dipping and tanning when you're itching to get off the float and avoid looking at everything you still need to do."

"That sounds fantastic." Murray's eyes sparkled with anticipation.

"It is. Farfar, that's Norwegian for Grandpa, built a stone firepit there. We often spent an afternoon around the bonfire in the fall when it became too cool to swim." Jenna climbed the ridge, occasionally looking back to engage the Greek God following her. "I take time out to enjoy life there. My favorite form of relaxation is kayaking. I'll pack a lunch, bring a fishing rod, and go where my heart takes me. Usually, it's Flores Island, but I often go to Whitepine Cove on the peninsula across from us or visit Terry or Wayne at his lease. Then the other summer inhabitants have cozy float houses in bays up here that will wave me in for a visit."

"So, you don't get lonely out here? Most women your age would miss the social life."

"Not me. I keep busy and go home for three to five days every second week." Jenna scrambled through the brush that had overgrown since her last hike and concentrated on the trail ahead.

Jenna could hear Murray clambering up the steep incline of the final approach to Paradise Pool, the name her mom called their swimming hole. She smiled, amused that he was finding it a challenging route. He was probably a city jogger.

"Ta-da!" Jenna stood on a rock ledge and spread her arms below her. Probably fifty feet wide by two hundred, the deep blue waters beckoned. The trickling sounds of a nearby waterfall proclaimed its source. To the right was evidence of vinyl hosing leading from the far edge of the pool through the bushes toward Westerlea Cove.

"That's amazing." Murray picked his way to the edge and looked inside. There's no shore. It's a canyon."

"More like a deep crevice, so we don't bring anyone up here who can't swim. That creek you hear becomes a good-sized waterfall in the winter. Over the years, my family has improved upon protecting the waterline that supplies our cabin, but occasionally, we still have to follow it, see where it's crimped, and fix it. Once in a blue moon, a tree will blow over and crush it, or a storm will pull it apart near the shoreline."

"I keep saying amazing, but I mean it. So much prepara-tion goes into a place like this, things I hadn't imagined." Murray sat down, removed his shoes and socks, and dipped his feet into the water. "Not bad. Not warm, but not freezing either."

"We call it refreshing. But in the winter, it's too damn cold. If your line stops working, you pray that it's nothing that you need to go underwater to fix." Jenna sat beside him and followed suit, her feet swishing the water back and forth.

"Uh." Murray's eyebrows lifted as he began a sentence, then stopped.

"What?"

"I'm embarrassed to ask, but who knows if I'll ever be here again."

"Well then, ask. What's the worst thing that could happen? I say No. That's it, end of story."

"When you put it that way, why not?" Murray turned to Jenna. "Would it be ok if I went for a skinny dip here?" Murray's expression changed as he watched for Jenna's reac-tion. "Or I could keep my briefs on."

His hopeful, bashful look reminded Jenna of kids she used to babysit, and she burst out laughing. "Strangers don't get to skinny dip. If you leave your briefs on, then go ahead. I'm warning you that it's colder than you think in October."

"I love cold water. I prefer it over warm water for swimming. It must be my Nordic blood, I guess. Will you join me?"

"Nope, afraid not. I'm not going back sopping wet, and I'm not going swimming in my underwear. Feel free to enjoy it. Do you want privacy? I can always head back." Embarrassed, Jenna cleared her throat and avoided eye contact.

"No, you don't have to. I'm not shy." Murray flung his jacket and T-shirt aside, removed his jeans, and stood up.

Jenna noticed his skin pebbling with the cool October air. She watched his lithe, muscular form follow the pool's edge several feet until he found a good toe hold. Lifting his arms straight ahead, he jumped high, grabbing his right knee to his chest, performing a perfect cannonball. Water splashed probably ten feet in the air. Surprised, Jenna clapped her hands in delight. This guy was a blast.

Murray broke the surface and bobbed up and down. "Woohoo! This is great. Are you sure you won't join me? It's so liberating."

"Not a chance." Jenna brushed the water droplets from her hair and swiped away the dampness on her clothes. She scrambled away from the edge before he decided to do something foolish.

"Fine. Chicken." Murray smiled, then turned and began swimming overhand from one end of the pool to the other. Five minutes later, he stopped, turned, and floated on his back, his arms slowly treading water to keep him in place. His eyes gazed at the trees around them and the blue sky above until his lips began to turn purple.

"Ready to head back?" Jenna decided he probably needed prodding even though he must've been freezing. "I've hot chocolate and peppermint schnapps to chase away the chills. What do you say?" Jenna began putting her shoes and socks on again.

Murray came to the edge, propped his elbows on the rock, and rested his chin on his hands. A daring glint came into his eye. "Come on, Jenna. Come for a dip. I won't look."

Jenna felt a tremor run through her body. "Not likely." She felt her face flush and noticed his lips curled upwards as he saw her face warm. With his looks and physique, she guessed he was used to women falling all over him. Jenna admitted he was a pleasure to watch, and she felt a stir of desire deep down in her belly. Jenna felt her pulse quicken and suddenly felt nervous.

What the hell? She didn't even know this guy. Jenna got to her feet and began heading down the slope. "Follow the trail when you're ready, and I'll meet you at the boat. You can't get lost." Jenna sprinted down the path, surprised by her jumbled feelings from Murray's teasing.

Once docked back at the cabin, Jenna went inside and boiled water in the kettle. Taking the Tim Horton's hot chocolate tin from the cupboard, she scooped three large tablespoons into mugs for her and Murray. She found the peppermint schnapps and waited for the water to boil.

Jenna could hear the men outside teasing Murray about his unkempt appearance. She hoped Murray wouldn't be embellishing the experience. That would be way too embarrassing. Jenna stirred the mix until it dissolved, added a generous dollop of schnapps, and then brought it outside.

"Murray's a bit of a daredevil, swimming at this time of year," Jenna commented after sipping her chocolate. "His lips were turning blue, for heaven's sake."

Vaughan laughed as he glanced back and forth between the two of them. "That's probably not the only thing that turned blue." The snide remark mortified Jenna, sending her back inside the cabin and making Vaughan laugh even louder.

Men. Sexual innuendoes at every chance. Jenna felt her face heat up at Vaughan's juvenile attempt at humor. She sipped the steaming hot chocolate, enjoying the peppermint after-taste as she gazed outside toward Flores Island. Jenna sat on the futon and wondered what she'd set herself up for. It would be a long weekend if that kind of talk kept up. Hearing a double tap at the door, she turned as Vaughan's head peeked around it.

"Is it safe? Can I come in?"

"Sure, as long as you leave your potty mouth outside."

"Sorry, Jenn. I didn't mean anything by it. Just guy talk, you know."

Jenna cocked an eyebrow at him, letting him know she knew precisely the sexist dialogue that happened out of earshot. "What can I do for you?"

"The guys want you to join them for dinner. Are you hungry?"

"I am, but I thought you'd eat later."

"All the fresh air has sharpened our appetites. I've your groceries inside the boat. Do you want me to bring them inside?

"Yes, that would be great. I harvested a few dozen oysters, then picked up fresh prawns and scallops this morning to share for your first night. How does that sound?"

"Scallops? It isn't often that I see those fresh."

"They appeared on a few of my outside stringers, so I've been saving them for a special treat."

"Awesome. You don't have to fuss over us, though.

Murray is an excellent cook. He told me that after university, he took a year off and went to culinary school, but Murray didn't like the chefs' hours. He joined the family business and said he's never regretted the decision. Although, I'll bet he'd jump at the chance to create a meal from your harvest."

"I'll show him what I have in the cooler. Maybe he'll let me watch, and I can learn a few things from him." Jenna rinsed her empty mug and placed it in the sink, listening to Vaughan get her supplies from the boat.

Jenna approached her cooler and opened it, beckoning the men to inspect the contents. "Have you seen anything fresher than this? I picked them this morning."

"Look at the meat on that scallop," Murray knelt on one knee to look closer. He touched the firm flesh and ran his finger around the side muscle. "It's almost peachy. I haven't seen that before."

"It happens. My dad calls them blushing scallops; as you can guess, they're the females. Their color varies in depth depending on the season. When you cook them, they lighten in color." Jenna snapped her fingers. "I almost forgot—Vaughan, if you go to the right side of the dock near the Adirondack, would you please pull up the bag net? Does anyone else have experience shucking oysters?"

"I'm not an expert, but I've used a shucking knife before. Let me handle that." Clint offered.

"Thanks. There's a stainless-steel bowl to pop our shellfish into." Jenna pointed to them on the picnic table.

Murray eyed the delicacies before him. "I've some angel hair pasta that would be wonderful with the prawns and scallops. Do you mind if I take over cooking duties?"

"Not at all. As long as I can watch you prepare. I have fresh garlic, lemons, and baguettes to go along with it if you like."

"Great. And I have shaved Grana Padano Parmesan. Clint can look after the oysters and wine. We'll light the barbecue and cook the oysters on the half-shell. Oh man, that'll be a feast fit for royalty." Murray gestured enthusiastically as he planned the meal, every inch the sous-chef he'd once thought of becoming. He looked over at Vaughan. "And you will be in charge of dishes and clean up."

"Don't you have paper plates?" Vaughan elbowed Murray. "I never wash dishes at home. I didn't think I'd need to do them here."

"Nothing tastes as good on a paper plate. Quit whining." Murray retorted.

Jenna entered the cabin for a large mixing bowl and sat beside the cooler. "Pull up a chair, Vaughan. We might as well start cleaning the prawns, and I'll let Murray finish shelling and cleaning the scallops."

"Let me get a beer first." Vaughan returned with an armful of Stella Artois, handing everyone a chilled brew. "To the best seafood available on the West Coast." Vaughan offered a challenge. "At least it should be if Murray's as good a chef as he professes."

Murray laughed and shook his head. "That, my friend, just earned you extra KP duties. Never, ever doubt my abilities."

The back-and-forth banter continued while everyone set to shelling and deveining the seafood. The prawn tails were longer than Jenna's index finger, and Jenna's mouth watered, just thinking how Murray might prepare them. It would be delicious. Murray presented Jenna with a misshapen pearl hidden underneath one of the larger oyster's flesh. She rolled it in her palm, feeling the imperfection and the coolness against her skin. That something as ugly as an oyster could produce wonders, even as imperfect as this one, never ceased to amaze her. Jenna looked up and saw Murray appraising her. She felt her cheeks warm. *Whew, that man was hot.* Quickly, she excused herself to bring the pearl inside to safety and calm her racing heart.

Jenna slipped on a jacket and rejoined the men outside. The chatter waned as the sun sank into the horizon, the colors overwhelming their senses. As the sun dipped below the slit of the horizon southwest of them, the water took on a purple hue. With the pinks and mauves painting the sky, the effect silenced them.

Murray was the first to break the hush from the incredible sight. "If I hadn't seen it myself, I wouldn't believe the water could turn that color."

"It doesn't often get this vibrant. The air temperature, time of year, and location dictate if and when it happens. Roy Vickers, a famous local First Nations artist, has painted a series of ocean scenes with similar tones. He paints with vivid colors like we saw tonight."

"I saw his gallery on Campbell St. but didn't go in. I certainly will when we drop Vaughan off. Maybe I'll invest in a few limited editions if they're as beautiful as you say."

"I think they're majestic, but each to their own. And speaking of taste, when are we going to start cooking?"

Murray laughed. "It sounds like you're getting hungry. Come on, let's get started. I have fresh herbs and spices in our galley that I like to use. Why don't you join me there?"

"Give me ten minutes. I want to clean up before heading over there. I'm feeling grubby." Jenna wiped her hands on her jeans with a half-smile.

"You got it. See you soon."

CHAPTER 8

The rumble of triple three hundred hp mercs penetrated Jenna's deep sleep. *Already?* She jumped from her bed, brushed her teeth, and threw her housecoat on, belting it as she exited her cabin. Jenna's heart palpitated with growing unease at their early departure. Was there a problem? She saw Murray place fresh ice and probably a fish filet in Jenna's cooler before closing it shut.

Murray wiped his hands on his jeans as he noticed Jenna's arrival. "Sorry if we woke you. When Clint decides he's had enough, he's ready to go instantly."

"That's ok. It surprised me that you were leaving this early." Jenna wrapped her unruly wavy hair behind her ears, folded her arms, and watched the men prepare to leave.

Vaughan unleashed the front cleat, then threw her the rope. "Hang onto that, will you?"

When Vaughan tossed the fenders in the boat, she glanced at Clint, staring at her. It gave Jenna goosebumps, and she rubbed her arms to banish them. Clint disembarked from the boat and approached Jenna.

"Thank you, young lady. You have a beautiful location

here, and I admire your work." Clint extended his hand to shake.

Jenna grasped his and felt him pull her to him. He leaned over and murmured in her ear. Flustered, Jenna stepped back. "I'm glad you enjoyed your time here. Maybe we'll meet again."

Clint nodded and retreated to the *Vagabond*, leaving Jenna speechless.

Murray approached Jenna, noting her uneasiness. "Time to head out. A couple of days flies by quickly. Maybe next time, we can extend the visit. Sorry that we woke you."

"Is anything wrong?" Jenna's eyes darted between the three men, two more nervous than the captain.

"No, but he has a few things he needs to check out. A problem with the supply chain. My uncle has a way of motivating people, so I'm sure it'll be fine."

"He's your uncle? He looks intimidating sometimes. Does he *ever* smile?"

"It's more professional if we don't advertise our relationship. That knowledge is for family and friends only. Not many other people know about it. But you're right. In the past few years, Clint has been more aloof than ever. Smiling doesn't get results in his books. He reminds me of Liam Neeson: tough on the outside, but when push comes to shove, he's there for his family. Although I must admit, sometimes he's so laser-focused on his businesses that he's oblivious to everything else."

"If you say so. I enjoyed this weekend. I've told Vaughan I'm too busy to have people moor here in the summer months. But if you're in the area in the spring or fall, maybe we can do a repeat."

Murray approached Jenna, putting an arm on her

shoulder and drawing her to him for a hug. "I've enjoyed it too. Do we have to go through Vaughan to see you?"

"Why not? He balances the two of you well—and he does dishes." Jenna pulled away from his hug and smiled.

"I'll be back in Tofino in about a month. Clint's interested in acquiring some property coming on the market soon. It's on the left as you come into Tofino. It used to be a private campground, and Clint wants me to look the place over. I want to take you out for dinner when I get a firm arrival date. Could you manage to be home for it?"

"Probably." Jenna's heartbeat quickened. Something was different with him. Warm and affectionate without the touchy-grabby routine. "Let me know the details, and I'll see what I can do."

"I respect you, Jenna." Murray paused as his gaze flitted over her features. "I want to be able to help you. Would you consider it?"

Murray's eyes held a hint of affection that made her skin prickle. Jenna wasn't sure what was behind his offer. *Hope? Desire?* "If you're considering purchasing it, the answer is no, thanks. I've something to prove here, and I don't see a purchasing scenario panning out anytime soon." Jenna spread her hands, lifted an eyebrow, and gave him a lopsided grin to remove any sting. "But, if you have a few weeks to spare and want to earn basic wages while working with me, I'd think about that. Although, I'm not sure if you could handle the callouses."

Murray's eyebrows raised, a tiny smile flitting across his lips. "Ha. I love challenges. We'll figure it out." He looked over at the captain's chair as the motors revved. "Time to cast off and head out. See you soon."

Murray winked at her, untied the rear cleat, and hopped into the Boston Whaler. Jenna gave the bow a push outward, then waved to the crew. The engine slipped into reverse and edged beyond the slow zone before the triple mercs growled powerfully and shot the boat forward.

WATCHING his nephew hop on board, Clint abruptly turned his face aside. Murray's blue eyes held a mischievous glint that clenched his guts. They were identical to his son's eyes and just as troublesome. Murray had his mother's curly blonde hair, thank God. Otherwise, he doubted he'd be able to spend much time with his nephew. It'd been three years since his son, Nate, had died. And at times, Murray's blue eyes tore open the pain Nate's absence inflicted.

Clint checked his instrument panel, then turned and skipped up the stairs to the command bridge to take over piloting from there. He heard Murray and Vaughan teasing each other and tuned them out. Searching the inlet ahead, Clint concentrated on his breathing to slow his thundering heartbeat echoing in his ears. The phone call he received this morning made him nervous.

Real nervous.

Clint thought of his son again, why he'd taken this risk, and wondered if he'd reacted too quickly. Absently, he rubbed his palm in a circle on his chest, easing the tightness that often overcame him.

It was too late now.

Thinking of Nate, so much like himself at that age, was sometimes a blessing, but his absence could also stab him with his irreplaceable loss. Always a bold and fearless risk-taker who loved to surf, Nate became a victim of a shark attack that mangled his right calf while waiting to catch a wave off Morro Bay in California. Nate was lucky not to have suffered more than flesh wounds and began rehab as soon as he was strong enough. Nate played the tough card, and Clint had no idea of the pain or the oxycontin medication that Nate relied upon. Thank God his mother, Melanie, had predeceased Nate. Otherwise, his wife would've probably shot him for putting business before their son's welfare – no matter how old their son was.

Clint covered the pain of losing his wife from breast cancer by going into overdrive. Too busy launching an international shipping enterprise to expand his business empire, Clint tossed aside the twirling unease when his son stopped returning his calls. Time flew, and when Clint realized that it had been over six months since he'd spoken directly to Nate, he had his office reach out first to his home, then to his physical therapist.

Clint deliberated his options when he heard they severed treatment because of several missed appointments. After all, Nate was an adult living in California. He should've been responsible for attending therapy without being checked on by his father. Clint told himself not to be a helicopter parent and that Nate wouldn't appreciate being nagged or cajoled into treatment.

Negotiating international shipping and environmental concerns was more stressful than he'd anticipated, and eventually, he let his office handle all personal calls until his return. NIMBY activists in southern California made the price of transporting rock between the western states shoot to astronomical levels. The new contract to ship bulk gravel fed by a conveyor belt from Indigenous Vancouver Island land to a deep-sea terminal in Desolation Sound, then down to Los Angeles, became a license to print money.

The volcanic makeup of the island rock made it dense, so less cement was needed to bind it, which meant less heating and shrinkage while curing. The product became the most sought-after commodity for high-rise buildings. Clint soon realized he needed Murray to take over the network of supplying anything and everything for landscape and wholesale centers, the original company started by his grandfather. This arrangement allowed Clint to concentrate solely on his new enterprise. The system worked well until three summers ago when Clint returned from his last series of business negotiations.

Sometimes, Murray's nonchalant attitude towards money and the family business reminded him of Nate, and he wondered if he could save his nephew from the temptations and arrogance of being rich. Nate and Murray thought they were above the cut, unanswerable to society's rules. In a rash decision, he had whispered a warning to Jenna, whom he believed was probably too naïve for her own good. One could only hope that would be enough. He didn't need to alienate his sister's only son.

Clint breathed in for a count of six, then exhaled until he emptied his lungs, then slowly sucked in another precious breath of oxygen, pushing the guilt away from overwhelming him. What a colossal mistake he'd made. It was a complete gut punch that still had him reeling at the most unexpected times.

If he could do it over, Clint *would* be the helicopter parent—at least he could've told himself he tried to set his son straight. Nate had needed him, and he'd been too busy building the family empire. He thought they had lots of time for Nate to grow up and become involved. But his only son died alone in his apartment, propped up in bed, with the television on. He'd never forgive himself or face his girlfriend Serena, who'd found him. *How's that for a father?* Clint growled his disgust yet again.

Regrets wouldn't make one bit of difference.

The pounding in his ears slowly subsided, and his hands steadied on the wheel as the trembling wore off. The *Vagabond* was Clint's release, his sanctuary where business was never allowed to intrude. It's where he went to relax and get lost in nature and the innocent beauty that made his life worthwhile. Now, he'd tainted the innocent pleasures the Vagabond offered him. Clint ran his hand through his wind-tangled hair, still struggling to control his anxiety.

Clint remembered Nate's therapist's pleas to help him build a supply chain to help others with no financial means or Medicaid get addiction treatment. At the time, his guilt for being an absent father made him eager to make amends, bend the rules, and help the less fortunate. He had to arrange the contacts, make the initial payment between parties, and then the Recovery Centre would take over. Getting the product from China to the shipping terminal in Canada and then transporting the product to Los Angeles on the bulk gravel ships was, no doubt, illegal. But, according to Dr. Norwell, *one* shipment could help finance several treatment centers the average person could afford.

So, he agreed. Clint took several months of discreet sleuthing to connect with a supplier for Dr. Norwell that would provide low-cost opioids similar to methadone and suboxone for those unable to afford addiction medication. He made an In Memoriam annual donation of a half million dollars, ensuring the long-term success of the Pacific Recovery Center, complete with a new wing named after Nate. The rest was up to Dr. Norwell and the Center. He wasn't sure how they'd manage it, but he didn't want to know. *God help him.*

"Hey, Unc." Clint heard the shout, then his nephew's quick footsteps climbing the command bridge, but refused to turn around and look. He kept his face forward into the wind and eyes on the horizon.

"Clint? Are you ok?" Murray stepped towards him and placed his arm around his shoulder.

"Yeah, I'm fine. What's up?" Clint's gruff voice displayed no hint of the anguish he'd wallowed in.

"You look angry about something. Who called you this morning?"

Clint glanced at his nephew, realizing that not much had gotten past him. He might as well 'fess up. "Delay in Desolation Sound. I have to do an intercept outside Port McNeil."

"That's too risky, Unc. I don't understand why you're doing this. Isn't half a mill enough for Dr. Norwell?"

"Half a million doesn't go far when you pay top dollar for drugs. I agreed to set this up for a one-time delivery. If the center needs more, they'll have the contacts and can do it themselves. I'm out of it."

"You know one shipment is just the beginning if they're focused on starting a chain to look after regular folks. I don't trust Dr. Norwell or his board."

"I've made sure everything is cash, and I trust my contact. He's in the same boat as me, a widower, even though he lost his wife to a fentanyl overdose. We both think too many Americans suffer from big pharma, and the government doesn't have the guts to do anything." Clint stretched his neck backward and rolled his head from side to side. "I don't like this any more than you do, but I'm committed to trying something drastic."

"Maybe so, but I'm afraid for you. We're not in the same league as these drug suppliers. They'd rat you out so fast you'd be in jail for the rest of your life. They could set us up, and we wouldn't know what hit us."

"You're not part of this, Murray. You may think you know

what's happening, but trust me—I've kept all the details to myself. If law enforcement gets a whiff of this, the only person they can reach is me. You know what to do if that happens."

"I know. The paperwork is set up for me to assume control of the company business in Seattle. The gravel import business is completely separate."

"And if it goes down, that's fine with me. You and the family will have plenty of income with the landscape and connected businesses that have operated for the last forty years. It will only be me and this operation that will suffer. Just do me a favor and don't take shortcuts—keep your nose clean."

"You don't need to worry about me. I know how business works. But what you should be worrying about is Dr. Norwell. What if he starts blackmailing you? Ever thought of that?" Murray growled.

Clint heard the frustration and concern in his nephew's voice. "He can't. I've got shit on him, too." Clint gave a deep sigh and turned toward Murray. "One-time assistance. That's what I told him through my lawyer, and then it's up to them to figure it out. A part of me is sorry for agreeing to this, but another part wants to make a difference."

"I know, Unc. But once you go through this, you can't undo it. You can't turn back the clock. It sounds like you're willing to take the chance of being caught and losing Prime Aggregates. So, why don't you set up a non-profit with the proceeds from this company? It's worth a bundle, so if you sell it, it should provide more than enough money to buy the drugs legally. Maybe you should let me fix this. I know several influential people in the medical field."

"Enough. It's too late. Leave it alone. Everything's been set in motion." Clint checked the readings on his GPS and then turned to Murray. "Grab me a double shot of Drambuie, will you? Then, get lost for a while. I need some space." Clint pressed the throttle for more speed, and the engines roared as the Vagabond's nose lifted, ceasing all conversation. Clint focused on the ocean and the horizon until he sensed Murray retreating downstairs. He let out a sigh of relief. *Damn.* All he needed was to have Murray stick his nose in this. Clint rubbed his chest again, easing the tightness. He should've kept his big mouth shut.

CHAPTER 9

Overall, Jenna mused, it had been a good weekend. She'd accompanied her visitors on a short cruise to Whitepine Cove, amazed by the speed and smooth ride the Boston Whaler 405 boasted. Extravagant and luxurious, it certainly made a status statement for Clint. No doubt, from the sounds of their conversations, he used the boat often. Nevertheless, it seemed a tad excessive for the typical tourists of the West Coast. Jenna had the distinct feeling that Clint wanted the evidence of his success to be impressive. Her questions about his business were sidelined, and rightly so. Nobody wanted to discuss commerce when they were on holiday.

Vaughan's mannerisms were tamer than usual, and Jenna found she enjoyed his company more. He interacted well with Murray and was respectful and almost deferential with Clint. A combination Jenna was surprised that he could pull off. She'd tell Carla how well her brother presented himself.

Jenna returned to her warm bed, thinking about the emotions Murray stirred inside her. Drew popped into her mind, making her feel guilty. The two of them were attracted to each other, that was for sure. Whether their bond would survive a long-distance relationship was still uncertain. It seemed a long time since she'd lain in Drew's arms, making love that felt safe and pleasurable.

This attraction for Murray felt nothing like it. Jenna wondered if a relationship with him would be the fireworks she'd always speculated about. Would mind-blowing sex be worth it? There was almost a month to think about him before she met him for dinner – *if* she met him for dinner.

Jenna tossed and turned as her mind flitted between the attractions until she gave up the attempt to capture more sleep. When the coffee finished percolating, she took a steaming mug outside and curled up with her cozy afghan. The silence was peaceful as she gazed over Westerlea Cove.

God, I love this place. She doubted that Murray could handle living here full-time. Unless she was wrong, he seemed the type to like the high life, only needing occasional flirtations with nature to ground himself.

The ocean was in Drew's blood. His high grades in microbiology and marine conservation proved that. While Drew was on a summer holiday this past summer, Lee had brought him to spend a week with her at the lease. They'd split their time, checking and replacing stringers, then kayaking throughout the Sound. Jenna shared similar interests, connected deeply with them, and greatly appreciated their support. Lee confided Drew's hope that there would be a re-ignition of their relationship down the road.

Jenna couldn't help but see how well Drew fit into this life, how much he cared about her and their environment. *Could it be love?* It felt like it. Yet, when Drew approached her with a romantic look in his eye, Jenna retreated, and Lee smirked. Love was so complicated.

Murray was a temptation. Plain and simple. Different lifestyles, most likely different values, too. Comparing Murray and Drew was like comparing apples and oranges. Frustrated, Jenna groaned and put her doubts behind her. Determined not to torture herself, she took a hot shower and dressed in jeans and a sweatshirt.

Jenna went outside and tidied the deck, pushing the Adirondacks to their usual position. Remembering the filet that Murray had placed in her cooler, Jenna smiled. She'd bring it inside to refrigerate and enjoy it for dinner tonight. Jenna opened the lid and lifted a Ziploc of quartered lemons they hadn't finished last night, along with the filet. Brushing the ice from it, she noticed another package underneath. Puzzled, Jenna fished it out of the melting ice. Wrapped in brown paper and sealed in a large Ziploc, the rectangular packet was heavier than she expected. Another one rested underneath.

What the hell?

Jenna returned to the kitchen and grabbed a towel to wipe them dry. She opened the plastic bags and tore off a wide strip of duct tape. After the first outer layer was unwrapped, Jenna noticed her name written in felt pen, with a happy face beside it, then the words "a gift from me to you." An "M" was scribbled underneath it.

Frowning, Jenna unrolled the package several times before she saw the contents. *Oh, my God. What was this supposed to mean?* Jenna's hands trembled as they glided over stacks of money. Her mouth fell open as her breath quickened. She opened the second bundle and saw the same content.

Jenna stacked *two bundles of brown strapped fifty-dollar bills and four bundles of yellow strapped hundreds. American, no less!* Jenna picked up a stack and riffled through it. She had no idea how many bills were in each package, but that was a shitload of money.

Stunned, Jenna collapsed on the kitchen chair. The bundles of cash spread out on the table in front of her. Her left leg bounced furiously. A wave of dizziness passed over her, making her drop her head between her knees. Jenna concentrated on breathing even, deep breaths, expelling the air through pursed lips until her mind cleared and her chest released the stranglehold on her lungs. She stood up carefully and then rushed outside. Pacing back and forth on the deck, Jenna wracked her brain for explanations. She hadn't asked for this. *Why, Murray? Why did you do this? I told you I wouldn't sell this place.*

Was it a gift, as he indicated? Or was it a loan? Or a way of tempting her to sell? She'd heard of super-wealthy people who didn't know what to do with their money, but really? Giving a stranger thousands of dollars—that was beyond her comprehension. It also made her suspicious. Who traveled with that kind of cash? Was he as trustworthy as he portrayed himself, or was this a setup?

Jenna ran inside the cabin to the VHF. Pushing down on the call button, she sent out her request. "Calling Murray on the Vagabond. Murray on the Vagabond, Westerlea Cove here. Do you copy?" Impatient, Jenna only waited a minute before repeating the request.

"Copy, Westerlea Cove. This is Murray from the Vagabond. Did you miss me already?"

Jenna's high-pitched giggle betrayed her worry. "I think you've forgotten your parcel here beside the cooler. It looks important. I think you should come back for it."

"Nah. I don't need it. Why don't you keep it, Jenna? I'm sure you'll be able to use it."

Jenna could hear the amusement in his tone. "I don't

think so. I'm worried you may need this, and I'm not returning home for another ten days. You'd better return and pick it up."

"I'm fine, honestly. Don't worry about it. I'll see you next time I come to town, and we'll talk, Ok?"

Murray's voice was firm but gentle. Jenna didn't want people listening to more details, and there seemed no point in arguing over the VHF. "Maybe I should pack things up here and head home early. We could arrange—" her voice trailed off.

"Jenna, please, we don't have time to wait for you. We're dropping Vaughan off and leaving immediately to head north and circle the island. We're on a tight schedule. It's no big deal, honest. I'll see you soon." Murray signed off the communication before Jenna could reply.

Jenna signed off reluctantly. Exhaling a long puff of air through pursed lips, she ran her fingers through her hair and began pacing again. *What the hell am I going to do with all this money?* Jenna picked up the stacks, brought them to her bedroom, and sought a container to conceal the temptation. Ahh. The antique brass chest where she kept photos and precious cards her mom had given her would work nicely. Jenna emptied it and filled the container with the bundles of cash before retrieving one.

Jenna flicked through the stack, counting the bills. One hundred. Wow. Five thousand dollars in one bundle. A quick calculation made her heart race and her hands tremble. Fifty thousand dollars plus the exchange rate. Almost a quarter of what her family's lease was currently worth. The heavy fear of their application for funding through the Oyster Recovery Fund slipped from her shoulders.

A flood of relief coursed through her—no more worries. Westerlea Cove would be solvent again. Jenna could explore more avenues of production, maybe even expanding into tray oysters, a hot commodity lately. Jenna worried her lower lip as she thought about the possibilities. She shouldn't look a gift horse in the mouth.

On the other hand—as her parents often told her, nothing in life was free. But waiting for the government fund to approve their application could take another year or more. There was only so much money to allocate each year, and she wasn't the only one who needed help. This cash could tide her over until she hopefully received her grant, then she could start paying Murray back.

Jenna returned the last bundle to the brass chest, latched it closed, and slipped it under the blankets in the linen closet. Passing a hallway mirror, she stopped and stared at her reflection. Her cheeks were stained red, and worry pulled her eyebrows together. She massaged her forehead to release the tension, then ran her fingers through her tangled hair. Jenna dropped onto the futon, pulled her knees to her chest, and laid her head atop. Knowing a lot of soul-searching was ahead of her, she sighed deeply.

As much as it would make her life easier, she didn't know these men. Murray was a charmer, Vaughan was an opportunist, and Clint? She had no idea if the vibe she caught from him meant anything. Just because she felt uncomfortable didn't mean he was a shady character, but it wasn't reassuring either. And his warning about Murray's charms not always being dependable. What was that about?

Was there an agenda behind his cash gift?

Double toots from a boat horn startled her, even though she immediately recognized it. Terry arrived, probably to get the lowdown on the weekend rental. Jenna returned to slam the linen cupboard closed and hustled to the bathroom, where she quickly brushed her hair. Jenna stared at her reflection. She looked guilty, yet she hadn't done anything wrong. The mirror reflected the surprise and anxiety of Murray's gift, nothing else. She hoped.

"Jenna? Hello, hello?" Two raps on her door prompted Jenna to throw it open. "Suffering from a hangover? You're usually an early bird."

"The guys left at dawn this morning, and I went back to bed." Jenna turned to the kitchen and filled the coffee pot with water. "Want coffee? I'm behind on my daily quota." Jenna added four scoops of MJB and turned on the gas.

"Sure, I'd love some." Terry pulled out a chair and sat down. "Are you ok? You look nervous."

"I'm fine. I've started going over my financials, which has me worried." Jenna shrugged, "I'll figure it out."

"I'm sorry about your money situation. This place has a good rep, so I'd be surprised if you couldn't get a loan to get you going again."

There was no use telling Terry that her dad was against the idea, so she followed his assumption. "Probably. Either that or apply for the recovery fund. I've got options and have to decide which route to go." Jenna brought the mugs, sugar, and Creamo to the table.

"So, what did you think about renting your dock out? Would you do it again?"

Jenna shrugged her shoulders. "They weren't any trouble. And the five hundred bucks came in handy, that's for sure. So, as long as it doesn't interfere with seeding or harvesting, I might agree to have them again. I don't want to open this place for just anyone, though. I've known Vaughan's family since elementary school, so I felt fairly comfortable that he wouldn't recommend miscreants."

"I'm glad you invited Wayne and me to come over and

meet them. We won't be alarmed if they come around when you're away."

"If I'm not here, they shouldn't be either. So, the same rules apply as before. Unless I tell you otherwise, no one will come and use the dock. Unless there's a helluva storm going on."

"Ok, message received. I noticed Murray watching every move you made. He seems like a nice guy." Terry's eyebrows danced questioningly.

Jenna shook her head as her heart thudded. "Quit fishing for info. He's a nice guy and a great cook. That's all." *Especially now that she had second thoughts about his true motives. So much for a budding relationship.*

"I heard you talking on the VHF. It sounds like you'll be getting together again when he returns."

"No secrets around here, is there, Terry?" The coffee pot percolated furiously, so Jenna turned the flame to a tiny blue glow. "Yes, we're going out for dinner. He says it's repayment for my hospitality."

"You don't believe that, do you?" Terry leaned his elbow on the table and cradled his head as Jenna searched the cupboards.

Pulling out a box of granola bars, she tossed them on the table. "That's the best I can do for breakfast this morning." She pulled one out, unwrapped it, and bit into the crunchy snack bar. "I don't know them well enough, so I'm not sure what to think. What was your impression of Clint?"

"It's too soon to tell. Clint seemed standoffish and didn't join in the conversation much. I felt like we weren't in the same stratosphere as he was. I thought Murray was ok, though. He didn't talk much about himself, which surprised me, but he asked a lot of questions about our lives and work."

"Yeah, he was fascinated by all the work it took to produce oysters, even though he thought it was too labor-intensive for the return. Strange thing, though—" Jenna switched gears and poured coffee for them before continuing. "He offered to help me financially."

"Already?" Terry leaned back in his chair, tapping his forefinger nervously on the table. "He barely knows you. Does he want a partnership? He doesn't look like a guy who'd enjoy doing this for more than a week."

"I don't know. I told Murray I wasn't interested in selling or having a partner." Jenna sipped the scalding coffee, then continued. "Murray said he admired me and wanted to help. He wasn't available for labor, so he wanted to gift me some money to help get this place back on its feet. He's loaded, and apparently, they've helped other people before." Jenna's knee began bouncing, and her gaze darted from Terry to items around the cabin, almost afraid of what she'd see in his eyes. "What do you think?"

"That's unbelievable. It's hard to understand why strangers would do that, rich or not. I don't get it. Sorry, but I smell an ulterior motive. Maybe he wants to build a fishing lodge here?" A sparkle appeared in Terry's eyes as he smirked. "Or maybe he's got his eye on you and wants to be able to spend the summers here with you?"

Jenna snorted with derision. "I doubt I'm his type. He's probably into the glamor girls, women who can be his trophy dates. His suggestion made me wonder what he was really after, and my temper flared. I put my hands on my hips while emphasizing my "no" answer."

"Ooh. I know that look. If Murray was smart, he probably backed off. I can't help but think he wants to ingratiate himself so that he could come around whenever he wanted."

"I hope not." Jenna laughed. "I made it clear that I didn't want help, so he backed off and told me it was worth a shot."

"And he left it alone, didn't bug you again?" Terry's eyes narrowed as he tried to figure out the reasoning.

"Nope, he didn't say another thing about it. I don't understand the offer. He doesn't even know me. Why would he do that?"

"I've heard wealthy people are a different breed. Either they're so cheap they squabble about the cost of everything, including toilet paper, or they don't blink twice at spending it. Of course, some use their money to benefit causes or help people." Terry slurped the hot coffee, then glanced back at Jenna. "I wonder which category Murray falls into? Maybe there's a plan we aren't aware of. Are you sure he didn't mention any business venture with you?"

"Nothing. Except that Clint might buy some property in town and develop it. But that has nothing to do with me."

"True enough. Well, I guess you'll find out sooner or later. But I have to remind you of the old saying, "*Beware of strangers bearing gifts.*"

"I know. Don't trust a stranger. I've heard it many times before. But wow, it's tempting."

"Especially if you're in a pickle. If Murray's a stand-up guy and you two develop a relationship, you'll soon know whether you can trust him."

Jenna sighed. "I admit he was intriguing, but something's holding me back. Even Vaughan was respectful to both of them. My overactive imagination screams at me to back away, even if he's rich and hot as sin." Jenna waggled her eyebrows at her description.

Terry drained the last of his coffee and stood to leave. "Listen to your gut, girl, until he earns your trust. I'm heading back to town for the season. Everything's secured for the winter, and there isn't much for me to do that Wayne can't handle. Unless, of course, a storm comes in and rips things apart. Make sure you call me when you come in. Maybe we could go for a few beers one night."

"I'll do that. Thanks for all the help you've given me. I couldn't have made it this far without you and Wayne." Jenna followed him outside and watched him untie his skiff. She held out her arms for a hug, and Terry grinned.

"No problem, you know I'm there for you anytime." He rocked as he hugged her, then ruffled his hand through her hair. "Take good care of yourself. I'll see you soon, I hope."

"Ok. I should be there in a week or so." Jenna pushed his boat gently from the dock and waved as he idled out of her no-wake zone. A double toot, then the engines roared to life, taking her friend home. The farther away Terry went, the more Jenna relaxed. As the tension eased in her shoulders, she sighed with relief. Jenna wasn't good at deception, so it was usually easy to choose the right path. She hated liars, or what some people called themselves—*dreamers*. Whatever the moniker, the bottom line was that they couldn't be trusted.

Jenna might not know what her future held or how she would handle the present, but one thing she couldn't do was deceive others or herself. Until her father's bout with alcoholism and his neglect of the family oyster lease, the Sorensen name carried integrity. If any of her family promised something, they followed through. That ingrained characteristic garnered respect and trust. It was in Jenna's DNA, and she wouldn't let anything justify a reason to associate or deal with shady characters.

CHAPTER 10

After almost a week of traveling an emotional roller coaster, Jenna tied the aluminum boat securely upside down on the deck, then stacked and secured the chairs and picnic table behind the cabin. She loaded two empty forty-pound propane tanks, her dirty laundry, and trash into her boat, then rechecked the place, inside and out. A storm was forecasted to arrive within the next seventy-two hours, and she wanted to get home to her dad before it hit.

Jenna kept her hands busy all week to quiet her racing thoughts. She sanded down the wooden deck chairs and re-stained them, then went to shore and began chopping her wood supply for winter. Going over and over the interactions with Murray, Jenna analyzed the tone of his voice, the look in his eyes, and the seemingly warm respect he gave her. She felt a mutual attraction and wondered if his emotions were real or contrived. Jenna woke up several times gasping in the throes of night sweats, the adrenaline rushing through her system.

Her appetite disappeared, and she lived on coffee. Thank God it was decaf. Retrieving the brass chest, Jenna counted the stacks of money every morning despite knowing its value. She thought about the pros and cons of accepting it. The temptation was driving her crazy. In the evening, she'd sit at the table and make lists. Lists of what she could do with the money. Lists of reasons she should use it or lists why she shouldn't. Jenna had many questions to ask Murray when they met for dinner, along with questions for Vaughan.

Clint and Murray were successful entrepreneurs, but of what? Were they honorable men, and could she trust them? Jenna needed advice but wasn't sure where to get it. And should she keep this a secret, or should she tell her father? So many problems to solve. If this was 'free' money, was it clean money? *Was there a hook attached?*

Part of Jenna wanted to return the cash to Murray immediately, yet another wanted to use the gift temporarily and pay it back when the Fund approved her application. The money could have the lease seeded and back in shape within a year, compared to waiting for another year—maybe even two, for the approval and dispersal from the Oyster Recovery Fund.

She could probably have her lease operational when her dad joined her again. How proud he'd be of her! Back and forth, back and forth. The indecision was killing her. Jenna bit her nails to the quick before she realized her childhood habit had returned.

Jenna decided to bring the chest home with her. She couldn't chance a theft while away. Thievery seldom occurred, but it did happen, even when neighbors kept an eye out for each other. In the dead of night, intruders didn't take long to invade the shed on the beach or the cabin for valuables. And knowing Murphy's Law, that's precisely what would happen to her. There'd be no chance of returning this money if it disappeared while she was gone.

It was time to focus. First things first.

"Millar Landing, Millar Landing, do you copy, Wayne? Westerlea Cove calling." This radio call was Jenna's third attempt to contact her neighbor before leaving her lease. If she didn't catch him now, she'd try again this evening from home.

"Hi Jenna, I just came in. What's up?" Wayne sounded out of breath as if he'd run to get her call.

"I'm ready to leave and wanted to let you know. Anything I can bring back?"

"Not off-hand. Can ya check the co-op before you return? It'll probably be the usual—smokes and fresh groceries." Jenna heard the flic of a lighter and a deep inhalation before Wayne continued. "Say hi to yer dad for me. I'll check yer place after the storm passes through."

"I will, thanks. I tied everything down tight, so you shouldn't have any problems."

"Ok, safe travels." Wayne signed off, and Jenna shut her VHF off.

Jenna did a slow tour around her lease, checking for anything amiss, but all appeared well. She stored her precious cargo under the pilot's seat and was ready to leave. Pushing on the throttle, the low burble from idling engines jumped to attention, popping the bow upwards before it leveled. A sigh of relief escaped her. Jenna was going home and prayed she'd have answers before her return.

The channel was choppy as Jenna turned on the GPS. November was unpredictable, so she followed her dad's instructions to plot a course to the lee of Monk's, then Vargas Islands, to escape the worst of the westerly winds. Concentrating on navigating the trip home would help keep her mind off her financial dilemma. She'd have a few days to look after laundry and focus on her dad while deciding whether to approach Lee for an opinion.

Cutting into the swells through Russell Channel took all her concentration. Her dad warned her that knowing what to do and doing it herself would be frightening, and he'd been right. She felt her pulse in her throat several times as she narrowly avoided floating logs dislodged from shore in the king tide. When Jenna slipped into a four-foot trench, the back of a wave threatened to spill over the stern. She felt a surge of power propelling her craft forward and glanced over her shoulder. The wall of water threatening to crest alarmed her, and she decelerated the engine to float atop the energy.

Feeling her boat lift in response helped to quieten her nerves. She'd heard her dad talk about trips like these and knew what she was supposed to do, but the reality was much more terrifying. Jenna felt the sweat trickling down between her breasts, dampening her bra. Trimming the tabs from left to right soon had her back in control. As she reached the protected waters of Maurus Channel, she gave a prayer of thanks and slowed her engines. The worst part of her trip was over.

Two hours later, Jenna had docked her boat and unloaded it using the wheelbarrows provided at the government facility on Second Ave. At this time of year, few people were sticking around and offering a helping hand. After dumping the trash in the appropriate bins, Jenna slid open the cargo door on the Dodge van, tossed in the dirty laundry she'd brought, and slid the brass chest underneath it. She hopped into the driver's seat, eager to get home. Blowing strands of hair from her eyes, Jenna made a note to get a haircut this time. A hot shower, fresh clothes, and a blazing fire beckoned.

"Dad?" Jenna flung the door open and dropped a hefty bag of clothes on the tiled entryway.

"Hey, sweetheart." Theo pushed his walker from the kitchen into the living area. "I'm surprised to see you. I wasn't expecting you for another few days."

"I wanted to get ahead of the storm and decided to come home early." Jenna removed her runners and hoodie. She hung it on the peg, then approached her dad with outstretched arms. "Besides, I missed you." Hugging over the walker was awkward, so she kissed his cheek and leaned back, assessing his overall health. "You're looking good. How are things going?"

"Not bad. I'll bet you haven't eaten dinner yet. Why don't you shower while I warm up the leftovers? Pat brought a shepherd's pie yesterday, and there's plenty in the fridge."

"Sounds good. I've been daydreaming of a long, hot shower all afternoon. I noticed the firewood on the deck— are you up for a fire tonight?"

"I never say no to a fire at this time of year, but you must be tired. We can build one tomorrow night."

"No big deal, Dad. I'll start it now, and it'll be blazing by the time I'm out of the shower."

Theo grabbed her cold hands and rubbed them briskly as he looked his daughter over. "Whatever you want, my dear." He turned her hands over and ran his fingers over her palms, shaking his head. "You're working too hard, Jenna. Look at this."

"Nothing wrong with calloused hands, Dad. Good, honest work is nothing to be ashamed of." Jenna withdrew her hands, smirked, and lifted her eyebrows, daring him to challenge her.

Theo's lips pursed as he recognized her attempt to get him riled. She knew he'd given up fighting her on this. "True. Shall I put a pot of coffee on while you do that?"

"I'd love some."

Jenna went outside for kindling and firewood. She made three trips, enough for the evening, then knelt on the hearth. Jenna reached for a newspaper and balled a few sheets up before arranging some kindling teepee style over the top. Striking a match, she blew softly until she heard the cedar crackle and watched the flames lick the dry edges. Jenna added three chunkier pieces of cedar before turning and checking on her dad's progress.

Watching him navigate the small kitchen brought a smile of satisfaction to her face. He was managing quite well. Shifting between the cupboard, coffee pot, and fridge, he seemed steady and sure of his movements. Raising his right arm, he retrieved the coffee and filters and set the coffee. He placed two cups and spoons on the small tray atop his walker and carefully headed to the kitchen table.

"See that? I'm becoming more agile every week. I couldn't lift this arm past my shoulder a month ago."

"I can see that. I guess you're still going to therapy, then?"

"Can't get away with not going. Your Aunt Pat, Fred, or Carla usually calls an hour before my appointment and coordinates the rides. And if they can't make it, they call Rollie. Even Vaughan has given me the odd lift." Theo shot a lopsided smile toward his daughter. "They can usually tell how well I've done by the expression on my face when they pick me up. At least I don't need a nap when I get home. PT doesn't exhaust me like it used to."

Jenna cocked her head as she eyed him over. "You look like you've gained a few pounds too. Your color is better."

She smiled and continued, "I'm proud of you. I'm glad you've developed a more positive attitude. I'll bet it makes a difference to everyone involved."

"Probably. I admit swallowing my pride and asking for help was tough, and I was miserable at first. But each bit of independence I gain as I heal makes me hope again. You don't know how liberating taking a shower yourself is—even if I have to sit on a shower bench."

"I can imagine. Good for you, Dad."

"Thanks. Slow but sure is my motto these days. Even Vaughan has been helpful. So, when he chops and piles wood on the patio for me, I slip him a twenty. Occasionally, he's a little cocky, but he's got a sense of humor. Once in a while, he'll sit and have a coffee or start a fire for me and challenge me to a game of crib." Theo paused, noticing her daughter's fatigue. "Enough chatter. Let's catch up later. Put another piece of wood on the fire and take your shower. You look beat."

Nodding in agreement, Jenna pushed her hair from her face again. She placed a log on the fire and then wrapped the screen in front of it. She was exhausted. All the worrying and not sleeping had caught up with her. Jenna grabbed her overnight case and backpack and trudged upstairs to the loft. It felt good to be home with her dad. She grabbed her housecoat and skipped down the stairs.

Jenna smelled the coffee percolating and grinned at her dad, who was putting a placemat on the table for her dinner. Quite the homebody he was turning out to be. *Thank God.* Jenna opened the window in the small bathroom and turned the water on. As the steam rose, she discarded her clothes, stepped into the pelting hot shower, and groaned with pleasure. She shampooed her hair twice and, using a scrubby, scoured her skin until it was rosy.

Brushing her hair and slipping on a bathrobe, she padded upstairs to the loft to dress in her pajamas. Her dad had his favorite CDs cued up to enjoy, and she smiled as she recognized Cheryl Crowe singing the blues. Her dad loved easy-listening music, but singers like Crowe and Cole were his preference, although Michael Bublé's music had recently caught his attention. Unfastening her overnight bag, Jenna removed the brass chest before opening her closet door. She laid it on the floor in the far corner and threw her backpack on top of it. Nobody but them and Carla's family would be near the cabin, and she felt confident that her treasure would be safe.

Jenna padded downstairs and took the shepherd's pie from the refrigerator, cutting herself a generous serving. She placed it in the microwave and set it for two minutes. "Want anything, Dad? A glass of milk or something else?" Jenna grabbed a jar of pickles and a tomato to slice up to accompany her meal.

"Only coffee, please." Theo pulled himself from the sofa with the help of his walker and took a chair at the table.

Jenna placed the steaming plate on the table and poured both cups of coffee. "Someone else's cooking always smells and tastes better than yours, right?" She picked up a fork and tasted her aunt's casserole. "Comfort food." Jenna rolled her eyes appreciatively as if it was the culinary meal of the month.

"Coming home makes you feel that way. Like many fishers who head out for a few weeks or longer, your mom and I had a different relationship than most couples. When I came home, it was like a second honeymoon. She was as excited to see me as I was to see her. And you too, of course."

"It was cute the way you two would fuss over each other. There were times I'd be jealous."

Surprised, Theo raised his eyebrows. "Honestly?"

Jenna shrugged. "I'm kidding you. My childhood memories are all good ones. I miss Mom, although probably not as much as you do. But sometimes, I wish she were here for me to confide in."

"You can always confide in me, sweetie. You know that, don't you?"

"I do, although now and then, I need a woman to talk with. They *get* all the emotional stuff that girls have."

"I'm sure Aunt Pat would listen if you needed her. Do you have a problem now? Is there romance in the picture these days?" Theo looked at his daughter with a puzzled expression.

"No, no. I mean, in general. Is there romance in the picture for *you*?" Jenna threw the comment back at her father, then watched as her father blushed. "Have you met someone? What's up, Dad?"

"Nothing." Theo tapped his fingers on the table nervously. "I've had a wake-up call with the accident and realized that I let my loneliness lead me into depression and the mess I've created. I've joined a support group Dr. Walker recommended, meeting every second week." Theo's eyes flitted from Jenna to around the room, looking slightly embarrassed. "I often sit next to a lady who's very interesting and observant. I've been reading a few books she recommended on overcoming grief, which is helping me a lot. She's very nice." A flush stole up her father's neck from his revelation.

"Great. That's really great." Jenna pretended not to see her dad's anxiety. "Mom used to say that we all need outside help now and then. She's been gone for over four years, and I'm happy you're starting to notice women again. What's her name?"

"Michelle. Michelle Browning." Theo sipped his coffee and raised his eyebrows, anticipating her next question.

"I haven't heard of her. She must be an import." Jenna noted the new sparkle in her father's eyes and approved.

"Yes, she's from Courtenay. She's younger than me and has a twelve-year-old daughter."

"Married?" *Hmm. This conversation was getting interesting.* The relationship probably wouldn't go anywhere because of the boundaries within support groups, but it was a step in the right direction.

"Widowed. Michelle's husband died in a freak skiing accident on Mount Washington. The sessions are usually over by 3:30 or 4:00. We've gone for coffee after our sessions a few times." Theo began drumming his fingers again on the table like Jenna did when she was nervous.

"Glad to hear that. Maybe I'll still be here for your next meeting, and I can meet your friend."

"Maybe. It's no big deal, but Michelle's easy to talk to and hasn't lectured me so far, which is a bonus. Are you ok with that?"

"Of course. Anything that brightens your day brightens mine." Jenna got up and put her plate in the dishwasher, then kissed her dad on the cheek. "Let's go sit by the fire."

Jenna added two pieces of alder to slow the blaze and curled up on the sofa. She leaned her head back and closed her eyes. Listening to the mellow tunes, the fire crackling, and her dad's steady progress into the room eased the tightness in her chest.

Initially, her father's progress was so slow that she thought he'd never completely recover. Was it because he had something to look forward to that there was an optimistic vibe about him? Probably. Her eyes became heavier, and she must've dozed off when she was startled by her cell phone pinging.

"Over here, Jenna. Catch." Theo threw the cell toward her.

"Hello?" Jenna rubbed her left eye as her senses returned to her. "Carla. Yes, I'm back for a week, probably. Maybe two."

"Great, I've missed seeing you. I hope it's two weeks. Otherwise, it seems you barely arrive and are gone again." Carla complained.

"I know. It all depends on the weather. No use going back in the middle of a storm unless Wayne calls with a problem."

"Vaughan said the weekend with you was fun. His friend, Murray, was impressed with you and Westerlea Cove."

"That place is hard to beat. You know that. Anyone who complains about Clayoquot Sound needs to have their heads examined. Their boat blew me away. It probably cost almost half as much as our house did. I can't believe the money people spend on those fancy toys."

"Yeah, it's got Vaughan all hyper." Carla laughed. "He wants one exactly like it, so he's building pie-in-the-sky plans. As if that'll happen. He might get lucky and charter for the big shots, but the goal of owning a boat similar to the Vagabond is out of his league." Carla sighed.

"True, but maybe he'll get fed up with restaurant managing and try day chartering. He could start small and see where it goes. It would be a good gig for him, doing something he loves. I have to tell you that I was impressed with his attitude. He wasn't the loudmouth he usually is. He was nice and only got on my nerves once."

"Whoa. I wonder what that was all about. Suck-holing

for another weekend on a beautiful boat?"

"Could be, I don't know. Your brother probably got paid well. Maybe that was the incentive. The younger guy, Murray, will be back in Tofino soon. He's invited me for dinner."

"Ooh. I take it you're going?"

"You bet—the Black Rock Resort in Ucluelet's a five-star restaurant. I can't afford dinner there, so you're darn right I'm going. Besides, I want to see what he cleans up like."

Carla giggled. "Don't tell me you're finally ready to start dating again?"

"It's only dinner, but you never know. We've got a few things to talk over."

"So, is there something brewing between the two of you? Let's go for dinner tomorrow night, have a few drinks, and catch up."

"Nope, and nope. Not tomorrow. Give me a few days with Dad, and then we'll meet."

"You're killing me, girl. My imagination's going wild."

"Then stop it. Wishful thinking hasn't produced a solid thing. We're only new friends, and I'm not sure I'd want more, even if he did."

Carla groaned. "Awe. One day, you'll fall in love like I did with Daryl. I thought it might've happened with Drew, but it doesn't look like that's possible anymore. I want you to find love in your life. Life's too short to be alone."

"Yada, yada. Goodnight, Carla. See you soon."

"You bet. Love ya, girlfriend."

"Right back at you." Jenna clicked off the cell, then glanced at her dad, watching him waggling his eyebrows and grinning.

"Don't you start too, Dad. Vaughan brought his two friends up for three days. He called and offered me five hundred bucks to let them moor at our lease. I couldn't refuse it."

"I heard. It's pretty hard to refuse that kind of cash for a weekend. It sounds like it was fun."

"Yes, a nice change. Murray's in his thirties, and his Uncle Clint's around fifty. They own a forty-foot Boston Whaler, which was all decked out. Very fancy."

"Nice people or snobs?"

"Murray was very friendly." Jenna saw the mischief gleam in her father's eyes. "Not *that* friendly, Dad. But he cooked dinners while they were there, and I learned how to make angel hair pasta with garlic prawns and scallops."

"Fancy, shmancy."

"It was awesome. Afterward, Vaughan washed the dishes while we sat on our dock and watched the sunset."

"Vaughan? Since when did he go domestic?"

"I know. It was weird watching him interact with those two. He couldn't do enough for them. It seemed like he was trying to get into their good books, or maybe he was trying to impress them. At least it was easier for me to have him around. Vaughan usually pisses me off with his attitude." Jenna stretched her arms, then drew her legs up underneath her.

Theo listened and offered an opinion. "Anyone who knows Vaughan long enough has the same problem. He keeps his good behavior for customers at the bar or the big spenders. The rest of us get to hear his make-it-rich plans— although I have to say, that seems to be changing. He's been popping by around here now and then. Maybe he's growing up."

"Better late than never. Vaughan's always reaching for the golden ring. I guess that's good. Better than being depressed." Jenna hated to speak ill of anyone. In her mind, she could be as catty as the next person, but not in conversation. "I'm getting another coffee. Want one?"

"There's iced tea in the fridge. I'll have a glass of that, please."

Jenna went to the kitchen and brought back their beverages. She added another log to the fire and settled with her knees tucked beneath her on the sofa. "So nice to be home, Dad. I don't know how I'll do in the winter at our lease. When the nights are long, I think it'll be harder. How did you do it for all those years?"

"It wasn't so hard when you have someone like Meg to talk to every night. I made sure to bring several books each time I went. And Wayne would come over now and then, play cards, and listen to some music. I'd usually be in bed by 10:00 p.m. I guess it's like hibernating. We work long hours from spring until fall, and it's probably our body's way of recuperating. Then, there was the 'honeymoon' to look forward to when I came home."

Theo paused, eyeing her pensively. "You know you don't have to do the same thing I did. You can take longer breaks and stay home. It would also help if you had someone to share your life. The guy you worked with would've been a good fit."

"That ship's sailed, Dad. Drew's up in Haida Gwaii, making the most of the transfer opportunity. We still keep in touch, or Lee fills me in when they meet at a Zoom conference. You're right, though. He'd have loved the lifestyle." Jenna paused. "You and Mom always told me things happen for a reason. If I'd gone with him, it would've been much harder leaving there and coming here."

Jenna decided coffee wasn't cutting it. "I think I'll switch to some wine. Now, don't you worry about me— I'm glad I was free to come home." She continued chattering while searching for the wine, finally locating a bottle in the pantry. "Regarding scheduling, we'll have to see how I handle it. During the winter, two weeks home at a time, then a week there would probably be enough, as long as I can have Wayne cover me." Jenna poured a goblet of red wine, added a log to the fire, and returned to the sofa.

"Talk to Wayne when you get back. I'm sure he'll be okay with that."

"I can offer to pay him for a drive-by check every few days. If anything needs attention, he can call, and I'll go back."

"That's what we sometimes did, especially during a cold winter when the weather flirts with frost. Clayoquot Sound usually has fewer storms when a northeast weather system settles in. I'd cover for Wayne and vice versa. You'll figure it out. Next year, if things continue to improve, I'll be the one to spell you off in the winter."

"I'm sure you will." Jenna's eyes grew heavy, and she leaned against the sofa. "Long day."

"Ready for bed?"

"Soon. Sitting here, talking with you, and relaxing in front of a warm fire feels so good."

"It's great to have you here," Theo paused. "So, Black Rock Resort? I overheard you saying that to Carla. That'll be an experience. Have you got a date yet?"

"Murray will call me when he knows for sure. Probably within a week or so—I thought I'd stay until after I see Murray if all's well at the lease." Jenna twiddled her hair around her finger as she gazed at the flames licking the cedarwood. Lost in the glowing embers of an established fire, she let herself zone out.

Minutes passed, and as the CDs completed their cycle, the room was quiet except for the crackling fire. Theo's deep, gentle voice intruded Jenna's zone, soothing her anxious mind. "A penny for your thoughts."

"Just thinking about the differences between Drew and Murray. They couldn't have more different lifestyles. It's hard for me to imagine being that rich and never worrying about money."

"Money isn't everything and has its own sets of problems. Everything is relative. The more important thing is enjoying the life you live."

"True. I love living on the coast and the challenge of Westerlea Cove." Jenna sighed. Slowly rolling the wine in her glass, her mind wandered.

"It looks like you're worried. Care to share?"

"I'm not sure. I could be worrying for nothing. Have you heard anything about our application for the recovery grant yet?"

"No. I can check online after January 1st for information on the process. Government things are usually long and drawn out. They don't like being hassled for an answer. You know that. We'll be lucky to know anything by the spring. And if we're approved, receiving the funds could take another six months or longer. Why?"

"I'm debating whether to call Lee or not. Maybe he can nose around and give us a hint on how things are going. Waiting and being unable to make plans seems like such a waste of time. I wanted to make my stringers in March and start seeding in April. Are you still against mortgaging our home?"

"Yes, there's no wiggle room there for me. I hope you understand."

Jenna saw the regret in her father's eyes. She knew he hated saying no to her. "I do. I can't entirely agree, but I get it." Jenna sat forward, elbows on her knees, and stole a deep breath. "I received a proposition lately. I turned it down, but sometimes I wonder if I did the right thing," her lowered voice echoed her uncertainty.

"Jenna, this lease belongs to both of us. Talk to me."

"Murray asked me if I wanted an investor. He and his uncle do this kind of thing now and then." Jenna puffed out a breath of frustration as her eyes darted around the room. "I freaked on him and said Westerlea Cove was a family legacy, and there was no way I'd sell the place. I was adamant that I wanted to restore it myself. Since then, I've wondered if I should've asked more questions."

"Hmm. It must've made you feel uneasy. Someone you hardly know offers to buy in. Do you think Vaughan had anything to do with that?"

"Who knows? But it did seem suspicious. Especially when I found the expensive gift he had left me. Once they departed, I started giving it more thought. Maybe there'd be a way I could borrow from them and then pay them back when we get our grant. It's tempting."

"I can see that would bother you. It also makes my skin tingle. How long has Vaughan known them? Who are they?"

"All I know is they're businessmen from Seattle. Part of me feels apprehensive about the offer. Another part of me wants to take a chance."

"We aren't gamblers, sweetie. We have what we have by the calluses on our hands. There are genuine people like —" Theo passed his hand over his chin as he searched for an example. "Like Oprah. And other philanthropists who help out individuals, but I think the reality of that happening to us is like winning the lottery. I'd rather mortgage the house than get involved with someone I don't know."

"Then that tells me to forget it." Jenna flopped backward

and raised her eyes to the ceiling before shutting them briefly. The room was quiet except for the crackling fire as they thought about the risks.

Theo leaned over and patted his daughter's knee. "You'll see Murray soon. Ask him questions about what he'd expect in return. What's his interest rate, or what would he expect as a return on a harvest? Twenty percent? Thirty? Or maybe this is a write-off for them, which benefits their tax situation. You won't know unless you ask." Theo paused. "Don't rush into anything. Do your research, and we'll discuss it again when you get answers. I don't want to be nosy, but what did he give you?"

Jenna's eyes fluttered downwards as she latched onto the first idea that came to her. "An intricately carved gold bracelet. It looks like it was probably an heirloom or something." Jenna reassured her dad, "I'll give it back to Murray at dinner, and we'll discuss his other offer." Jenna hated to lie to her dad, but she knew his views well. He wouldn't want her to have dinner with him if he knew of the fifty thousand dollars. She clasped her dad's hand that still sat on her knee and winked. "Has anyone told you you're pretty smart for an old man?"

"Legions have expressed their awe at my insights, my dear," Theo panned.

Jenna laughed, "I hope it's hereditary. I'm done for tonight. I think I'll hit the hay." She leaned over and kissed him on the cheek. "Thanks for listening."

"You're welcome. I'll stay up a while longer until the fire dies out. I might even play another CD."

"You can play a marching band, and I wouldn't hear it. See you in the morning."

"Goodnight, sweetheart. Love you."

"Love you more," Jenna repeated the familiar response.

CHAPTER 11

Leaning into the mirror to check her mascara, Jenna felt a flutter in her chest, quickly moving up her throat. It had felt like Saturday would never arrive as each day she waited seemed to crawl. She swallowed nervously and chastised herself.

For God's sake, it was only a date.

Jenna added a coat of lip gloss to her siren red lipstick and sprayed a mist of *Fifth Avenue* on her wrists and behind her neck before she returned to the full-length mirror in her bedroom and considered her appearance.

This look was as glamorous as she could get. If Murray wanted more sophistication, then he'd better look elsewhere. Her three-year-old black dress looked new, with the spaghetti straps and fitted bodice. A side slit to mid-thigh showed her long, lithe legs. Jenna padded down the steps and twirled in front of her father.

"Well?" Jenna lifted her outstretched hands in the air, waiting for his response.

"Wow." Theo's eyes said it all. "You're beautiful. My little girl has grown up. Your mom would be smiling and very proud of you."

Jenna noticed the brightness of her father's eyes, saw the love shimmering within, and felt her eyes misting. Their relationship had become so much closer as they verbally shared their feelings. If this was the silver lining to the black cloud that had hovered over them, she welcomed it. She leaned into her dad and kissed his cheek. "Thanks, Dad. I bought this dress for the university's New Year's Eve dance. Since then, I've lost a few pounds, but it still works, right?"

"Most definitely." Her father approached her and took her hand. "I still have your mom's black diamond pendant and earrings if you want to wear them. It may be too old-fashioned, but they're yours if you do." Now, it was Jenna's turn to be surprised.

"Really? I forgot about them. I remember Mom wearing them at Christmas. I'd love to have them." Jenna reached behind her neck, unclasped the gold chain, and removed the matching hoops from her ears.

"I bought the set for our tenth anniversary." Theo rolled his walker toward the bedroom when the doorbell rang. "That must be your date. Get that, will you? I'll be right back with the jewelry."

Jenna slipped on her three-inch heels and then went to the door. She opened it wide to see Murray holding a bouquet of yellow roses. "Wow. Thank you. Come on in."

"I hope you like roses." Murray handed her the flowers entwined with baby's breath and greenery. His navy blazer and crisp, grey dress trousers called attention to his physique. He was sporting a new one-inch scruff that shrieked sexily and sent a shiver down to her toes. His eyes were bright with a hint of anxiety, surprising her.

"Roses are one of my favorite flowers. These are beautiful." Jenna sniffed the fragrant bouquet and smiled. "I'm almost ready. Please make yourself comfortable while I put these in a vase. My dad will be out in a minute."

While arranging the bouquet, Jenna heard her father call her. She turned to Murray and held one finger up. Two minutes later, Jenna returned with her cheeks rosy as her fingers caressed her necklace.

"Dad, this is Murray Meadows. Murray, this is my dad, Theo Sorensen."

"Nice to meet you, sir. I suppose you've heard how your daughter and I met. You raised a beautiful and impressive woman. After her generous hospitality, I wanted to spoil her with dinner at the Black Rock. I hope it's as good as 'they' say."

"She's my pride and joy. I'm sure you'll love your evening there. The resort wouldn't get five-star accreditation otherwise. I understand you like cruising around our Island home." Theo lowered himself to the armchair and gestured for Murray and Jenna to sit.

"Every chance we get. We usually take a few trips a year in the summer to enjoy Vancouver Island's east and west coasts or head to Haida Gwaii. If we're not too busy in the winter, we head toward San Diego for a month, where our family flies down to join us."

"You're a lucky man to be able to do that." Theo fluttered his hand towards the door. "Well, you didn't come here to entertain an old man. Off you go now. Enjoy the evening—don't waste a minute of it."

Jenna leaned over, pecked his cheek, then smoothed off the lipstick with her thumb. "I'll tell you all about Black Rock later, Dad. Love you."

Murray stood up, leaned over to shake Theo's hand, and exchanged pleasantries. He placed his hand on the small of Jenna's back and followed her. Jenna reached for her long red woolen coat and handed it to Murray. Helping her into it, he then followed her outside.

Murray guided Jenna to the passenger side of the white Lexus SUV, opened the door, pulled out the seatbelt, and handed it to Jenna. Impressed with his courtly manners, Jenna saw another glimpse of Murray and his luxurious world. He lived a privileged life, yet he seemed so down-to-earth with her.

"Are you cold? I could flip the switch on for the seat heaters if you need it."

"No, I'm fine. Maybe on the way home tonight, it might be nice." Jenna watched him press the ignition button to the electric-powered vehicle. "This vehicle is so quiet that I can't hear it running."

"It takes a while to get used to it. At first, I'd hit the ignition twice because I hadn't heard the usual hum of motors running. EVs are the way of the future."

"I agree. Too bad it took us so long to wake up. It's easy to stick our heads in the sand and pray we're mistaken." Jenna shifted in the butter-soft leather seat and watched Murray's expression. "You know quite a lot about me, but I know very little about you. I hope you don't think I'm nosy, but what business do you and your uncle operate? Do you have a lot of employees?"

"We're distributors for landscape supplies across the Pacific Northwest. We import slate, marble, and decorative supplies like sculptures and fountains. My uncle also has a business supplying gravel by barge from the Desolation Sound area to California."

"Not a Home Depot type of operation, I gather."

Murray slid a glance over and gave a lopsided grin. "No. We cater to a much higher-end market. I'm in charge of the landscape side, and Clint keeps himself busy with his project."

"From the look of things, it's a profitable enterprise."

"Yes, very. My grandfather started with one distribution location, and each generation expanded it. My father died of a heart attack about six years ago, and that's when I began working with Clint, my dad's brother, in the family business. We have a very competent board of directors that I rely on to keep it running smoothly."

"I'm sorry to hear about your dad's passing. My mom died five years ago, so I understand how much you must miss him. How old was he?"

"Fifty-six. It's made me appreciate my mom and my sister more. We're a close family."

"My mom was forty-eight, and I'm an only child, so it's been hard for my dad and me."

"Shared experiences. Maybe we'll find happier ones ahead."

"Maybe, in time. Although truthfully, we lead such different lives. It's hard to imagine what we'd have in common." Jenna fiddled with her pinkie ring, twirling it around her finger. "We might as well get this out of the way so we can enjoy our dinner tonight. About the money you left me—".

"Jenna, please. Leave it alone. I wouldn't have done it if I couldn't afford it. There are benefits to being rich. We aren't all assholes. I like to contribute to worthy projects when I see an opportunity to help someone who deserves it. That's it. That's all there is to it."

"It's hard for me to believe you have no ulterior motives.

Since you left, all I've done is worry about it." Jenna presented her hands for emphasis. "See these beautiful nails? I bit my nails down to the quick and needed to invest in a gel manicure for tonight."

"I'm sorry, Jenna. That wasn't my intention." Murray pulled her left hand to his mouth and kissed her fingertips. "Does it help if I tell you how sexy they are?"

"No. Well, maybe." A smile tugged at her lips at his compliment. "You can't imagine how tempting it is for me to accept your offer, even though it goes against my principles," she said as she pulled her hand away.

"If you're worried about whether any strings are attached, don't. I admire the work you're doing there and the effort you've gone through to rebuild your family's name. You deserve a break." Murray flashed a smile her way, then continued. "My uncle may disagree, but my money is mine to do with however I choose. He keeps a tight rein on his investments, demanding top interest. But that's not me. You'll have to trust me on that."

Jenna cocked one shoulder and permitted a small smile to cross her lips. "I haven't known you long enough to do that."

"Then hang onto it until you do. In the meantime, let's enjoy getting to know each other better. Deal?" Murray reached over and clasped Jenna's hand.

A zip of heat surged through Jenna, momentarily blocking her verbal response. She licked her lips nervously, then cleared her throat. "I-uh-I guess so. At least for tonight."

"Smart move. Why ruin an evening with money talk?" Murray turned Sirius on. "What's your preference? Soft rock, jazz, new age or ?"

"I've grown up on soft rock, although I'll listen to almost anything except hip-hop."

Murray tapped the screen a few times. "How about Eric Clapton?"

"Sure, sounds good."

The mellow, caressing tones of *'Wonderful Tonight'* flooded the vehicle, making Jenna's heart flutter. This guy was something else. Everything he'd done had set off fire-crackers inside her with minimal effort, yet there was a hint of danger behind it. Or was it anticipation? She leaned back in her seat and pushed her annoying thoughts aside. She slipped her hands underneath her coat and dried her damp palms discreetly. A handsome and attentive man was trying to impress her, spoil her with flowers and dinner in the most elite restaurant on the West Coast. *Quit looking a gift horse in the mouth.*

Murray parked his Lexus, walked around to the passenger door, and opened it for Jenna, offering his hand to help her step down. Jenna was thankful for the subtle lighting that hopefully hid her blush. She felt breathless with his sexy, lopsided grin concentrated on her. He lifted her fingers, grazing them with his lips, before enveloping her hand in his large, firm grip.

Jenna brought her other hand to her chest, "I'm not a princess, Murray. Cut it out."

"Let me spoil you, Jenna. Somebody should. Life isn't all hard work. There's so much you haven't seen, so much you haven't experienced. Let me introduce you to it."

The doorman ushered them inside the Black Rock Resort with a welcoming smile. Murray slipped an arm around Jenna's waist. They walked toward the Currents Restaurant, where another employee checked their reservations. The attendant took their coats, then ushered them toward a table for two beside the panoramic windows. A lit candle in hurricane glass greeted them.

Jenna's eyes widened as she absorbed the presentation. A white linen tablecloth with forest green napkins, gleaming silverware, crystal water and wine glasses triggered a hushed 'wow' from Jenna's lips. As Murray pulled out the chair for Jenna, he bent close to her ear and whispered. "Just for you, Jenna. I hope you'll love our evening."

"This place is amazing. I don't know where to look first." Jenna turned to view the ocean crashing on the islets below, the white crests and surf highlighted by discreetly placed lights shining from the shore. "I've often walked the Pacific Trail nearby, but this is another perspective entirely."

"Romantic, isn't it? I love this place. When I come alone, this is where I stay. They've beautiful suites here, with glassed wrap-around patios. Black Rock Resort is the next best place if you can't be on the *Vagabond*. After dinner, I hope you'll join me for a nightcap and judge for yourself."

"Hmm. That might be very nice."

A waiter came to pour ice water into their crystal glasses, diverting Jenna's attention. Murray ordered a Middle Loire wine when Jenna opted for red wine over white. "I hope you'll like it. Chinon is a French wine with hints of black currant and anise. It's one of my uncle's favorites when he orders meats, and it's fast becoming mine, too."

"That sounds unusual. I'm not a wine connoisseur, but I'll try it." Jenna gazed into Murray's dynamic blue eyes. It was hard to believe, but she could swear that he was smitten with her. His focus was solely on her, a situation Jenna seldom found comfortable. She could almost feel the heat emanating from his eyes that ignited each part of her they caressed. Slightly nervous, her eyes darted around the restaurant, avoiding his intense gaze. His hand reached for her fingers, rubbing them slowly, causing her to relax as a glow spread throughout her. Jenna's anxiety subsided, allowing her the confidence to concentrate on his features.

The waitperson approached with a linen towel over his forearm and poured an inch into Murray's glass. Murray swirled the contents, inhaled the aroma, quickly checked the legs, and sipped. Nodding with appreciation, the waiter poured wine for both before disappearing.

"Here's to getting to know you better. I'm sure it'll be even more adventurous than it has been so far." Murray lifted his goblet and tilted it toward Jenna.

"Thank you. To new friends." Jenna clinked hers to his. "How did your business meeting go today?" Jenna needed to start a conversation about anything else but herself. "I didn't know you were interested in acquiring property here."

"Clint always has an eye out for opportunities. Sometimes, it works out, although sometimes, it's not worth the effort. The property for sale here has seen better days, so the value's merely in the land. Water views would be possible on the second and third floors of a development we're considering. Retail businesses are on the main level, and luxury timeshares are above. There are two older homes beside it that we may also approach to buy."

Jenna caught herself frowning before noticing the question in Murray's eyes. It was none of her business what his intentions were. She stretched a smile on her face, picked up her wineglass, and wished him luck. "To the future, Murray. I hope it works out for you."

"You don't look too excited about the idea. What's wrong?"

"Nothing." Jenna squirmed in her chair, her fingers fluttering around her wine glass.

"Spit it out. It wouldn't hurt to get a local's opinion on this. Honestly."

Jenna blew out a breath and rolled her eyes. "Call me old-fashioned. My town has changed so much in the last ten years that it's almost unrecognizable in some areas. I was born here, and watching our community develop luxurious, high-density developments bothers me. How can locals find reasonably priced housing when these extravagant resorts and subdivisions have skyrocketed land values? I know business ventures are about making money, but things are becoming unaffordable for ordinary people."

"It's called progress, Jenna. If we don't invest, someone else will. This place is wild and pristine, a real jewel. And people want to get away from busy city life. With an increasing number of employees able to work from home, the population has become more mobile. And they're choosing destinations like these." Murray spread his hands before him. "You can't blame them. You can't hide this place forever. You need to look at the big picture."

"I know, I know. Look, let's drop the subject. What will be, will be." Jenna looked around to catch someone's attention. "I'd love to see the menu."

Murray glanced toward the center of the room and gave a quick nod. Immediately, a waitperson materialized and presented their menus. After giving assurances he'd soon return, Jenna and Murray perused the limited but mouthwatering concoctions.

"I think I'll go with the lamb chops, celeriac, and saffron rice." Jenna closed the menu. "It's hard to beat the freshness of the seafood I can get, so I seldom order it in a restaurant."

"I agree. How about an appetizer first? The food is

amazing here, but the portions are small. A Charcuterie would be nice to start. We're in no hurry for the main course, are we?"

"No, not at all. I've never had that for an appetizer, so that sounds good. What tempts you for the main course?" Jenna asked.

"I'm going for the Roasted Duck. I've enjoyed it before, and the spiced honey and fennel accent the bird perfectly."

Another bottle of wine appeared shortly after, along with the Charcuterie board, and the conversation became more intimate as they delved into each other's past. Jenna learned that Murray had been married for five years but had divorced. "She loved the high life, always on one committee or another. She'd never step foot on a boat unless it were a cruise ship. We had very different tastes about what we preferred to do in our leisure time." Murray smirked. "You can guess how much she resented it when Clint and I would plan a trip on the *Vagabond*. I hate arguing, so I didn't spend much time at home in the last year of our marriage. We drifted apart and finally agreed we'd be happier alone."

Jenna told him of her two years at the University of Victoria and her job in Nanaimo afterward. He already knew she'd quit her job to come home and said he approved of her family commitment.

Murray often touched her hand to make a point, creating a buzz that gave her goosebumps. Their shared parental loss created a bond of empathy that bypassed their short acquaintance. When dinner was savored and completed, Jenna surprised herself by occasionally reaching for his hand.

The thrum of passion enhanced by the expensive French wine heated Jenna's cheeks with heightened aware-ness. Murray's adoring gaze skimmed over her features, from her eyes and hair to the swell of her breasts and the thin straps of her slinky dress. The first pass of his leg against hers made her instinctively pull back as her words wavered. Flicking her eyes to his, she saw an intensity brewing that she suspected wouldn't be quelled quickly.

Time to be brave. She slowly moved her calf up and down against his at the next pass. This time, it was her smiling as his conversation briefly faltered.

"I can't stop admiring you tonight. I know you're shy, so I hope it won't make you uncomfortable when I say this, but I find you incredibly sexy. I hope you're ready for a nightcap?" Murray murmured as his splayed fingers entwined with hers. Using his thumb to create circular patterns on her palm, he grinned when he saw Jenna suck in a breath.

Jenna lowered her eyes a moment and gathered her feelings together. Spontaneous had never been in her vocabulary, but she tossed caution to the wind tonight. Was it his smooth sophistication or the cobalt blue eyes framed with thick, smoky lashes that tempted her? Or could it be his chiseled features now encased in a sexy scruff in his hot-as-sin face?

Jenna was captivated. Her eyes flickered over his perfect features, returning to his full lips. Whatever it was, she needed to feel those lips against hers and the rasp of his scruff against her hypersensitive skin. She wanted to taste him and nip at the fullness his lips offered. And feel them nibbling and tasting her. Soon.

"I have to say your new scruff adds something to your good looks. You've hit "hot" on the sexy scale." Jenna teased back bravely. She hid her nervousness behind a smile as she decided to throw herself out there and see what would happen. Jenna threw a mental wall up, refusing to let thoughts of what would happen afterward change her mind.

Knowing what was ahead, her nipples grew hard under the thin crepe bodice, and Murray's observant eyes became molten.

Murray searched for their waitperson, who immediately appeared with the bill and a payment terminal. His eyes never left hers as he swiped his American Express card across it. He reached into his wallet, took a hundred-dollar bill, and slipped it onto the tray.

"An excellent evening. Please give our compliments to the chef." Murray remarked as he pushed his chair away to help Jenna out of hers.

"Thank you. I hope you continue to have a memorable one." The young man backed away, smiling. Murray nodded, but his concentration was solely on Jenna.

The touch of Murray's hands on her bare shoulders sent an intoxicating thrill spiraling through her that quickened her breath. As Jenna retrieved her purse, she turned and lifted her hand to his, accepting his courtly manners.

"Let's get your coat. I'll give you a tour of my suite."

"I'd like that." Jenna's whispered response ignited a low growl from Murray's throat, weakening Jenna's knees. The heat between them reached an explosive point that required privacy—*as soon as flipping possible*. As their vibes intensified, Murray propelled her across the restaurant.

Draping Jenna's red coat over his forearm, Murray whisked her to the elevator. As the door closed behind them, he pressed the fourth-floor button, wrapped his hand in Jenna's hair, and pushed her against the wall. Plundering her mouth ravenously, he moaned as her lips opened to grant him access.

A feverish need overtook Jenna, and she hooked her leg over his to hold him tight against her. She felt the hardness of his passion rocking her to her core. Jenna pulled back, gasping for breath to calm her racing heart. They stared in wonder at each other.

"Wow," Murray whispered as he ran his fingers down Jenna's bare arms, causing goosebumps. "I don't think either one of us expected this tonight."

"That's for sure." Jenna searched Murray's stormy blue eyes for the answers to why her emotions catapulted into a volatile, lusty embrace. Her pulse was racing as fast as a marathon runner's while this burning passion raged within. *This was so not like her.* A craving unlike anything she'd ever experienced shook her previous perceptions of her sexuality. Jenna closed her eyes for a moment as she struggled to make sense of her reaction.

"Remind me to buy a case of Middle Loire to have on hand." Murray joked. "When I tried to entice you to skinny dip at your lease, you seemed timid."

"I should hope so. I'd known you for almost an hour by then." Propped against the elevator wall, Jenna's knees were trembling and weak from desire. Her lips were still tingling from their combustible connection with Murray.

The elevator door whispered their floor number, and the doors quietly eased open. Murray cupped Jenna's elbow and steered her to the left. He retrieved his key card, and once the keylock turned green, he flung it open for Jenna to enter.

"Please, make yourself at home. Would you like another glass of wine or maybe a cocktail?" Murray flicked the dimmer lights on, hung up her coat, and motioned her forward to explore the suite.

Jenna passed the fully contained kitchen with marble countertops, stainless appliances, and a Barista coffee station. She gasped when she entered the rectangular living room with floor-to-ceiling windows facing a dark expanse of the Pacific Ocean. Jenna heard these suites were spectacular, and now she believed it. She could only imagine how impressive the daytime view might be.

Stepping to the sliding glass doors, Jenna cracked them open a few inches. A chilly breeze assaulted her, making her shiver, but she didn't close it. The pounding of waves invisibly crashing below was music to her tumultuous feelings and well worth the goosebumps.

Warm hands on her shoulders and hot kisses on her neck invited Jenna to lean backward, secure in Murray's embrace. He wrapped his arms around her, as mesmerized by the booming crescendo outside as she was. "Alexa, play my favorites song list."

As the mellow tunes of Rod Stewart's Great American Songbook drifted throughout the space, Jenna turned to face this man who turned her world upside down. Her brazen fingers traced his full lips, then caressed their way up through the scruff on his face before threading through his curly blonde hair. Jenna stood on her tiptoes and leaned into his neck, nibbling and kissing her way to his ear. Then Murray took over, his lips and hot breath trailing down her neck, and she felt his hands on her ass, pulling her closer to him. Taking a deep breath, he drew back to search her face.

"As much as I'm enjoying this, I need to be sure you're on the same page. I don't want you to have regrets tomorrow."

"I'll probably have a twinge or two, but I know what I want." Jenna's eyelashes fluttered downwards as if embarrassed. "If you haven't guessed, my reaction tonight is unusual. I don't sleep around, and I've only had a few short relationships. It feels like a long time since I felt this way, and I want more." Jenna returned her gaze to his mouth, pulled Murray's face down, and sucked on his lower lip, flicking her tongue in his mouth. "No regrets. I promise," she whispered.

WESTERLEA COVE

Jenna giggled as Murray groaned, picked her up in his arms, and brought her to the bedroom. The liquor buzzing through her system encouraged her, making her eager to participate. He placed her in the middle of the king-size bed, removed her heels, and tossed them onto the floor in the corner. His eyes watched hers as he explored the length of her legs, hooking the nylons and slowly peeling them off her. Jenna clenched the bedsheets and squirmed as his fingers stroked her thighs, reaching higher to her apex before pausing.

"Tell me what you want," Murray whispered.

Jenna's grin turned shy as she shook her head, her face flushing. "Not yet. It's your turn. Take your shirt off. Slowly. Or would you like me to do the honors?"

Murray chuckled, whipped the tie from his neck, then slowly unbuttoned his shirt and let it drop to the floor. "Any other instructions, ma'am?"

"Let me explore you." Jenna got to her knees and approached him. Her hands climbed his thighs to his waist, where she heard him suck in his breath as he waited for more. Lingering there, she teased him with feathering kisses across his hips and up his muscular chest to his neck. Her imaginative fingers explored hidden territory.

Murray's breaths were coming short and ragged as he struggled to control his response. He slipped the spaghetti straps off her shoulders, then let his fingers skim the top of her bodice. His lips tasted her skin, making Jenna shiver with anticipation.

His touch lit her skin on fire and took away all thought. Her breath hitched as she willed him to go further. *Fever. That's what this is,* Jenna thought. A white lightning desire to touch and be touched, taste and be tasted overcame her. *So, this was passion. This is what sex was supposed to be*—an inferno of need that demanded to be tamed.

JENNA DIDN'T KNOW how to describe their interlude. The sexual attraction was more potent than she'd ever experienced, but her mind searched for a description that fit her feelings. Jenna couldn't describe it as her idea of love. What she'd taken part in was mind-blowing. Initially embarrassed to open herself to the sexual fantasies Murray introduced her to, Jenna couldn't deny the pleasures and blissful release she felt. She was grateful for his skill, patience, and ability to arouse and bring her to multiple orgasms, an event she previously believed to be exaggerated fiction. She finally understood what her high school girlfriends would swoon about.

But they were worlds apart in their life perspectives. She wondered if they could stay friends, maybe even lovers. Tonight, he made her feel sexy and desirable. But Greek gods weren't for everyday people like herself. Jenna dropped her hand over her eyes as confusion threatened to overwhelm her. *Why did she constantly analyze things to death?*

"Jenna? Come and join me outside."

Startled, Jenna cleared her throat. "I need water first. Do you want any?"

"There's Evian in the fridge. Grab one, and I'll have mine later. If you're hungry, I ordered a platter of hor d'oeuvres delivered to the fridge. There's a chunk of brie there, too, and the crackers are in the cupboard beside it. Help yourself."

Jenna slipped on a thick cotton bathrobe and then padded into the kitchen. She caught a reflection of her mussed hair and swollen lips, then blushed as she remembered the pleasures she'd discovered. She retrieved the water and grabbed the platter before she wandered into the living room. Jenna nibbled at the assortment, cracked the Evian open, and drank deeply. She thought of Murray's sensual attention and how he'd stripped away her shyness. Jenna hoped she'd given as much as she received—he'd certainly looked enthralled with her explorations of him. If the heavy snoring afterward indicated his pleasure, Jenna was pleased.

She looked around the beautiful, luxurious suite. Money meant everything and nothing to people like Murray. There was so much potential to make a positive difference in this world. Jenna wondered how she'd handle it, then shrugged her shoulders. It was a different lifestyle, yet would she give hers up for his? *No*. Would she want a repeat performance of tonight? *Yes*. The experience was amazing. But a commitment? *Not likely*. Jenna suspected their clashing perspectives would probably cause more friction than benefit.

Murray had turned on the gas fireplace earlier, and the welcome heat counteracted the incoming draft from the open sliding door. He stood outside in the pre-dawn light, leaning over the balcony stark naked. Jenna giggled despite herself and admired the muscles that flexed as Murray paced the patio. He was a modern-day Apollo, not someone she ever imagined being involved with.

How this night ever happened was beyond her. He'd shown his prowess more than once, as witnessed by the aftershocks still lingering in her lady parts. Her passion ignited as never before, freeing her from inhibitions she'd always struggled with. His patience to pleasure her and his intense concentration to bring them to nirvana together spoke of his experience, for which she was thankful. He was a great teacher—quite the combination.

Murray turned and grinned as he saw her watching him. "Come on outside, baby, the water's great."

Baby? "Ha. It's too cold out there—even your friend has disappeared."

Murray looked down and shrugged. "At least one of us is smart. No worries, though. He always returns. Come and warm me up."

Jenna took another large gulp of her water, placed it on the coffee table, and joined him outside, wrapping herself around his chilled body. "Better?"

"Much." Murray kissed the top of her head. "Thanks for staying tonight. What's your father going to think of this?"

"He'll probably approve. My dad hasn't understood why I haven't been in a serious relationship. He was already married at my age, and my mom was pregnant."

"Good. You're an adult capable of making your own decisions without his approval. Look what you've managed to accomplish at Westerlea Cove." Murray lifted her hands and kissed each calloused fingertip before licking her palm. "That's why I left you the money so that you can hire someone for the hard work." Murray trailed a finger down her nose, then traced her lips. "Your intentions are great, but you're a woman first. My woman."

"Excuse me? Your woman? I think you're getting ahead of things, aren't you?" Jenna took a step back. "Tonight was a lot of fun, and I appreciate every bit of it—but you're jumping the gun. Before tonight, I wasn't looking to get involved with you. We hardly know each other."

"I knew when I saw you that you were the one. Do you think I'd give just anybody fifty grand? I wanted you to know

I could look after you. You and I have a chance for a great life together. I can see us traveling—"

"Hang on, hang on. You're going off the deep end here, Murray. I wasn't asking you to come into my life and make it better. I wasn't flirting with you." Jenna could feel her blood pressure rising and struggled to maintain her temper. "I admit the *fireworks* tonight were spectacular, but there's more to sharing life than great sex. I love my independence. I'm quite capable of fixing the situation my family is in. I'm far from ready for a relationship."

Suddenly, Jenna felt a hot flush of anger sear through her. *Nobody, but nobody, tells me what to do.* So why was she explaining herself? Did he think that giving her money gave him the privilege? Even her father knew enough not to give her ultimatums. He'd ask, they'd talk, and then they figured it out together. No way would she settle for less from anyone else. She stomped from the patio and gathered her clothes from the bedroom.

"What's the problem here? What are you getting all worked up about?" Murray followed her and stood, hands on his hips as he watched her shed the bathrobe and slip on her thong and dress.

"In case you haven't noticed, I've got a mind of my own and a temper to go with it. I don't like people planning my life for me. Did you really think leaving me money would cause me to drop everything important to me and run away with you?"

Jenna pointed a trembling finger at him as her voice rose with anger. "You don't get to make plans and decide what I'll do without talking to me first. No one does. It shows that you don't know me at all." Jenna slammed her hands into his chest and pushed him out of the doorway. "I don't care how fantastic this night was. My opinion needs to matter. I'm a person, not chattel."

"Jenna, baby, that's not it at all. I love your independence and your attitude. I wanted to make your life easier and show you a better life." Murray lifted his hands in supplication. "Listen to me—please—I'll make you happier than ever. I'll set your dad up, make your oyster lease the jewel of Clayoquot Sound. We'll have a great life together. Let me do this, please."

"If I were you, I'd back off right about now. I think we both need time to figure *this*—" Jenna pointed to herself and then to him. "Whatever *this* is, out. I don't feel like we're on the same page." She stormed to the door, grabbed her coat and purse from the foyer, and flung it open.

Jenna lowered her voice into a slow growl to avoid ambiguity. "As I've explained, I'll do whatever it takes to make our family's lease profitable and in top shape again. And I'll do it *on my own*. I don't *need* you to make me happy with your money." Jenna lifted an eyebrow, daring him to convince her otherwise. Hearing nothing further, she entered the hall and marched toward the elevator. Glancing behind her, she saw a bewildered, naked man spreading his hands in front of him, his eyes wide open, and his eyebrows stretched almost to his hairline.

"Get inside, Murray, before someone calls the cops on you," Jenna whispered loudly. She turned away from him and leaned against the elevator wall. What was the matter with her? Jenna was sure her outburst had shocked the hell out of him, yet not half as much as she'd surprised herself.

The elevator pinged its arrival, and she entered without another word. Digging in her purse for her cell phone, she texted for a taxi to pick her up, then slid on her heels. Jenna saw her reflection on the mirrored wall surface and groaned. Her hair was messy, her eye makeup smeared, and she was barelegged. She looked like she'd been screwed royally.

And she had. But then, so had Murray. It seemed that she panicked anytime money was involved in her adult life, causing her temper to explode and creating more problems. Had she ruined a chance to repeat the best sexual night of her life?

What the hell have I done?

CHAPTER 12

J enna knew her late arrival after her date hadn't gone unnoticed, so she didn't have to say a word when she trundled down from the loft looking like death warmed over. Her father pushed the button on the coffee machine, sat at the table, and waited. Jenna headed straight for the shower.

When she emerged twenty minutes later, she felt human again. Jenna poured herself a coffee and gestured the pot to her dad, who refused the offering. She sat across from him and sighed. "What do you want, good news or bad?"

"Let's start with the good. I imagine you were impressed with your dinner?"

"Definitely. The ambiance was luxurious, the food and wine were unbelievable, but things soured later."

"Figured something happened, or you'd be up early bubbling with information."

"Yup, that's how I usually roll." Jenna shrugged. "It started well, and I'll skip to the end. You know that funny feeling I had about him? I figured it out. Before I left, he'd created a future all mapped out for us."

"Uh-oh. Let me guess. Murray didn't ask your opinion first?"

"Nope, he didn't. And this was our first date, for heaven's sake." Jenna took a deep breath and slowly exhaled. "It was the red flag I thought might pop up. He assumed that whatever he wanted would be so good for me that I should be pleased and thankful to go along with it."

"He's only known you for a few days and thinks he knows what's right for my girl? He didn't look that stupid."

"I know, right? I lost my temper and huffed out of his suite. I'll bet any money that he's waiting for me to call and apologize. After all, what girl wouldn't want to be looked after like he suggested, especially after the expensive gift he left me?"

"I imagine some women want that life, but you're too headstrong and independent. If Murray is truly crazy about you, he should consider your feelings before making decisions. Theo shook his forefinger lovingly at his daughter.

"You're exactly how your mom and I raised you to be— self-sufficient and confident. But it would help if you also learned *not* to jump to conclusions. Instead of exploding and storming out, you should've talked and cleared things up that you disagree with."

Jenna nodded, her eyes downcast. "I know. By the time I entered the elevator, I was already feeling awful. Not to get into details, but it's a night I won't soon forget. I didn't stick around to find out his end plan, but I'm sure he won't give up the high life in Seattle for Westerlea Cove. And I'm certainly not the type to enjoy his standard of living and the social events he's probably accustomed to." Jenna took another sip of her coffee and sighed. "Give me Tofino any day. A week's holiday now and then is enough for me."

Jenna cocked an eyebrow at her dad, then smirked, "but

I wouldn't say no to another night at the Black Rock." After following that thought through, Jenna frowned and shrugged. "Although I probably screwed up that possibility. Oh well."

"You never know. Maybe not. You know who you are and what you want in life, but don't shut out future opportunities." Theo sipped at his coffee and cleared his throat. "As you've recently reminded me, relationships aren't as traditional as they used to be nowadays. It's more common to be together while living apart at least some of the time, especially with the age of technology and instant communication."

Theo shifted in his chair and drew his hand over his chin as usual when thinking. "Feelings and situations change, so always trust your gut. You may not understand why you feel a certain way. Sometimes, the reasons take time to percolate from feelings to understanding. Human instinct is a precious tool, and too many people ignore it. I hope you won't."

"I'm trying not to." Jenna popped the dishes into the sink and turned around. "I think I'll go for a long walk on the beach and clear my head. I might go to Ucluelet later and visit with Lee, so don't wait for dinner because of me. It could end up being a long night."

"Whatever you need to do, go for it. You don't need to explain yourself to me. I'll see you when I see you."

ANOTHER TEXT—THIS time pleading for answers. Jenna frowned. Without any response from her, Murray changed tactics. He'd left her alone for three days, probably thinking she'd come to her senses and call him to apologize. She almost did, but she resisted the temptation. No amount of talking would change things right now.

When that didn't work, the texting began, acknowledging his stupidity and declarations it would never happen again. Jenna refused to get into it with him and pleaded with him to give her time. His idea of time certainly didn't jive with hers, as the texts became more frequent, so she'd blocked him until she could figure out her feelings. Now, he began to text Vaughan messages to relay for him.

That wouldn't work, either. Despite Vaughan's pleas to call the poor beggar back, Jenna refused to bow to his demands. He might as well get it through his thick skull that their brief night together might not be repeated. Yes, she enjoyed dinner with him, and yes, she was thrilled with his sexual expertise. But that funny feeling in the pit of her stomach only became stronger.

Seriously, what was wrong with a guy who spent one night with a woman and decided she should spend the rest of her life bowing to his opinion? No. Jenna would never be controlled by someone else. All this texting pressure did was create more tension between them and lessen the likelihood she'd give him a second chance.

Spending time with her father and taking solitary walks along Chesterman Beach in the blustery early winter weather grounded her. Why was she nervous about meeting Murray again? For a man his age and status, why didn't he have a steady girlfriend? What did he want from her? She might not have the answers to her ambivalence, but that wisp of fear prevented her from reaching out.

Money matters always made her nervous. Instinct warned her to break free of the tie that bound them. She admitted it didn't make sense that his gift should cause her so much anxiety, but it was. If the money were gone, maybe they'd have a chance. With the decision to get rid of his unwanted gift made, Jenna felt much better.

Jenna returned home, hung up her jacket in the foyer, and sat beside her father. "I called Wayne at his lease, and everything is fine over there, so I thought I'd spend another week at home. I'm going to stay with Lee for a few days. I need a break and more buddy talk. Are you ok with that?"

"Of course. Lee will probably perk you up and get you back on track faster than I can."

"Probably. A few bottles of wine will have Lee psychoanalyzing me, and we'll solve the world's problems before I come home." The attempt at humor fell flat, and Jenna grimaced.

"Then go have fun. How about you and I go for dinner at the pub when you return? It's been a while since I've gone out."

"Great idea. I texted Lee that I wanted to spend time with him, so he's arranged to take a few of his sick days off and return to Ucluelet this afternoon. Yay." Jenna danced a jig, which made her dad smile.

"Go on, get out of here. This is what you need right now. Buddy time."

"I know." Skipping up the steps to the loft, Jenna quickly filled an overnight case and the cash in a backpack, then bounded back down to the bathroom for toiletries. She was packed and racing out the door in ten minutes.

Laughter, a best friend, and wine truly were the best medicines. After a slow start, Jenna confided the details of her night with Murray to Lee. He gasped, commiserated, and laughed appropriately. Revealing her father's wise observations, Lee was impressed.

"Your dad really has his life turned around. You must be so proud of him. Too bad he didn't get counseling right away after your mom died. It would've saved a lot of grief for both of you."

"So true. A woman in his support group may have something to do with his progress. Her name's Michelle, and I think she's inspired my dad to become healthy again. I'm thankful for whatever triggered the change in attitude." Jenna yawned.

"Me too. I love a happy ending." Lee stretched his arms and rubbed his eyes. "You've got me yawning now. Ready for bed? I'm done."

Jenna nodded, followed him down the hall, and entered the guest bedroom. She thought she'd be too wired to sleep with all the chatter and thoughts running through her head. Over a week of very little sleep finally caught up with her, and she was out like a light.

THE AROMA of fresh coffee filtered through her senses, bringing Jenna to consciousness. She stretched out and sighed. The weight on her shoulders was gone. She had a plan. She flipped the duvet off and padded into the kitchen.

"You slept well. It's after ten o'clock. Ready for coffee?"

"I haven't slept so well in, like, forever, it seems. Ever since that money appeared in my life, it's controlled me." Jenna's voice dropped as she sank her head into her hands. "I'm so confused."

"What do you know about Murray? Have you checked him out on Facebook or Instagram? Maybe he's not the guy you think he is." Lee went to his home workstation and grabbed his laptop. "Let's check the guy out."

"I don't know. It doesn't seem right. Isn't there a law about ghosting people?"

"Don't be silly. Everybody does it. Murray's from Seattle, but what's his last name?"

"Meadows. He and his uncle have a landscaping empire, although I don't know what it's called."

Lee typed in the info and hit enter. Several Murray Meadows popped up, and she arrowed down until she found Seattle, then clicked on it. "Is that him?"

Jenna leaned forward and verified the photo of Murray shaking hands with someone as the man she'd met. "Scroll down, see what else we can find." As Lee scanned the photo album, Jenna pointed out the *Vagabond*. "That's the boat his Uncle Clint owns. See the older guy in that photo? The grumpy one? That's him.

Lee and Jenna began scrolling through the posts, giggling about their detective skills, until a picture of a voluptuous red-headed woman leaning on Murray's arm caught their attention.

"Wow, she's beautiful. Look at the clothes and the jewelry on her. That must be his former wife. He said she liked society life." Jenna noted the diamond and sapphire necklace glittering against her skin. "Can you tell me the date of this photo?"

"Just a sec. Hmm... it looks as if Murray likes the event, too. He looks extremely sexy in that tuxedo." Lee was a speed reader and began to scan the article about the charity event they were at. "Uh-oh. Did you say he was divorced or something?"

"Yes. Murray and his wife were only married for a few years. Why?" Jenna grabbed the laptop closer so she could also read it. "Oh shit. This photo was taken only a few months ago." Jenna looked at Lee, confused by what she had read. "He must've been escorting her to the gala. Maybe something he was involved with, and they went together."

"Maybe. Take another look at the woman and check out her left hand. That sure looks like a wedding ring to me." Lee zoomed in on the photo, then zoomed in on Murray. "And he's wearing one too. I'm sorry, Jenn. Something's fishy here."

"I can't believe it! That lying sack of shit." Jenna pounded the table, then stood and paced the kitchen. "Why would he do that?"

"That's obvious. You're a challenge. A beautiful, naïve young lady living on the Canadian west coast. Who would ever know about you besides his uncle?"

"Oh, my God." Jenna closed her eyes and fisted her hands. "That's what he meant." Jenna flushed at the memory. "Clint warned me. He whispered in my ear when they left Westerlea Cove. Something about watching out for the charming ones. They can't always be trusted."

Lee guided her to the living room and gently pushed her onto the sofa. "I'm so sorry, Jenn. What a con artist."

"I can't believe I fell for him." When Lee shot her a distressed look, Jenna backpedaled. "I didn't fall *in love* with him, but I did let him get under my skin." Jenna put her head into her hands, tears rolling down her eyes. "I knew something wasn't quite right, but I couldn't figure out what it was."

Lee went to the fridge, pulled out a bottle of chardonnay, and grabbed two glasses. "It's not your fault. He buttered you up slowly. You didn't stand a chance. You saw someone sexy and adventurous, and you ignored your intuition. You hear of this kind of thing happening all the time. There's one good thing—at least he wasn't after your money—you don't have any." Lee grimaced.

"No, he was after my body. But why would he give me fifty thousand dollars?" Jenna's eyes went wide as she contemplated his reasons. "He was going to set me up, wasn't he? Make me fall in love with him, then set me up as his mistress away from home. Or maybe he was after the lease?" Jenna reviewed their night together, cringing at her naivete. "We weren't making love that night. We were having sex. Lust--that's all it was."

Lee massaged Jenn's back as Jenn's tears welled up again. "It's okay, sweetie. We all make mistakes. We'll look into this further, and maybe there's an explanation. Do you want to call and ask him about it? Make sure we're not blowing this out of proportion?"

"No, I'm not calling him until I check this out more. But my gut is telling me this was why I held back. Tempting as everything was about Murray, I had an uneasy feeling." Jenna felt her temper warm up, and she smacked the coffee table. "That's it. I'm done with him. I'm calling Vaughan today and arranging a pickup and delivery as we discussed." Jenna tilted her wineglass toward Lee, indicating she needed more wine. "I'm getting a refill, and then I'm going to end this nightmare now. Can I top you up?"

Jenna filled her friend's glass and her own, returned to the living room, and got comfortable on the sofa. She picked up her cell and turned it on. Ping after ping rang as message alerts sounded. Jenna rolled her eyes.

"Is that Murray again?" Lee draped an arm around Jenna, plunked down beside her, and watched her friend's eyes flit through the messages. The edges of Jenna's mouth turned down with aggravation as a groan escaped her lips.

"Well, it's Vaughan relaying his messages. Murray wants to meet for coffee before flying back to Seattle tomorrow. He's so pushy. He says I owe him at least that much."

Lee abruptly stood up and began pacing the living room. "You don't owe him jack-shit. He'll be out of your hair in one more day, and you can relax." Lee was as shocked at his audacity as Jenna had been. "Although," Lee paused and cocked his head to consider his thoughts. "If you do meet him, you could drop the package in person. I mean, what's he going to do when you drop it on a table and walk away? Leave it there? No one deliberately leaves behind that much cash, even if he is stinking rich."

"Call me chicken, but I can't even look at him right now. The thought of being face-to-face with him makes me angry and nauseous at the same time. I don't want to cause a scene or fall for his excuses." Jenna took a deep breath to calm herself. "I thought of sending the money via courier, but I'm scared. What if there are laws about sending that much money over the border? Or, with my luck, the package might get lost."

Jenna slapped her hand on her knee and applied pressure to still the frantic bouncing it usually did when she got stressed. "I don't want to see him, listen to his apologies, or get conned by his charm again. I've contacted Vaughan. He's agreed to help and return my gift for me."

"But can you trust Vaughan with that much money? I can do it for you. Murray means nothing to me, and he won't be able to reach you through me."

Jenna noticed Lee's clenched jaw and reassured him. "Murray knows Vaughan and trusts him. He's Carla's brother, and I doubt Vaughan would do anything to jeopardize his sister's best friend. He may be my only chance to get Murray to stop pressuring me."

Jenna spread her hands before her. "You get that, don't you? I'd rather not involve you at all. I want Murray to accept the money and stay out of my life."

"You're frustrated with him, but I sense passion mixed up with your anger. Are you positive that's what you want?"

Jenna squared her shoulders and lifted her chin. "He destroyed my trust. He doesn't get another chance to do it again." She paused a moment before continuing. "I admit the night Murray and I spent together was eye-opening. That man is *good* at what he does." Jenna slowly rocked her head from side to side. "But great sex isn't everything. What do you have after you leave the bedroom? And reading his texts almost scared me with his intensity." Jenna fumed at the memory. "The way he looked at me, his tenderness, was unbelievable. That man is an accomplished liar. If you don't have honesty and trust, the rest doesn't matter."

"And now he's texting you that you 'owe' him an explanation. You could take that as proof that Murray *was* manipulating you."

"I honestly don't know, but I won't take any chances. Murray fooled me twice, and I can't let it happen again. I'm bringing the parcel to Vaughan on my way home tomorrow. He promises to give it to Murray when he meets him for coffee before Murray flies out. Vaughan doesn't know how much cash is involved. I told him it was only an expensive gift that I was uncomfortable accepting."

"I imagine Murray is a man used to getting his way. He must be frustrated that he doesn't have any influence over you despite the money he gave you. As far as Vaughan goes, that's probably a smart evasion. I don't know Carla's brother, only what you've told me. Somehow, I think he's an opportunist. A wannabe."

Jenna laughed. "You've got him pegged already. Although to give him credit, he's a hard worker like the rest of his family. He's just a dreamer—nothing criminal about that."

"Hmm. Another interesting word you've used

concerning that cash. *Criminal.* Do you think that cash is dirty?"

"What do you think? Who travels with that kind of money? What would be the purpose? Nowadays, with credit cards and PayPal, cash like that isn't necessary. I seldom have even a hundred bucks on me. Why would they?"

"I don't know. It seems strange, but I don't know any wealthy people. Be careful, Jenna." Lee's eyes watered, and his lips thinned. "I've got a bad feeling that Murray's interest was more about your isolated location than you. What if he's picking up drugs or whatever?"

"Look at the two of us—all caught up imagining a criminal conspiracy. Murray may be manipulative and a liar, but I can't see him being a crook. Too much risk at stake for him and his family."

Jenna's right knee began bouncing again. She groaned and ran her fingers through her messy hair. "I think I'm going off the deep end because I'm second-guessing everything he's said or done."

Jenna began to pace the living room like she'd done so many times in the last three days. November rains were legendary on the West Coast, and they'd spent most of their time inside Lee's condo, and it was starting to get to her.

Lee looked worried, the big softie. Jenna held her arms out and pulled Lee in for a hug, wrapping him tightly. "Once I get rid of the cash, things will return to normal. One more night, then I'll get rid of that albatross so we can concentrate on what we'll do at the Westerlea if we don't get the funding."

"You'll get it. I'll make sure of that. In the meantime, we'll focus on estimates, fill out the paperwork, and prep a professional proposal."

Jenna pulled back from the embrace, studied Lee's face,

then leaned her forehead on his, their eyes searching each other. "You're always there when I need you, yet you never smother me."

Lee broke away. "It's about time you noticed. I'd do anything for you."

Feeling a warm wave of emotion flood through her, Jenna nodded. "You can always count on me too. Even if we don't—" Jenna's eyes darted around the room before continuing. "Cross the line. You mean the world to me. You know that, don't you?"

"Silly lady. Of course, I know that. Early in our friendship, I realized I wanted more than you could give in that department. You're a hard act to follow, but I've been trying to find a partner."

"What about Sandi? I liked her when I met her last summer. Is she still in the picture?"

"Yes, she floats in and out. Neither of us is ready to commit to something permanent, but we enjoy what we have. Don't worry about me. By the way, Drew has taken a three-month temporary posting in Bamfield. He's taking Tom's position while he's going through some chemo. I plan on having him for dinner to welcome him. You're invited."

"Hmm." Jenna felt her heart flutter. "That'll be nice having him closer for a while. You'll love working with him. All his research is carefully documented." Jenna felt her face flush and watched Lee's eyes widen. "I'll join you for dinner, but don't go planning anything else to get us back together. That part is over."

Lee smiled as he winked at Jenna. "Sure, it is. Nothing wrong with reconnecting with an old friend, right?"

"Right. The look on your face tells me you hope for more between us. Please don't push it, Lee. I've got enough on my plate."

"Never. Both Drew and I are here if you need us. Let's leave it at that."

"Good. I'll be happy to see him. I've always known you understood my feelings, even when I didn't." Jenna smiled at her friend. "My emotions are all over the map right now. Connecting with Drew just because I'm in trouble wouldn't be fair. Drew deserves the best in a woman, not a bunch of drama. And that's all I am these days."

"No problem. Drew, you and I are forever friends. We can count on each other. Whatever happens between the two of you happens. I won't get involved. Trust me, okay?"

"Absolutely. I love you, and you love me. Unconditionally. I think Drew might fall into that category, too. We'll see." Watching a blush cross Lee's face made her glad. They had each other's backs. They cared deeply about one another. The present connection between Drew and her was probably better than a romantic one anyway. Time would tell if it'd stay that way.

"VAUGHAN, OVER HERE," Jenna yelled, waving him to her van. Vaughan finished the early shift at the Black Fin pub, usually by 2:00 p.m.

"So, what's going on, Jenna?" Vaughan spread out his hands, palms upwards. "Murray's texting me like crazy, wanting to know what's happening. He wants me to bring you to the airport. Why don't you answer his calls?" Vaughan seemed hyper and anxious, likely due to the pressure Murray was applying. "So, Murray pushed you too hard, too fast—I'll bet he won't make that mistake again."

"Forget it. I'm not going with you. There's a lot more going on between the two of us than you need to know."

Jenna's shaky voice made Vaughan stop short and assess his longtime friend. "One day, you'll hear the whole story, but for now, just trust me that this is the right thing to do. Ok?"

"Are you sure? Whatever you're going through, you're not the only one with problems. Murray got a call this morning from his mom. Clint's been pushing himself hard since his son died, and he's had a heart attack. I'm betting that Murray could use some TLC right about now. It might be a good time for you two to iron things out."

"OMG, that's awful. Pass on my wishes for his uncle's speedy recovery, but Murray can't use that as an excuse to have me back in his life."

"You're a tough broad, aren't you? Where's your compassion?" Vaughan's eyebrows almost jumped into his hairline at Jenna's insensitive remark.

"It's alive and well, thank you. But I can't get sidetracked, and with his uncle now recuperating, neither can he." Jenna's voice quickened, and she folded her arms. "Money isn't always the answer to every problem, yet both he and his uncle seem to think it is. And look at the trouble that attitude's brought."

"I guess so." Vaughan shifted from one foot to the other, struggling to devise a compromise.

"Don't bother trying to understand, Vaughan." Jenna reached into her backpack and pulled out the wrapped shoe-sized box. "I'm glad you're bringing this back for me. Murray bought me a beautiful antique gift, and it's too valuable to keep if I've no intention of seeing him."

"If it were me, I'd keep it. Isn't it bad luck to return a gift?"

Jenna smirked. "No, you idiot, it isn't. Good try. His expensive gift feels like an anchor that links us. I don't want that kind of connection, so the anchor's got to go." Jenna handed it to Vaughan. "It's fragile, so please be careful. You'll bring it back to Murray now?"

"Yes. I'm meeting him in an hour for a drink before he flies out."

"Thanks, Vaughan." Jenna pulled out her wallet and gave him a folded fifty-dollar bill. "I hate sticking you in the middle of this, but I appreciate your help. Buy yourself a bottle of Crown Royal, ok?"

"Thanks. I guess the *Vagabond* isn't welcome at Westerlea Cove anymore?"

"No, I'm afraid not. But anytime you're in the area, you're welcome to call and stop by."

Vaughan shook the box, gauging its weight and what could be in it. "What is it?"

"Girly stuff. Nothing you'd be interested in, trust me." Jenna winked, then headed back to her truck. "Let me know how it goes, please."

"You bet. Later, Jenna." Vaughan returned to his Toyota Rav 4, opened the door, and carefully placed it on the passenger seat before offering Jenna a nod and his usual two-fingered salute. Jenna waited until she saw him leaving the restaurant parking lot and heading toward the airfield before breathing a loud sigh of relief. Mission accomplished.

THE MORNING after Jenna delivered the tightly wrapped parcel to Vaughan, she returned from Lee's. She parked in the driveway and brought her overnight bag into the house. Jenna felt a lot lighter than four days ago, that's for sure. A heavy weight fell from her shoulders as she handed the money to Vaughan, making her feel...safer? Maybe. Life would return to its complicated normal. She, her dad, and Lee would figure out a solution to Westerlea's financial situation. It wouldn't hurt that Drew was also here. Hopefully, he'd be an added voice to approve the oyster fund application.

"Hey, Dad, how are things going?"

"Same as usual, can't complain. How was your visit with Lee? It looks like it's perked you up. Any more word from Murray?" Theo was refilling his coffee and tipping the pot to her. Jenna nodded her assent, and he retrieved her mug, filled it up, and passed it to her.

"He's tried, but I blocked him, so I think he's got the message." Jenna blew on the steaming brew and sipped the potent blend. She paused and then cleared her throat nervously. "You might not approve of something Lee and I did. We felt we didn't know enough about Murray and decided to become amateur detectives. There's no such thing as privacy on Google if you're in the public eye. The truth was tough to swallow, but pictures don't lie." Jenna paused as she wondered what her dad's reaction would be. "Remember I told you he was divorced? He's not. We saw several recent pictures of him and his wife posted at charity galas. They were both wearing wedding rings and looked very happy."

"You're right. Normally, I don't believe in scouting personal info online, but there are always exceptions." Theo's voice shook with anger for his daughter's obvious distress. "Awe, sweetheart. I'm sorry." Theo's eyes glittered as he raised his voice. "What a jerk. How dare he lie and flirt with you like that. You must be pissed. I would be." Theo shook his head in disbelief, then reached over and patted Jenna's forearm.

"I am. I'm so angry I could spit." Jenna used a phrase her

mom would often say when frustrated. She swallowed a lump in her throat as tears welled up. "I should've listened to my gut like you advised me. I believed him, fell for his charm, and ignored my intuition."

"So now what?" Theo began drumming his fingers on the table.

"I called Vaughan for a favor. He's bringing my 'gift' back to Murray at the airport. I've asked him to emphasize that I don't want any further contact, although I doubt I'll hear from him anyway. At least, I hope not. His uncle had a heart attack, and Murray will probably have to take over his uncle's business operations for a while." Jenna shrugged her shoulders as if shucking off a cumbersome weight. "Just as well."

"I'm sure you've looked at every angle, Jenn. Could there be a mistake? Looks can be deceiving. Maybe there's an explanation."

"Thanks for trying to give me hope. Like Mom would say, 'You can tell the same truth over and over, but lies only get tangled up.' I don't want to listen to excuses or his justification for seducing me." Jenna lifted an eyebrow as she noticed her dad's reaction. "I know, I know. I'm a grown woman, and I went out with him with my eyes wide open."

"Yes, you did. But you were still disadvantaged because you didn't know the truth. Everything that happened after your dinner wouldn't have if you'd known."

"That's true." Jenna puffed out a sigh. "I learned something valuable, though. It's what you told me a while ago. You may not know why you feel a certain way, but there's a reason, so listen and proceed carefully. I didn't, but I won't make that mistake again."

Theo slid his chair closer to his daughter and wrapped his arms around her. "Life isn't fair, pumpkin. Don't let this bad experience make you bitter. There are nice guys around. When the time's right, you'll find yours."

"I know, Dad. More than anything, I'm disappointed in myself." Jenna disengaged and brought their coffee cups to the dishwasher. "I'm now focusing on my family, friends, and Westerlea Cove. Nothing else matters." Jenna forced a smile before continuing. "Let's change the subject—what do you have planned today?" Jenna sat down and snagged a shortbread cookie.

Theo nodded. "I'm going to physical therapy at 3:00, which takes about an hour. Then I have a coffee date with Michelle at the Patisserie. You're welcome to join us. I've talked a lot about you."

"Of course, but not today. I need to visit Carla in the early afternoon for a visit, then dinner."

"No problem, we'll get together another day."

"Thanks, and tell Michelle I'd love to meet her when things calm down around here. Maybe next time I come back from the lease." Jenna looked at the time. "I better get moving. This week, Daryl is working out of town in Ahousat, so Carla and I plan to catch up with her wedding plans. And if I know the Walsh family, she already knows about the drama in my life. I'm sure she'll want some explanations. Vaughan's supposed to join us for dinner. I'm dying to find out how Murray reacted. I'll see you tonight. Is that okay with you?"

"No problem. Enjoy your visit, and try not to get upset. Things will settle down eventually, so be patient."

"I'm trying, Dad. You have no idea—" Jenna ran upstairs to change into jeans and a sweatshirt. She pulled her still-damp hair back into a ponytail, then swiped on mascara and lip gloss. Good enough.

JENNA PULLED into Carla's visitor parking spot. She hadn't seen Vaughan's vehicle yet, but he was often late. She knocked several times before she heard the thumping steps of someone going downstairs. The door flew open, and Carla rushed to hug her friend.

"So glad we're having dinner together tonight. It's been way too long. Are you sure you didn't want to go out and eat?"

Jenna slipped her shorty boots off and followed her into the dining room, where Carla had set the table for three. "No, I'm sure you've heard about all the crap going on with Vaughan's friend. I figured we'd be wiser to talk about this in private."

"Holy shit, Jenna. Vaughan says this guy is loaded. I mean *loaded*. And he's driving my brother up the wall with texts about you. Tell me all the juicy details." Carla sat on her chair with her elbow on the table, supporting a curious face. "Come on, spill it."

"Don't I get a coffee or a soda first?" Jenna teased. "I smell baking. You went all out."

"Of course, I made your favorite—a raspberry cheesecake. The main course is marinated chicken breasts and stuffed potatoes. I'll turn them on an hour before we're ready to eat. A Greek salad's waiting in the refrigerator. Whatever's leftover, I'll send home for my parents with Vaughan." Carla jumped to her feet and into the kitchen. "Coffee's about half an hour old, and I've ginger ale and sodas in the fridge. Unless you need wine, which I'll get from the pantry."

"Let's save the wine for dinner. Ginger ale's good for

now." Jenna accepted a can and poured it into a glass. "How long before Vaughan gets here?"

"Anytime, I guess. You know my brother. He was supposed to pop over and see the folks last night, but he didn't show. Probably work, but he could've phoned them and apologized."

"Agreed. That wasn't nice. Although, I'm glad we've got some alone time first. There's stuff your brother doesn't need to hear. But if I know you, you'll want all the details about our date at the Black Rock."

"You bet I do. And whatever happened afterward that had Murray in a knot." Carla's eyebrows waggled as she giggled. "I can't believe it. My buddy snagged a hot one."

"Maybe Murray snagged the hot one," Jenna shot back. "For the record, once and only once will I say this –but no wonder you never stopped talking about sex when we were in high school. *Wow.*" Jenna smiled as she remembered her initiation to heightened passion.

"I knew it! I knew that your story would change when you found the right person. So, did the earth shudder?" Carla took a drink of her soda and then started to laugh, almost choking on it.

Jenna popped up and smacked her on the back a few times. "You're getting a lot of pleasure out of this, aren't you?"

"Damn right, I am. Have I ever told you how much I hated your eye rolls? Whenever I met a new guy and went goofy on him, all you did was roll your eyes each time I mentioned their name."

"Could be because you never shut up about them. You never had a filter—whatever you thought came out of your mouth. Most of the time, it was too much information. Thus, the eye rolls."

"Whatever. Spill. Vaughan tells me that he's a hunk. Blonde and tall. And rich. What more could a girl want?"

"Really? What would you say if, after the best sex of your life, your partner starts telling you what to do or what he's planned for the future? What if you found out later the same guy lied to you?"

"No! Best sex of your life?" Carla's mouth fell open, her eyes shining with anticipation of the juicy details.

"Oh, for heaven's sake, that's what you're getting out of that statement? Ok. Here it is, Carla. Yes, twice in one night. It was incredible. Heart pounding, thrilling, and exhausting all in one."

Carla was slapping her palm on the table, celebrating the breakthrough. "Awesome, I'm so excited for you." Carla paused, her eyes wide. "Hold it. He lied to you? About what?"

"I better give you some background first. I must admit I was floating on cloud nine for a while. But after the fun was over, it was a different story. We'd only known each other for four days. We spent three days at the lease together and one night at Black Rock. Then he tells me how he'll set my dad up on the lease, and as his girlfriend, he expects me to take it easy there."

Jenna shook her head and pulled her knee underneath her as she became comfortable on the chair and leaned forward. "Talk about going overboard and taking over my life. It scared the shit out of me. I mean, who does that?"

"After sex-glow is a powerful emotion, Jenn. He must've been over the moon with plans to improve your life." Carla fidgeted in her chair, trying not to ask questions but clearly wanting more information.

"Maybe so, but that's not all. Long story short, nobody tells me what to do and when."

"Miss Independent. Vaughan tells me that Murray's realized his mistake and wants another chance, and you keep saying no."

"That's right. Murray gave me a ridiculously expensive gift, and then he began to say things like I owe him." Jenna paused and took a deep breath. "Well, I packaged it up and gave it to Vaughan yesterday. They met for coffee at the airport before his flight back to Seattle. That ought to emphasize how I feel." Jenna sipped her soda, squinted at her friend, and wondered how much to tell her.

"There's something else too. Murray told me he was divorced. Lee and I checked him out on social media and found out differently. He lied to me, Carla. He was so charming and attentive I ignored my initial doubts. He had me completely fooled, and I feel so stupid now." Her eyes searched her friend's, looking for reassurance. "You know me. I have no tolerance for guys like him, no matter how special they think they are."

"Wow. Aren't you going to confront Murray with what you found? Maybe there's an explanation?" Carla's surprised look soon turned practical. "I don't know many women who wouldn't give a guy like him a second chance. I probably would. Hell, I might even give him a third." Carla teased as she patted her heart, indicating her probable reaction.

Jenna raised her voice, smacked the table, and sputtered. "Really? You'd have to be there to hear and see what I did. Controlling men, especially those who are liars, aren't my cup of tea, no matter if they *are* rich. I don't need to get first-degree burns to avoid a roaring fire."

"I'm sorry." Carla's eyes became somber as Jenna paused to catch her breath. "Your evening started so great—too bad it didn't work out as you hoped."

"But that's the problem. I didn't hope for anything. I

wasn't looking for anything. I accepted Murray's dinner invitation, which was an amazing experience. We drank too much wine, and all the attention he gave me went to my head. So, we went to his suite. He was a great lover and teacher. I don't regret that. But Murray wasn't quite the gentleman I thought he was. If I'd known the truth, I wouldn't have slept with him."

"I really am sorry. I thought Murray might be the one for you. And you're right. Relationships are doomed right off the bat if honesty isn't there."

Jenna shrugged her shoulders. "I know. Maybe it's our small-town upbringing, but I can't trust a guy like that. I don't even want to give him a chance to explain."

Carla smiled and patted Jenna's hand. "It was like the Cinderella-type story that everyone wishes might happen to them or someone they know. Too good to be true."

"Yes. I'm still processing what happened. One thing that the fiasco made me appreciate was my friend, Drew. Maybe we didn't have fireworks, but there's something to be said for loyalty and respect. I never doubted anything about Drew." Jenna finished the rest of the ginger ale and sat quietly. "Where's that brother of yours? I'm getting hungry."

Carla turned the oven on. "Won't be long. If he's not here in an hour, we'll eat. He can nuke his own when he arrives. Are you ready for a glass of wine before dinner, or wait until the meal's served?"

"Sure. Now that we've discussed my love life, let's catch up with your wedding plans." Jenna looked at her watch. "How's it going? I can't believe you haven't let Daryl move in with you. Talk about old-fashioned."

"No, only good common sense. It'll be easier to renovate if we aren't living in a mess. Daryl will tackle the renovations after returning from our honeymoon in August. We'll stay in his apartment until the restorations are completed, then hopefully, move into our forever home in the new year."

"You're very lucky that your family figured out a way for you to buy this place. It's hard to find anything affordable." Jenna injected a tone of interest even though she only wanted to concentrate on Vaughan and the package delivery.

"I know." Carla crossed her fingers and kissed them, an old expression of thankfulness she'd always used. "Mom and Dad cashed in my life insurance they'd started when I was born, then added the balance needed for the ten percent down payment as our wedding gift. With no real estate fees and their financial help, we now own our first home, and everyone's happy that it's staying in the family."

Pointing to the dated wallpaper border below the ceiling and the pink carpet on the floor, Carla complained. "Daryl calls this the *Pepto-Bismol Palace*. There's so much pink in this place that getting rid of it'll be a relief. There are even pinky-beige kitchen counters—yuk." Always demonstrative, Carla stuck her finger in her mouth, indicating a gagging reflex.

"Daryl's a good electrician and handyman, and you've got a good eye for putting things together, so you'll transform this place beautifully. You're lucky."

"I am. We *are* blessed. We'll have a work party when it's time to paint, so prepare for that event."

"Good luck. Give me a job for the outside."

"You have to paint too. We're giving you the closets, though." Carla laughed at the expression on her friend's face. "If you make a mess, no one will notice. You should get experience painting. One day, it'll be your turn to renovate." When Jenna stuck her tongue out at her, Carla continued. "What about your dad's place? One of these days, he'll want to move back in. It might be smart to paint the place at least and re-finish the floors there. It wouldn't bring back so many painful memories."

Jenna's rueful expression turned thoughtful. "You know, that might be a good plan. I'll bet it'll be easier on Dad if we change things around. Not a bad idea, Carla."

"I've been known to have a few. And one right now is to enjoy our dinner. I'll give my brother another text with a five-minute warning, and then he can fend for himself."

"Sounds good. I hoped to talk to Vaughan about his meeting yesterday. I asked him to call and tell me how it went, but he didn't."

"Something must've happened at the restaurant that's got his attention. He could never do more than one thing at a time. I'll get him to call you or pop over tonight if you want."

"That'd be great," Jenna agreed. But inside, her heart was beginning to trip hammer. Although she hoped there was nothing seriously wrong with the pub, it might be preferable to the wrath of Murray's anger. *Oh, stop overreacting*, Jenna scolded herself. *Do you honestly think Murray would take his anger toward her out on Vaughan?*

The dinner was a success, and Carla packaged portions for her parents and two pieces of cheesecake for Jenna to share with her dad. In the meantime, Jenna checked her cell several times, waiting for contact from Vaughan. The gnawing feeling in her gut warned her that something might be off. By the early evening, she stopped hiding her anxiety, thanked Carla for the hospitality, and returned home. She begged Carla to have Vaughan call or text her, no matter the time.

At 11:00 p.m., Jenna couldn't help herself and called Carla again.

"I'm sorry he hasn't called you, but I don't know where he is. Vaughan isn't responding to my parents' texts either. We're starting to get worried. A day or two incommunicado isn't unusual if he's on his days off, but you're right. Something seems off."

Jenna heard the tension in her friend's voice and attempted to soothe her. "Maybe he decided to go with Murray at the last minute. You know your brother. He wouldn't turn down a free trip."

"That little beggar will get a tongue lashing from us if he's gone on a joy ride without letting us know. If we haven't heard by Saturday night, please do us a favor and text Murray. Maybe my brother joined him, and they're partying it up in Seattle."

"Oh, gosh, Carla. I don't know. I don't want to open that can of worms again."

Carla blew out a long sigh. "You're probably right. My brother will arrive home with a ton of excuses and a hangover. I'll make sure he contacts you as soon as I hear from him."

"Ok, let me know what the troublemaker's been doing," Jenna said before clicking off the cell. *Damn.* She'd have to consider contacting Murray if Vaughan hadn't reached his family or returned to work on Monday. What the hell were the two of them up to?

CHAPTER 13

A week had passed since Vaughan disappeared. Frantically, the family called all the hospitals on the Island, fearing he'd taken a joy ride and crashed somewhere. On Monday, Carla's parents went to the RCMP detachment and filed a missing person's report. The police performed their due diligence and contacted all the detachments with Vaughan's name, description, and vehicle information. As they reassured the family, it takes time for patrols to be on the lookout for abandoned or crashed vehicles. There was rough terrain on Vancouver Island in every region. He could be anywhere.

Their inquiries were in vain. There was no report of Vaughan receiving or requesting medical assistance. The RCMP wondered if Vaughan's disappearance had a logical explanation, like him going on a trip. The Walshs reassured them he'd never leave for more than a few days without informing them or his employer.

"Jenna? Jenna?" Theo raised his voice to break through his daughter's woeful trance. "I think it's time to contact Murray. It isn't fair for the Walsh family to be worried if

Vaughan joined him in Seattle. We all need to know one way or another."

"I was awake half the night, thinking the same thing. I was on a group text with Lee and Drew yesterday discussing the best action plan. Contacting Murray is the next step. We've got to know if Vaughan is with Murray before we do anything else." Jenna retrieved her cell, unblocked Murray's name, and then took a deep breath. "Who knows if he'll even accept my call? I'm afraid I was firm about the no-contact rule."

"You won't know until you try. Murray might be ecstatic to see you reaching out." Theo tilted his head to one side and offered an encouraging smile.

Jenna remained silent as she thought of the secret she'd kept from her father. "Maybe, but I think I'll go outside. It might get ugly, and you don't need to hear that." She slipped on shoes and a heavy sweatshirt and went onto the patio to sit on an Adirondack chair. She began her text.

> Hi Murray. I wanted to check that you received my package from Vaughan before you left.

Jenna bit her lip as she waited for a response. He was probably working or busy, so she'd wait a little longer. After ten nerve-wracking minutes, Jenna tried again.

> I'm sorry to bother you, but there's a problem here. Please text me as soon as you have a free minute. Thanks.

Jenna sat quietly for a few minutes, wondering how he'd react to her messages. She couldn't blame him one bit if he ignored her. As she waited, she drum-rolled her fingers on the chair to release her restless energy.

When her knee began to bounce, Jenna jumped to her feet. *This could be a long wait.* Jenna stepped down from the verandah and headed between the evergreens toward the beach. The sky matched the grey seas, a study in tranquility, something she was currently lacking. Jenna flipped the hoodie over her hair when she neared the beach to keep the damp air from chilling her, then slipped her phone and cold hands into the fleece-lined pockets.

Jenna concentrated on stepping through a three-foot section of washed-up seaweed from the last storm. Breathing the salty tang of ocean air slowly calmed Jenna's anxiety. Low tide stretched a half kilometer from shore, and Jenna made her way close to the barely discernible surf. So many scenes played out along the west coast. Wild and stormy, sunny with surf, or foggy and preternaturally calm. Jenna was glad that the weather today mirrored her mood.

A pang of guilt stabbed through her. She used Vaughan to solve her problem, and her request to deliver the package to Murray might be why he was missing. Would Murray tell her the truth about Vaughan and the money she returned? She hoped so. Jenna thought of Murray holding her that night, his blue eyes suffused with desire. Her pulse quickened before she chastised herself. She was so naïve. She mistook his lust for passionate love.

If it weren't for the truth she'd discovered, would she have found the strength to resist Murray? Thank goodness, the dishonesty made that question moot. Oh, Lord, what a mess. Reigning in her growing panic, Jenna lifted her eyes to the sky, begging for help from a Higher Power. Her inner compass had lost true north, causing her to make poor decisions. She prayed for courage to help her fix the crisis she had set in motion. Jenna closed her eyes, breathing deeply, and calmed her racing heart until she felt a state of serenity overtake her.

Minutes later, Jenna became aware of her surroundings as her senses awoke one by one. Fear had disappeared, and confidence flooded her senses, causing her to smile and experience the fullness of gratitude. She whispered a thank you to her mom for her guidance in her hour of need. With help, she'd find Vaughan and the missing money and make amends.

Jenna turned her attention to a distant dog barking as its master tossed a stick into the water. A couple enjoyed the game with him, probably trying to tire him out. Jenna smiled at the domestic scene and wondered if she'd ever find a partner to share her life with. A tinge of sadness made her turn away and retrace her steps toward home.

Contradiction warred through her emotions again as she compared her relationships with Murray and Drew. Truth be told, there was no comparison. The crucial values she'd grown up with were those that Drew presented. Morals that would stand the test of time. She'd never have to question his loyalty or his truthfulness. They shared common interests on the West Coast, and Jenna finally recognized their mutual beliefs formed a strong bond between them. As thrilling a temptation as lust was, it was a fleeting emotion with no substance.

She might've thrown away a chance for true love by alienating the first man she'd trusted implicitly. Sorrow threatened to engulf her as her eyes moistened at the possibility that she and Drew might never return to the relationship they had. Blinking quickly to avoid the sadness from overcoming her, she pulled Kleenex from her pocket and blew her nose. She needed to get a grip on her emotions and deal calmly with a man she'd grown to dislike.

A vibration from her cell phone set her heart racing. She looked at the sender and exhaled a breath of relief.

(M) Jenna. I'm surprised to hear from you. What's up?

(J) I need to talk to you about Vaughan. Do you know where he is?

(M) Why would I? He didn't show up at the airport when I left, and I haven't heard from him. He isn't answering my texts either. And I do have a few other important things on my plate these days.

(J) I heard about Clint's health problems. I hope he's recuperating well. You must be overwhelmed with everything.

(M) Not as much as I thought I'd be. My uncle's a perfectionist and has his businesses running smoothly. But I'm sure that's not why you reached out. What's going on?

(J) I'm in big trouble. Oh shit, I don't know how to say this.

(M) What do you mean? What's wrong?

(J) I wrapped up the money you gave me and told Vaughan it was an expensive gift I wanted him to return to you. He promised he'd give it to you at the airport. He's been missing ever since.

(M) What's the matter with you? Why would you do something like that? Do you despise me so much that you couldn't deliver it yourself?

> (J) I'm sorry, Murray. I don't know what came over me. I freaked out. I imagined you had ulterior motives, and your gift was part of it.

Jenna's phone rang. The caller ID said *M. Meadows.* Jenna's heartbeat raced with the fear of what Murray would tell her.

"Hello?" Jenna's voice wavered.

"I can't continue texting. I needed to hear your voice."

"After my outburst, I'm surprised you'd want to hear it." Jenna sniffled as her voice shook.

"If only you'd listened and met me to discuss our night. We could've talked this through. We could've avoided all of this."

Now was no time to tell him of her detective skills or accuse him of lying. If she wanted his help, it was best to have him think she had feelings for him. "I'm sorry. I should've delivered it myself and prevented this nightmare. And now, if anything's happened to Vaughan, I'll never forgive myself." Jenna's voice quivered. "And the money? I don't know how I'll do it, but I'll pay you back. That's a promise," Jenna's voice dipped to a whisper as she struggled with the apology.

"Jenna, slow down. We'll figure it out. I'll check the airlines and find out if he bought tickets to go anywhere. If he had opened that package, it might've been too tempting. He might've decided to take a free holiday." Murray paused as he considered other reasons. "Or if someone was with him, they could've robbed him, and he's too ashamed to come home."

"I never thought of that. I assumed Vaughan went to Seattle with you, and maybe you offered him a job he couldn't refuse. I know the RCMP tried to track him by his credit card, but Vaughan had some financial issues about a year ago and cut them up. They're going through the process of obtaining his banking history to see when and where he last used his debit card." Jenna's voice deepened as she tried to control her emotions. "What a mess I've made. I've always had hang-ups about my independence and money. Now, look what's happened."

"Don't take all the blame. If Vaughan hadn't opened it, I'd have received the package and taken it home. You're right when you said I was rushing things. If you'd known me better, you would've trusted me."

"What are we going to do? My dad and the Walsh's will be so disappointed in me." Jenna broke down and sobbed. Even though she knew the kind of man Murray was, his compassion seemed genuine.

"We're going to find him. I've security on staff, and I'll have them dig into it. I'll take the first available flight to Tofino, and we'll talk."

"But you can't do that. You've got Clint to cover for."

"My uncle has all the best care money can buy, and he's already feeling better. And my mom and sister are spoiling him rotten. Our board of directors is excellent and knows what they're doing. No one will even miss me. Besides, you need me more." Murray inhaled deeply, then puffed out a breath. "Ok, back to Vaughan. I assume you've checked hospitals and the police station?"

"Yes, the family has. Nothing's surfaced. That's when I decided to call you. I'm sorry, Murray. It's my fault he's missing, and so is the money."

"I'll be there soon, Jenna. Tomorrow afternoon at the latest. Send me a recent picture of Vaughan that my staff can use to look for him. Also, I want the make and model of his car." Murray paused a moment before continuing. "Neither your dad nor the Walshs needs to know the full story. Their main concern is Vaughan's safety; the rest is none of their business. We'll figure it out."

Jenna listened to Murray's reassurances that no one else needed to know exactly what was in the package. They'd decide what to do when Vaughan and the money were recovered. Numbly, Jenna promised to text him the information he requested and agreed with his every suggestion even though she disapproved.

WHEN JENNA RETURNED HOME, her breathing was under control, and she was ready to tell her dad the truth, no matter how much it hurt. "Dad?"

"In the laundry room, Jenna. I'll be right there. I set the coffee pot, so push the button for me."

"Thanks." Jenna blew on her fingers to warm them. She turned on the coffee and placed two mugs on the kitchen table. The gurgling and aroma from the Cuisinart settled her and made her feel safe. Between her dad and Lee, Jenna knew she'd have moral support to handle Murray and the missing money. She just hoped no one would hate her. Jenna sat at the table with her head in her hands as she struggled with her confession.

"What's up, sweetheart?" Theo massaged Jenna's shoulders in an attempt to ease her obvious distress. "Did you get a hold of Murray?"

"Yes, he returned my call. He says his uncle's getting stronger."

"Glad to hear that." Theo poured them coffee and then sat beside her. "Did he know anything about Vaughan?"

"No. Vaughan didn't deliver the package, and Murray

hasn't heard from him since he left here." Jenna's eyes filled with tears as she looked into her father's trusting eyes. "Oh, Dad—I've made a mess of things. And on top of it, I'm ashamed to admit I lied to you. I'm sorry." Jenna grabbed a napkin from the holder, wiped her eyes, and blew her nose.

"I've never known you to lie, Jenna. Avoid a truth occasionally when you were younger, but nothing worse. What's so bad that you couldn't tell me?" Theo reached over and covered her hand, his voice gentle.

"The package I wanted to return to Murray wasn't a bracelet." Jenna's eyes darted about the kitchen while she built the courage to disappoint her dad. "I trusted Vaughan not to open it." Her hands shredded the tissue she'd been using, and she grabbed another. "I'm scared stiff that he did, and now he's in trouble." Jenna began to hyperventilate, sniffling and wiping her eyes throughout her explanation. Her tearful voice became shrill. "I'm so f-frightened for him."

"For God's sake, Jenna," Theo said, gripping his daughter's hand tighter. "Get control of yourself. Take a deep breath and count to four, then exhale." Theo hobbled to the kitchen sink and dampened a paper towel to place on the back of her neck. He coached Jenna through deep breaths until the tremors, tears, and hiccups subsided.

"There's nothing you can say that will change our relationship. You should know that. So, spit it out. What the hell was in it? Not drugs, I hope."

"No! Never!"

"I didn't think so. Tell me everything, sweetie. Don't leave anything out." Theo scooted his chair close to his daughter and put an arm around her. "I'll do everything I can to help you, but it has to start with the truth. Together, we can fix it."

Jenna nodded and took a sip of her coffee, then another one. She looked into her father's hazel eyes, now haunted with fear. "Remember when I told you that Murray offered to help me, and I didn't know his motives?"

"Yes. You were anxious and confused when you got home, and I told you to trust your gut."

"I was stressed about getting the oyster lease operational again. And when Murray offered to help, I refused." Jenna's gaze left her father's face and darted around again, ashamed of what she was about to confess. "Before he left, he placed two Ziploc bags in my cooler that I didn't see until afterward." Jenna paused and turned to face him again. "It contained fifty thousand dollars, Dad."

Theo's eyes popped open; his eyebrows raised. "Fifty thousand dollars? What the hell? No wonder you were nervous. What's the matter with him?"

"I know. When we went for dinner, Murray insisted I consider the gift philanthropy. He said he could well afford it and liked to help deserving people reach their goals. He told me to use it, and if I still felt strongly about it, I could pay him back after we got the Oyster Recovery Fund. It was so tempting, Dad."

"I'll bet it was." Theo let out a whistling sigh. "That was wrong of Murray to tempt you, especially since he hardly knew you. No wonder you were conflicted." Theo looked at his daughter, whose eyes were downcast. He lifted her chin, held her gaze, and smiled tenderly. "How were you to know if he was trustworthy or if the money was illegal? So, the 'gift' you sent back with Vaughan was money? You did the right thing, giving it back to Murray, although you should've returned it personally." Theo hugged his daughter to his side and kissed the crown of her head. "That's why you've been so edgy lately. You're worried that Vaughan got nosy and looked inside."

"Why didn't Vaughan listen to me?" Jenna swiped at the tears threatening to slip down her cheeks. She took a stabilizing breath before slapping the table. "I told him it was expensive girly stuff, so I don't understand why he'd bother opening it." Jenna looked at her dad, searching for understanding. "Who knows what kind of trouble he's in now? I'm so worried and embarrassed that I feel sick." Jenna's face was blotchy from crying, and her hands shook. "This will destroy the Walshs if they find out their son stole the money. I don't want them to know that, Dad. It'll break their heart, and they'll hate me for getting him tempted and involved with that much cash."

"They'll have to know if Murray reports the theft to the police. Now or later, it's going to come out." Theo limped over to the counter and refilled their coffee mugs. "Is Murray coming here or dealing with it from Seattle?"

"Murray has his security team working on finding him, and he's arranged to come tomorrow. Murray doesn't want to say much about the money until he finds Vaughan. Then he'll make a decision. He says it's no one else's business how much was in there, and if we can recover most of it, he won't report it." Jenna's puffy, red eyes begged for understanding.

"But, if something terrible has happened to Vaughan, Murray will have to tell the police, and then you'll also have to tell the Walsh's."

"Yes. Although Vaughan probably couldn't control himself when he saw the money, he wasn't stupid. We're hoping he comes home with his tail between his legs and a rags-to-riches story to tell."

"So, you're thinking Vegas or Reno?"

"Probably. Hopefully, we'll know soon." Jenna sighed

and closed her eyes for a moment. "I don't know what I would've done if Murray hadn't accepted my call. He was frustrated but kind despite having family issues at home." Jenna's voiced her confusion. "He's such an enigma. I can see both sides of him, and it shakes me up. I hope the kind side of him will be here tomorrow to help me make things right."

Jenna threaded her fingers through her hair as she struggled with possible scenarios. "If Murray reaches out to kiss me, I won't be able to hide my feelings. Once he realizes I know the truth about his marriage, I wonder if he'll continue to be helpful or walk away." Jenna's eyes filled with tears as she searched her father's face. "I'm scared, Dad." Jenna pushed her cup aside, put her hands on the table, and rested her head on top, exhausted from the confession.

"He's bound to be defensive, but don't let him sidetrack the issue. It all started with a relative stranger giving you a huge amount of cash. Then bad decisions from you and Vaughan have created this crisis." Theo gazed at the collapsed form of his independent daughter, stroked her hair, and whispered. "We'll get to the bottom of this soon, Jenna. I promise. It'll all work out."

JENNA, her father, and the Walsh family gathered Thursday afternoon, drinking coffee and waiting for Murray to arrive. His approximate arrival time would be 5:00 p.m. at the Tofino airport, barring delays. It was only a fifteen-minute drive from their home, and he'd call Jenna once he landed from his chartered flight. Jenna would pick him up, and they'd have time to talk privately before meeting with the Walshs. As the time neared, Jenna couldn't sit still.

"I can't take it. I need to walk this off, or I'll explode."

Mrs. Walsh's nervous smile was encouraging. "Go ahead —it's been a long day, and some fresh air will do you good."

"It will." Jenna dressed in her down-filled coat and went outside, zipping it closed against the brisk wind tearing off the ocean. Jenna constantly checked her watch and cell phone and then paced the verandah. Looking inside at the family preparing for answers, she couldn't stop feeling guilty and made a split-second decision.

Screw this.

Jenna could wait at the airport as easily as here, and at least she could pace without being stared at. Jenna knocked at the window and waved, indicating she was leaving. Blowing them a kiss goodbye, she scrambled down the steps and jogged to her Dodge van.

Driving the narrow, already dark highway to the airport, Jenna felt the van buffeted by the wind. Murray chose the quickest route by flying to Victoria, then boarded the VIH Execu-jet to the Tofino airport. In December, the days were short, with dawn arriving around 7:30 in the morning and setting by 4:30. Jenna parked near the arrival gate and kept the vehicle idling to stay warm. Several people were waiting inside, but she didn't want to be around them when Murray arrived. Jenna didn't know what her reaction would be. She felt ashamed and guilty and prayed she wouldn't burst into tears.

Jenna wondered how he'd greet her. He sounded worried but could've become angry at her stupidity by now. No doubt she deserved it, but to have their possibly stormy meeting witnessed by strangers was more than she could handle.

At 5:15, Jenna saw the flashing wing lights heralding the inbound flight. She shut off the van and waited as she watched Murray disembark with a travel-on suitcase. Jenna left the vehicle and slowly walked toward the sliding glass doors with mixed feelings. Relief saturated her body that he'd come to help, yet she was nervous about how she'd be received. His tall form, wearing a black winter coat and navy-blue scarf, strode quickly through the lounge. His eyes scanned for her. As their eyes connected, he nodded and smiled.

Thank God. Her eyes noted the nervous energy reflected in his features. He opened his arms, and Jenna stepped into them, giving him a quick hug. "Thank God you're here."

Murray kissed the top of her head, draped an arm around Jenna, and strode toward the van. "I'm glad you called me. We've lots to discuss before meeting your dad and Vaughan's family. Where can we find privacy?"

"If you haven't eaten, let's go to the Black Fin Pub where Vaughan worked. We can get a quiet table and talk while we're eating. I'll call Dad that you're here, and we'll bring home a pizza for them."

"Stop a minute." Murray stilled and tilted Jenna's face to his, his eyes drinking in her features. "I'm here now, Jenna. You can relax. Don't worry. We'll find Vaughan and straighten it out. Trust me." He bent to kiss her, then looked at her questioningly as she sidestepped his attempt. "I see we still have some issues to iron out." His eyebrows lifted.

"I know. If it makes you feel any better, my dad and Lee have given me some tough love. They told me things I didn't want to hear, which wasn't easy to face." Jenna gazed into the tempting blue eyes that captivated her from their first day together and steeled herself to follow through with the charade for a bit longer.

Murray nodded. "I want to take my time and discover who you are, what you love, and where I fit in. You floored me, and I moved too quickly, which scared you. I hope you aren't frightened of me now?"

"How could I be? You dropped everything to come and help, no questions asked." Jenna pulled away, clicked her key fob to unlock the van, and busied herself with the seatbelt. "What're you waiting for? Hop in." Jenna put the key in the ignition and started the van.

Murray slipped his overnight bag into the back seat. "Let's find a quiet place where we can reconnect." He tilted his head and grinned at her, daring her to accept his offer.

Jenna felt her face flush. "First things first. Let's have dinner and find the troublemaker. Then we can figure out our next step."

After Jenna and Murray ate their burgers and finished their beer, Murray clasped Jenna's hand. "I suppose with all this worry, you haven't had time to think about us." Murray's melodious voice was almost as hypnotic as the blue eyes staring at Jenna. "Our dinner and early evening at the Black Rock were a happy experience for both of us, but it didn't end well. I hope you've had time to think about that night. I wasn't trying to boss you around, Jenna. I'm not that kind of guy. I like your independence. It may be old fashioned, but my hope to make your life easier was grounded in good faith."

"There's no excuse for my rudeness when I left your suite. I can only blame it on my gut. I couldn't understand why you'd given me so much money and what you wanted in exchange. Too much wine didn't help my reasoning faculties either. So, when you made remarks about fixing my life, it hit me the wrong way." Jenna paused as a ring tone alerted Murray to an incoming call.

"Talk to me. What've you got?" Murray listened intently,

asked questions, and then disconnected the phone. "We know where Vaughan is. Stupid ass."

"Where? Is he ok?" Jenna's voice trembled as she saw Murray's jaw tense. "Murray?"

"Yes, he's fine. Well, maybe not fine, but he's alive. As I suspected, he opened the package and must've decided to double his money. The good thing is he didn't go to Reno or Vegas. He played the big shot at the Gateway Casino just outside Maple Ridge."

"Oh, my God. What happened? Will he be ok?" Jenna gripped Murray's hand tightly as she waited for his answer. Her heart was pounding so hard that she felt the beat in her ears.

"He will be. I gather he was unconscious when maid service entered the room. The ambulance took him to the Peace Arch Hospital under a John Doe moniker, as he had no wallet or ID. He was in an induced coma for three days. I can imagine him drinking too much, then feeling impressed with a beautiful woman coming onto him and following her to her suite. He doesn't have experience with cons. He just thinks people are being friendly."

Jenna's hand clapped against her mouth in horror. "Does that mean he's lost all your money?"

"I don't know yet. The hospital won't release Vaughan for possibly another week. We'll find out more soon."

"So that's why the RCMP couldn't find him."

"Probably. My staff faxed Vaughan's picture to all lower mainland hospitals in BC and the Pacific Northwest and offered $500.00 for any information. That must have caught some attention, and thankfully, he was recognized. The admitting staff alerted us and the RCMP. So far, no one has located his vehicle. It's probably in a chop-shop, and he won't see it again."

"His parents will be glad he's coming home, but they won't be surprised that he got conned. By the way, I originally told my dad that the package contained a valuable heirloom bracelet. He would've tried to talk me out of seeing you if he'd known about the cash." Jenna paused, worrying her lip and searching Murray's eyes. "It was hard, but I told him the truth yesterday. He was very disappointed in me and you, for that matter, for giving it to me. I haven't told Vaughan's family. Do we have to?"

"I'm glad you came clean with your dad. I'll have to apologize and explain my reasoning later." Murray ran his hand through his hair as he digested the news. "Regarding the Walsh's, we'll minimize the amount in the package. No one else needs to know how stupid we all were, especially as we won't be filing criminal charges. There's no advantage to anyone knowing the entire situation. They're upset enough as it is."

"True enough. I feel so stupid, and it's my fault Vaughan's in trouble. I wish I could turn back the clock." Jenna felt a wave of dizziness overcome her and closed her eyes. "But why'd you have so much cash with you? It made me suspicious, and my imagination went wild. After the first flush of temptation, I wanted to get rid of it as quickly as possible."

Murray raised his eyebrows. "Honestly? I didn't think I needed to explain myself. We don't advertise that we often travel with twice that amount of money—that would be asking for trouble. But you never know when you'll find someone tired of struggling to make their business work or ready to give up their isolated life on the coast. Giving them a cash offer is often the best way to acquire property at a great price. Then we fix it or sell it to other investors for profit."

Reaching for Jenna's hand, Murray squeezed it gently.

"These transactions are normal for us. I should've realized it might not look that way for you. No wonder you didn't trust me." Murray brought her fingers to his lips, grazing them lightly.

Jenna shivered and pulled her hand away. "My dad always told me to trust my gut. I doubted my instincts and let you under my skin. Now look at the trouble that my family's in."

"You're not blaming me for all of this, are you?" Murray's eyes widened, and his eyebrows lifted in surprise. "All I did was try and help you. If anyone's to blame, it's Vaughan for being nosy. I rushed over here to try to smooth things out for you, and now you think it's my fault?" Murray's voice rose an octave, and his eyes were stormy.

Jenna shook her head and retreated quickly. "We all made mistakes. No one person was totally to blame. I'm thankful you've found him, and we can get to the bottom of this and put it behind us." It took all her willpower to keep her face neutral and her eyes on his deceptive face.

The boxed pizza arrived at the table, along with the bill. "Good. Let's go and get this over with. I've got your back on this, Jenna. You lead the way, and I'll jump in whenever you want."

"I'm scared to face them." Jenna's voice shook with anxiety. "The Walsh family was supportive after my dad's accident, and then I thank them by getting their son involved in an issue I should've handled myself. Now, he's hurt, and you've lost a ton of money." Jenna lowered her eyes, and her hands trembled as she reached for her purse.

Murray helped Jenna with her coat, then slipped an arm around her shoulder and hugged her reassuringly. "Let's go and deal with this. Time to clear these issues up." After tending to the bill, they left the Black Fin. Racing through the wind and heavy rain, they returned to the van.

Jenna started the ignition, then turned to Murray and burst into nervous laughter. They both looked like drowned rats. "Could tonight get any worse?"

Murray used his scarf to wipe his face, then brushed off his wet wool coat. He turned the van's heater on high to defog the windows and watched Jenna turn the rearview mirror toward her, wipe her face, and comb her fingers through her wet, tangled hair.

"Not for long. The first part will be the hardest, but I'm right here with you. I'd preferred that you'd have used the money as intended, but once I gave it to you, it wasn't mine anymore. So don't let that overwhelm you. Whatever's missing will be Vaughan's responsibility, and we'll figure out a solution eventually."

Jenna couldn't delay her response any longer. She turned to stare at Murray and frowned. "I won't let it overwhelm me because I'll return it all to you, one way or another. You see, the money wasn't mine either. I didn't accept it. You left it for me." Jenna tapped her chest. "I didn't earn that money, and I'd made it clear to you before you left the lease that I didn't want to have any outside interest." Jenna glanced away from Murray's stony stare and took a deep breath. "Let's get this straight. I won't discuss this before the Walshs because we don't know how much we'll recover. But rest assured. I'll be giving you back the full amount."

"Jenna, you're overreacting here. I understand you're frustrated, but you don't need to do that." Murray paused as he saw the resolve on her face and wisely switched the subject. "Now, after you introduce me, you can start the conversation and explain, but I'll jump in whenever you want. Concentrate on the good news—we've found Vaughan, who'll be home soon. His family doesn't need to know what was in the package he was delivering other than it was a gift from me to you. If they ask, I'll step in and be evasive. The stolen money will be dealt with between Vaughan and us, and we can go from there."

Jenna was confused by Murray's refusal to acknowledge and accept her intentions, so she didn't reply. The drive home was strained, and as they pulled into the driveway, Jenna glanced at Murray and then back to the figures highlighted in the window. "Here we go." A frown creased her forehead as she took a deep breath. Murray nodded his encouragement, then dismounted from the vehicle, picked up the fresh pizza in one hand and his overnight case in the other. He hipped the door closed and followed Jenna inside.

JENNA MASSAGED her temple in a circular motion, trying to eradicate the headache that attacked her an hour ago. Listening to Carla's impassioned anger toward Vaughan and at herself broke her heart. They'd both made poor decisions and who knew what shape Vaughan would be in when he returned. Murray listened to all of them before stepping in.

"All right, all right." Murray stood up, crossed to Jenna's chair, and massaged her shoulders as he saw her struggling with tears. "If there's blame anywhere, then look at me first. I didn't mean to upset Jenna and put her in an impossible position, which proved irresistible to Vaughan. All three of us made mistakes, and I'm sure Vaughan's equally sorry for his actions as Jenna and I are." Murray scanned the table, assessing the emotional damage around him.

"Let's be thankful that we found Vaughan, and he's in

relatively decent shape. Tomorrow, Vaughan will undergo more tests and X-rays, and then I'll have a chartered flight bring him home as soon as possible. He'll finish recovering at home, and we'll all go from there." Murray paused, making eye contact with each one of them. "No criminal charges will be filed. Our main concern is getting Vaughan home and healthy again."

"The flight home won't be necessary, Mr. Meadows." Mr. Walsh spoke firmly. "We'll head to the hospital tomorrow and see his condition ourselves. Maybe we'll get a better idea of when he'll be released. Thanks for your offer, though."

"Of course. If you change your mind and think a quicker mode of transport would be more beneficial, my offer still stands. I also feel some responsibility here."

Murray ran his fingers through his hair, sighed, and gazed at the shocked expressions around him. "We need to put this in the past. Depending on how you deal with this, your lifetime connections with each other will either be gone or they'll be stronger. So, let's break for tonight and think about this. All right?" Murray's left eyebrow raised, waiting for a response.

Carla reached over, grabbed Jenna's hand, and squeezed it tightly. "I don't blame you, Jenn. We'll always be best friends. I love my brother, but he's an idiot sometimes. Hopefully, that'll wake him up. We'll get through this mess."

"Thanks, Carla." Jenna cleared her throat, but her voice still shook. "It's heartbreaking to have brought this on your family, especially when your family has so generously helped us. I promise that we'll fix this mess."

Still dumbfounded by the situation, Mr. and Mrs. Walsh agreed, then stood and hugged the group before heading home. Daryl put his arm around Carla and followed the Walsh's.

"That was a hell of an evening," Theo spoke as he tapped on the table. "I'm glad Vaughan's recuperating, and I'm proud of you, sweetheart. I know how hard it is to admit you're wrong, but you did the right thing." Theo stood and used an arm crutch to get to Jenna and hug her. "You did well tonight. I love you and always will. Remember that." Theo turned toward Murray. "Thanks for finding Vaughan and admitting your part in this disaster. I'm sure everyone's learned a valuable lesson." Theo shook Murray's hand and carefully walked toward his bedroom.

Murray turned to Jenna, eyeing her weary features. "We've probably talked ourselves out tonight, so I'm going to call myself a taxi. You look exhausted, and I'd rather you got some rest. We can continue our conversation tomorrow."

"That's a good idea. I'm exhausted. Now that the hospital knows the next of kin, we'll probably get the medical updates that way. I'll text you if I hear anything more from the Walshs."

Jenna gathered the mugs and put them in the dishwasher while waiting for Murray's taxi. The evening's stress and resulting fatigue had taken its toll on them, and they exchanged only the barest of conversation.

"THANKS FOR MEETING ME, Jenna. I wasn't sure you would." Murray was quieter than Jenna had ever seen him. "You were right about the money being the root cause of so much trouble for you and your friends. I'm sorry."

"We live in different worlds, Murray. I think your gift to me was a token of your respect for my efforts at the lease.

When you justified planting it in my cooler, you told me it wasn't a big deal." Jenna's face flushed as she remembered her battle with temptation. "I tried to convince myself I could use it as a loan, but I would've had to lie to my father about how I paid for supplies. As he reminded me, the Sorensens have earned that lease by the callouses on their hands and the legacy our values brought us. That kind of money changes lives like ours, so no wonder I was nervous about it."

"I understand, but it doesn't mean we're completely different. Look how well we connected at the Black Rock. That had nothing to do with how much I had in the bank. It was a passion I'd like to explore more."

"Exactly. I noticed the word 'love' wasn't included, which is truthful. That night was proof of chemistry. I'll grant you that the fireworks were spectacular, but by the time I left, I felt empty and confused."

"That's only because you got your back up by thinking I was trying to impose my dreams on you," Murray reached across the table and put his hand over the top of Jenna's. "I'm crazy about you, Jenna, and I think I scared you off."

"I'm actually glad you did. That white-hot anger I felt signaled something was off. I ignored my instincts because I couldn't pinpoint a reasonable answer to why I was uneasy." Jenna's eyes flitted about as her anxiety rose to another level. "It was too easy to blame it on my independence and the unexpected cash that could've solved the problems at Westerlea Cove."

"Or maybe you were nervous because you've never had a relationship with a wealthy person. You challenged me like no other woman. You may not consider that valuable to a guy like me, but trust me. It's an aphrodisiac like nothing I'd experienced. And very, very valuable." Murray's eyes flitted from her face to her body before returning to conquer her eyes. "I want you in my life, Jenna. I hope you'll let me start over."

"You want me in your life?" Jenna tilted her head to the side and pulled her hand from his. "How would you manage that?"

"It would be tricky. I know your life here with your dad is extremely important to you, just as the oyster lease is. But we could make it work." Murray lowered his voice to a soft croon. "I could fly in regularly. We could take holidays together." Murray reached over and began massaging his thumb in circular motions on her forearm. " I know we'd make each other happy."

Once again, Jenna pulled away, tucking her forearm under the table—*the unmitigated gall.* Anger simmered within, making her face flush. Her breath quickened as she attempted to control the words that begged to explode. "That's interesting. However, I don't think your wife, Susan, would appreciate me. How would you explain your absences? Another business trip? You lie to me, and then you lie to her. Who else do you lie to? What were you planning—to set me up as your mistress? Were you ever going to tell me the truth?"

The angry questions spewed across the table, probably shocking Murray. Jenna hoped so. She scraped her chair away, gathered her purse, then paused and leaned forward until she was inches from his face. "A word of advice. I may be a small-town girl, but the internet's available here too. You might want to be careful about what you post online." Jenna smirked at the surprised look in his eyes and the stunned look on his face.

"Close your mouth, Murray. That's probably the only

way another lie won't come out." Jenna growled as she held her hand up for him to stop him from replying.

"I'm done. Don't ever contact me again. I don't accept money that I don't earn. You'll get your money back, but don't expect interest."

CHAPTER 14

A week later, Jenna carried two bottles of red wine up the steps to Lee's condo. Drew and Lee insisted that a prime rib dinner was to celebrate an important announcement. They were secretive, and no amount of cajoling would loosen their lips. Whatever it was, Jenna was excited to feel happy and as light as a feather.

The heavy burden of responsibility that she'd carried for almost three weeks disappeared. A heated argument about her intentions to return the money Murray had dumped on her led to another one about the true state of his marriage. Afterward, shaky and defiant, Jenna confessed to her dad that she'd never felt so powerful, so in control as she had that night. Jenna doubted she'd ever see the arrogant jerk again. Her dad congratulated her and told Jenna she inspired him. He would fight to bring their lease up to standard again and restore the Sorensen name.

Yes.

If she had a free hand, she'd do a fist pump. Jenna grinned. She'd have to toast that accomplishment tonight, along with whatever Drew and Lee's surprise was.

Leaning against the doorbell while balancing the wine and dessert, Jenna waited impatiently for the door to open. She thrust the fruit flan into Lee's hand and slipped inside, relishing the warmth of the condo. Scents of garlic and roasting meat made her mouth water, and she giggled as her two friends began talking over each other.

"Hey guys, I'm happy to see you too." Jenna bussed Lee's cheek, then approached Drew and handed him the wine. "I hope the cabernet will work with beef. I asked the liquor store clerk and went with his advice."

"Perfect." Drew took the bottles to the kitchen, uncorked them, and set them aside to breathe. "Give me your jacket, Jenn. Make yourself comfortable."

"So, what's the big surprise? I've been dying to find out what all the hoopla's been about in the last few days." Her eyes darted between her two friends, who were beaming with excitement.

"Let's see. We have a few things to celebrate." Drew counted them out on his fingertips. "We know Vaughan is safe. Murray's gone home. The Walshs have returned from seeing their son and are satisfied with his progress. You're looking great." Drew paused.

"Definitely all worth celebrating, I agree. But so far, nothing that I didn't know about earlier." Jenna agreed. "Spit it out—I can't take the suspense any longer."

Lee and Drew exchanged glances. "Let's wait until dinner to make a toast."

"Screw that. You two have been holding out on me, and I deserve to hear some great news." Jenna spread her hands before her. "What do I have to do? Beg?"

Lee laughed and nodded to Drew to give the news.

"First of all, you have awesome friends. They've got

brains, they've got connections, and they're just about to make your day."

Jenna growled, warning she was running out of patience. "I agree. You're both smart and wonderful; I'm lucky to have you. Although, if you want to stay happy, you'd better make your announcement."

Lee grasped Jenna's hand, then reached for Drew's. "Say what you want, but small towns care for each other. Several people have been watching you work hard at helping your dad and getting Westerlea Cove going again. They're rooting for both of you to succeed. Some community leaders have contacted everyone they can think of to help you with the necessary funds to rebuild your lease."

Drew and Lee exchanged happy looks. "You have an appointment on Tuesday to see the manager of the Pacific Financial Group. Bring the proposals we've been working on, and Mr. Davies will take it from there. You have the backing of the whole community, and Mr. Davies is willing to finance a restructuring of Westerlea Cove. Congratulations!"

Tears sprang to Jenna's eyes as they jumped up and down together, laughing excitedly. "This is almost too good to be true." Jenna swiped a tear from her eye, then clapped her hands together. "I can't believe it. Thank you." She grabbed her friends, hugged them, and kissed them soundly.

"That's not all," Lee sing-songed. "This part is unofficial —you didn't hear it from me. But it looks like you'll be able to pay off the business loan with the oyster recovery grant. Westerlea Cove's application is at the top of the list. I'm not sure of the date, but it's yours."

"Oh, thank heaven!" Jenna exclaimed and fanned her flushed face. *Could it really be true?* The Sorensens were on their way to reclaiming their reputation. "Grab the wine glasses. We're not waiting for dinner for a toast. Let's celebrate."

After toasting each other and finishing their glasses of wine, Jenna set the table as Drew and Lee put the finishing touches on their gourmet creation. Drew's prime rib was perfectly cooked, well roasted on the outside, and medium rare inside. The baked potatoes were hot, buttery, and fluffy inside—a combination Jenna could never attain. Lee had sauteed peppers and vegetables on the outside grill. Jenna poured their second glass of wine as her friend set the dishes on the table. Drew lit the single candlestick and was the last one to sit. "Are we ready now for the official toast?"

All three friends lifted their glasses, gave thanks for the power of friendship, and drank to the positive developments announced tonight. Finally, the future looked promising. Jenna lay back against the sofa a few hours later and watched her friends relax. Drew and Lee had also enjoyed wine while prepping dinner, and now, with their tummies full, they were having trouble keeping their eyes open. She was so fortunate to have them in her life. Not for the first time had Jenna wondered how she would've fared without their support. Not well, she surmised.

Jenna was blessed with friends and family surrounding her. Her mom would be proud of the progress her daughter and husband made. Jenna had often turned to her mom for guidance in the past several months, talking to her and feeling her responses. Without a doubt, Jenna knew her mom steered her when she was most conflicted and influenced the optimistic outcome tonight.

Grabbing a lap blanket, Jenna draped it over Lee and whispered good night. When she approached Drew, she stopped momentarily and contemplated the life she had walked away from. *Everything happens for a reason*, Jenna reminded herself. But damn, she missed this rock of a man. His wavy brown hair curled over his forehead, and Jenna yearned to run her fingers through it as she had once done. As if feeling her intense gaze on him, Drew opened his eyes and nodded. "Come here, Jenn. I've been waiting."

"I better not." Jenna blushed at the possibilities. "I've called a taxi, which should be here any minute. I won't forget tonight. Thanks, Drew."

"My pleasure. You deserve it." Drew stood and gently drew Jenna into his arms. "Whenever you're ready, I want you to know I'm here for you. No pressure. I get your reasons for not joining me in Haida Gwaii and your commitment to your family. That's all good. But don't forget about us because I haven't."

Leaning her head against Drew's shoulder, she breathed in his scent and felt the warm feeling of belonging, of being in the right place. "If you only knew how often I thought of you and wished things had been different. I don't know if we could return to how we were." Jenna felt her eyes moisten, and her voice trembled with the effort not to cry. "I'm almost scared to give it another shot. As it is now, at least you're in my life. If it didn't work, I might lose you altogether."

Drew pulled back and lifted her chin so she could see his eyes. "Silly girl. After all you've been through, you're afraid of dating *me*? Don't you feel the link between us? We've never had trouble trusting each other. Give me a chance to show you I haven't changed. We love each other as friends, and it's time to move on to the next phase. Let's take a chance." Drew stepped back. "I'll text you tomorrow. Maybe we can go for a trail hike and get to know each other again. Think about it, ok?" Drew cocked an eyebrow and held up crossed fingers.

Jenna couldn't help but grin at his old mannerisms for asking favors. "Ok. It does sound good. Let's give it a try."

"Thatta girl." Drew retrieved her coat and watched Jenna slip outside to a waiting cab.

⁓

THE TWENTY-MINUTE RIDE to Ucluelet on Saturday passed quietly. The light rain eased as the winds slowed, allowing the evergreens to stand tall again. Drew cracked open the side window to let the chilly air snap Jenna back from her snooze.

"Sorry, Drew." Jenna yawned and sat up straighter, stretching her arms ahead, then tilting her head from side to side. "I can't seem to get enough rest during the night. I toss and turn and seldom get more than a few hours of sleep before I wake myself tossing and turning again. No wonder I need these power naps during the day. My internal clock is out of whack."

"Gee, I wonder why. The past month has been a nightmare for you. No wonder you're not sleeping soundly." Drew reached over and clasped Jenna's hand. "I'm glad Murray's gone. Once we pick up Vaughan and bring him home, I think you'll see your anxiety will dissolve. It's the not knowing that's hard."

"I'm glad the Walsh's have agreed to let us pick Vaughan up. The trip his parents took to visit him was exhausting for them. Plus, we'll learn more about the missing money when it's just the three of us." Jenna sighed. "Once we get that straightened out, I'll sleep well again."

"I don't know what mental shape Vaughan will be in, so we should be careful," Drew said. "I hope retrieving the money and knowing the story behind Vaughan's escapade will be the last piece of the puzzle to clear the financial mess Murray caused. We'll need to be tactful with Vaughan because I don't want to create more stress for him while he's still so fragile."

"I agree, but I'm keeping my fingers crossed that he wants to get this episode off his chest. I can't wait to hear the story. I hope this cures Vaughan of the pie-in-the-sky deals he always dreams up." Jenna worried her lip as she thought of the conversation. There was no way of knowing how Vaughan would react, so she shrugged and continued. "The second half of my stress with the oyster lease has eased, too. You have no idea how relieved I felt since you told me about the contacts you and other community members made by contacting Mr. Davies. I never imagined that kind of support would happen for my family."

Jenna squeezed Drew's hand tightly. "I can breathe now without my chest hurting. Honestly, I can't say thank you enough. It's been a long-haul planning to get the lease operational again, but I can see a brighter future now."

"I'm happy for you." Drew pulled into the public parking lot and grabbed his backpack. "Let's get some fresh air and exercise. It'll re-energize you."

"It always does. Particularly this trail, it's my favorite."

Walking briskly to the start of the Pacific Trail, Jenna anticipated the release of tension. The Lighthouse Loop was one she often used when short on time. She paused, took a deep breath, followed Drew's lead, and began her stretches. The wide, well-manicured trails wound through ancient cedars and rocky bluffs. The paths were damp but not muddy even after the morning's heavy rains. Fat drops of rain showered down when a puff of wind shook the evergreen branches, reminding them of the recent storm. Usually, less than a forty-five-minute hike, she'd take advantage of the many viewpoints where she could sit and lose herself in the beauty of the wild West Coast. Nothing soothed her nerves better. Today, it would be even better, as Drew planned to extend the hike to its entire length. He'd surprised her by packing a picnic lunch to balance the trek with a leisurely break.

Breathing the cedar scents and the salty tang of the Pacific, Jenna was excited to start hiking. Finishing her stretches, she found her pace, swinging her arms vigorously. Shivering after raindrops snaked through her scalp, Jenna pulled her sweatshirt hood over her hair. Jenna glanced back and giggled as Drew struggled with the bulky backpack and scampered to catch up with her.

"Sorry, I couldn't wait any longer." Jenna was sure happiness must've shone from her eyes as the freedom she experienced was unparalleled. "I can't believe how good I feel. It's like I don't have a care in the world." Her lips pursed as she thought about her statement. "I mean, I do have challenges ahead, but they're minor now that I know the finances will be in place."

Impulsively, she leaned forward and planted a kiss on Drew's lips. "Thank you for this day. It's exactly right. You know me so well."

"Of course. Together, we make an awesome team." Drew held his hand out for her to clasp.

Jenna paused and momentarily considered his offer before she smiled and clasped his. She hadn't dared hope it would be this easy to resume their relationship. Today's hike was a great way to start. As they approached the first incline, they quietened as the majesty of the forest left them speechless. Jenna peered high into the giant evergreens, appreciating the angle of the windblown branches and the freshly exposed wood ripped from the last storm. Jenna pointed to an ancient cedar tree, where a deep, empty eagle's nest sat cushioned between the trunk and a thick branch. Drew followed her sightline and nodded his appreciation.

Speech was unnecessary, as no words could effectively describe the beauty of nature. Jenna dropped her gaze to where thick moss, clumps of salal, and bracken ferns carpeted the forest floor. The flora created a perfect hiding spot for the common chickadee, red crossbills, and chattering squirrels.

Jenna's eyes darted about, looking for treasure, and spotted an eagle feather near the base of a Sitka Spruce. She bent down, picked it up, and ran her fingers over the silky vane. As Canadian law permits only Indigenous peoples to keep them, Jenna sighed and replaced the feather. Jenna heard Drew's camera snapping shots, saving a new memory, and smiled.

A faraway screech caught Drew and Jenna's attention. They searched the skyline and found an eagle circling a tall snag on a rocky bluff before gracefully landing. It perched and called again while they stood mesmerized. Minutes later, the mate arrived, landing on a branch a few feet lower, their sharp eyes trained on the waves and beach, searching for their next meal. Drew crouched at different angles, aiming his camera for the perfect photo.

Jenna and Drew whispered between them, reluctant to spook the eagles and spoil this perfect view of nature at its best. Reluctantly, they resumed walking briskly. The overcast sky reflected in the ocean, and the breeze was almost non-existent—unusual and short-lived at this time of year. Jenna felt her heartbeat increase and her breath quicken as she climbed the next hill to the viewpoint atop the Rocky Bluffs.

"Are you going to make it without a break?" Drew teased.

"No problem. I'm taking my time and enjoying the fresh air." Jenna refused to admit her breathlessness. A grunt of derision from Drew told her she hadn't fooled him one bit. "It always takes me a little while to get into the groove of a hike. Don't worry. I won't hold you back."

"I'm not worried. I like to tease you." Drew winked, picked up his stride, and reached the summit first. He surveyed the panorama before him while waiting for Jenna to join him.

Jenna stood beside him and caught her breath. After a few minutes, they headed to the wooden bench perched atop and scanned the vista, the waves breaking gently on the beach below. Drew pointed out two otters who floated on their backs, then disappeared, probably to fetch clams or mussels to crack open and eat.

Further out beyond the surf, Jenna watched several seals roam the waters, bobbing underneath the waves and returning to the surface fifty feet or more away. She'd spent many hours doing this when her mom died—burying her sorrow while watching nature perform. Her dad called it *putting life in perspective*. It never failed to heal her broken heart or calm her worries.

Drew passed Jenna a bottle of water and took one for himself. Half an hour later, they approached the Amphitrite Lighthouse, where they'd enjoy lunch.

"You're looking much more relaxed, Jenn. More optimistic." Drew removed the hoodie from Jenna's hair and reached to pull a twig from it. His hand returned to her thick hair, and he ran his fingers through the tangles before pulling her toward him. Jenna wrapped her arms around him, and Drew closed his eyes momentarily before he bent and kissed her gently.

A warm surge of emotion flooded Jenna as Drew

embraced her before increasing his lips' pressure on hers. Being here with him felt like a homecoming, and Jenna realized this was the love she'd been looking for. A true love whose loyalty she'd never have to question. A cornerstone to build a future. The knowledge reverberated within her, weakening her knees. Jenna gathered her wits about her and stepped back, searching Drew's serious face. *Had he felt it, too?*

Drew nodded her unvoiced question. "I told you nothing had changed between us, but I was wrong. What we have is stronger than it's ever been. We understand each other completely, and it's almost like we can read each other's minds. Your troubles are our troubles, and your joy is our joy. Can't you feel it?"

"I do. It's amazing." Jenna reached to touch his face and trace his lips with her fingertips. "I love you, Drew. With all of my heart."

"I love you too, Jenn. Always have, always will."

Jenna giggled and broke the intensity of the moment. "I can't imagine what my dad or Lee will say."

"They'll probably ask what took you so long to realize it. I'm a patient man, but I'm not a saint. Your heart's journey sure took a long way around to find mine."

"True, it's had a few bumps in the road, but I got here." Jenna slid a teasing glance his way and skimmed her hand over his ass. "What do you say about finishing this day off perfectly?"

"I'm way ahead of you. I tentatively booked a reservation at the Francis Boutique tonight. It's their low season, so it wasn't a problem."

"A little sure of yourself, were you?" Jenna's eyes danced mischievously. "I approve. That sounds wonderful." Jenna stood on her tiptoes and kissed his lips. "What are we waiting for?"

Drew quickly picked up the remnants of their lunch, grabbed Jenna's hand, and kissed it before challenging her to a sprint. They jogged alongside one another and covered the distance in less than half an hour.

"Can you bring me home so I can get ready for tonight? I can meet you back here around dinner time?"

Drew chuckled. "I'm not giving you a chance to chicken out. I'll pick you up at 4:00. We'll go for a drink and dinner, then head to the Inn."

"Ok. Just so you know, I wasn't going to chicken out. We have history, and although this second chance has come together quickly, I'm not worried. I know this is right for us." Jenna leaned over and kissed Drew long and slowly, promising an unforgettable night.

Drew's face flushed, and his breathing hitched as the searing kiss ended. "You won't be sorry, sweetheart. Our life together will be awesome, I promise. I'll be your rock that you can always depend on." Drew winked. "I'll rephrase that. I'll be your diamond in the rough, which will also make you sparkle."

Jenna felt her eyes tear up joyfully. "Right back at you. The past is behind us, and I'm happy we're together."

"I was hoping this was where you'd be." Drew peeked into the bedroom and smiled as he saw Jenna waiting.

"You've brought the wine in with our overnight bags?"

"Yes, we're all organized. I'll pour us a glass and join you in a second."

Drew brought a tray with two filled wine glasses and

placed it on the side table. He passed Jenna a glass. "You're beautiful, do you know that?" He crawled into the king-sized bed and cuddled up to Jenna. Drew traced his hand up her arm to her neck, lifting her hair to expose her delicate ears. He leaned in, kissed her shoulder, worked his way up to her ear, and sucked the lobe. "You drive me crazy."

"Likewise," Jenna's husky voice quivered. She felt her face flush, so she pulled away and tasted her wine. "A toast?"

Drew flopped back onto his pillow and reached for his glass. "Yes. A toast to a great day on the West Coast, with you in my bed tonight." Drew tipped his glass to hers. "And to Vaughan being found alive and recuperating."

"Perfect." Jenna tipped her glass to his again, then drank. "I'm glad you suggested we stay here."

"Me too. It's not luxurious like the Black Rock—"

"Stop right there; this is very romantic and more our style."

"I'm glad you feel that way. We're ordinary people and don't need to prove anything to anyone." Drew took another drink, set the glass down, and turned toward Jenna. "Our only needs are to focus on our feelings for each other. The rest will fall in place." He slipped his hand under the duvet and found her midriff, then traced the curve of her hips. "Agreed?"

Jenna followed his lead and turned towards him. Her voice dipped to a sexy purr. "Agreed. Get your hot body over here. It's been a long time since we've been together like this." Jenna's hand slid up his muscular back and through his hair. The fire was building quickly inside both of them.

Drew returned to her face, peppering her lips and each feature of her face with quick, breathless kisses. He paused and cocked his head to the side, smirking. "Now, do you believe we're perfect for each other in every way?"

"Yes. Yes! Now stop talking and make love with me."

Drew looked after the *protection*, then moaned with pleasure as he pulled her close. "Whatever you want, my love."

Jenna placed her hands on his chest, her eyes boring into his. Feeling Drew's gentle hands roam her curves and watching his eyes cloud with passion filled her heart with tenderness. Her lips traced along his neck and chest before Jenna snuggled into him and listened to his quickened heartbeat. Her love for him flooded her senses as she felt his gentle and caring caresses, and tears filled her eyes.

Drew pulled her alongside him and wiped a tear from the corner of Jenna's eyes. "No regrets?"

"None. Not really. Not moving away was the right thing for me to do, but sometimes—" Jenna's eyes dropped away from his as she struggled to explain.

"I know, sweetheart. We've got lots of time to make up for. Don't apologize; we did what we needed to do, and we're stronger for it." Drew slipped his fingers through her hair and kissed her gently before trailing kisses down her neck and arms.

Jenna and Drew rediscovered each other slowly and lovingly, comfortable with the other's responses. As Drew guided her to completion, Jenna bit her lower lip as her eyes shuttered before collapsing against him, her mane a tangled mess across his chest. Gasping for breath, they separated and gazed at each other.

Jenna smiled at her lover and shook her head with wonder. "Is it my imagination, or are we better at this?"

"We're better—maturity has its benefits." Drew winked, then left the bed and passed Jenna her wine before going to the washroom to freshen. When he returned, she was waving an empty glass. "I think we may need refills," Jenna giggled.

"I'll be right back." Drew returned with another full bottle of Copper Moon and a small fruit and cheese platter.

"My, you've been busy," Jenna teased.

"Not really. Before we arrived this evening, I arranged for room service and ordered a few things to be delivered. Good idea?" Drew refilled both glasses before jumping into bed and placing the food between them.

Jenna nodded. "You do know how to treat a woman." She snagged a grape and then sipped her wine. Jenna popped a piece of Brie on a cracker and sighed. "You, monsieur, have wonderful taste."

"Yes, I do. You're here, aren't you?" Drew cut a piece of cranberry and pecan-covered goat cheese onto a thin wafer and fed it to her. "This is even better." He watched Jenna's eyes roll back in appreciation. "Told you that stuff is delicious." Drew and Jenna chatted as they devoured the appetizers and drank their wine until drowsiness pulled them to sleep.

∼

TWO DAYS LATER, Carla called Jenna with welcome news about her brother. After a week in the hospital, the critical part of Vaughan's injuries passed, and his surgeon's office called to make arrangements for him to come home. He would be tested for cognitive damage in his hometown at regular intervals. That sounded worrisome, but the joy of having him return home in one piece was more important.

Jenna called her dad immediately to update Vaughan's care. She explained the possible brain damage from the concussion that the beating incurred. Vaughan was currently experiencing aphasia, but he'd probably return to normal with therapy and healing. How he sustained a fractured left tibia was anybody's guess, but that, too, would eventually heal. All things considered, Vaughan was lucky.

Theo remembered his brush with critical injury and knew the journey involved. "He isn't alone, Jenn. Vaughan has many people around him to support his recovery. Me included. We'll do everything possible to get him back on his feet."

"I know. We'll see how Vaughan's coping before we talk to him about his foolish escapade. Drew and I have decided not to stress Vaughan out by giving him the third degree about the missing money if he doesn't want to discuss it. My priority is helping him get strong again to help me find a solution."

"You've got a good man, there. Drew's a good fit for this family and our lifestyle." Theo said.

"I agree. I'm glad we reconnected." Jenna's voice quivered. "Drew and I are more committed and in love now than ever."

"I'm glad you see things differently. Lessons learned all around. You know that all I want for you is to be happy doing what you love. I hope Drew feels the same way."

"Time will tell. We'll take it slow and find out. See you tomorrow around noon?"

"I'll be here. Love you." Theo said.

"Love you more, Dad."

CHAPTER 15

Vaughan was happy to see Drew and Jenna pick him up at the Peace Arch Hospital on the lower mainland. They delivered him to the Tofino General Hospital for observation to save his parents an exhausting trip. Because of a small seizure suffered during the journey home, his local doctor extended his stay to four days while assessing the scope of his injuries. A physiotherapist and a speech pathologist ensured that Vaughan understood his limitations before allowing him to go home.

During the trip home from the lower mainland, Drew and Jenna kept the conversation away from his escapade, which probably relieved Vaughan. Although dying of curiosity, they kept their word to keep stress to a minimum and let Vaughan adjust to his new situation.

Jenna reviewed her conversation with Carla at the Patisserie as her friend devoured an apple turnover. Jenna sipped her latte and patiently listened to the information she'd already heard from her father about Vaughan's return home to live with his parents until he no longer needed crutches.

"How's your brother handling the idea of living with your parents?"

"He's a little cranky, but I'm surprised he hasn't made a fuss about returning to his apartment. He'll be eligible for a medical benefit while off work, but it's only sixty percent of his wages." Carla cocked an eyebrow. "You can imagine how Vaughan feels about that. He'll also miss the tips he used to pocket each night. But until my brother gets stronger and can fend for himself, he knows this is his best option. We're subletting his apartment for six months to offset his reduced income." Carla polished off her pastry and wiped her mouth before continuing.

"I'd have him live with me, but our condo is two levels with upstairs bedrooms." Carla waggled her hand from side to side. "We aren't sure if he'll continue to have seizures. The last thing he needs is to have one and then fall downstairs. Better safe than sorry."

"I've heard it's unusual for concussions to cause seizures, but hopefully, as the neurologist theorized—it's a short-term side effect of the brain trauma he experienced. Drew and I offered to pick him up from the local hospital and bring him to your parent's home, and he agreed. We wanted to catch him while he's alone so we can talk privately."

Jenna saw the puzzled look on her friend's face and the frown developing. "Don't worry. We aren't going to give him the third degree, I promise. We need to know anything he might remember that he's too embarrassed to tell anyone else."

"Fair enough. We appreciate that Murray found him, although I'm glad we don't have to deal with him anymore. I don't know what my stupid brother did with the package he never delivered, but I hope it won't cause too much financial damage. My parents will help him cover it, but he'll have to pay them back eventually. You'll let us know, right?"

"I will, but I've decided to help cover the loss, too." Jen's eyes darted around the café while twiddling her pinkie ring around her finger. "I shouldn't have asked Vaughan to be a go-between, but I was so angry at Murray. I couldn't face him, and that was wrong of me. I can't afford much, but I'll contribute something."

"That's not your responsibility, but I'd probably feel the same way. Let's wait and see what we're dealing with, alright?" Carla patted her friend's forearm.

"Alright. I can't believe I was attracted to Murray and thought he might be the answer to my problems." Jenna blew out a breath after her admission. She focused on her friend and shook her head slowly from side to side. "I didn't listen to my gut, and the result was frightening."

"I have a feeling Murray fooled a lot of people. Although, from all appearances, you've moved on. Maybe the experience has shown you what you truly want." Carla waggled her eyebrows. "How's things going with Drew?"

"Fantastic. Better than ever. And Drew refuses to let me feel guilty about my night with Murray. I feel great—as if I'm exactly where I need to be with the right person. Money and charm didn't deliver what fairy tales promised. I've got what's real, and I'm so happy."

"I'm glad. You deserve to have a man like that in your life. As you've discovered, lust is a helluva lot different than love and passion. Some people can handle lust without love, but not many. There's quite a difference." Carla squeezed Jenna's hand.

"You bet there is. I feel strong and confident about myself. I don't have to worry about what Drew thinks or what he might expect." Jenna spread her hands, encompassing the wonder of her emotions. "He accepts and loves me for who I am. We're on the same page on almost everything we do." She grimaced before continuing. "Not like my time with Murray. That was a confusing, emotional roller coaster."

"My roller coaster with Daryl's still fun, although tamer than it used to be. You'll be fine, Jenn." Carla paused and patted her friend's hand. "You've had a tough time since we left school, with your mom passing and your dad's troubles. Now everything's falling into place." Carla retrieved lip gloss from her purse and swiped a coat on before pushing her dishes away with a sigh. "If I keep nervous eating like this, I'll need to alter my wedding dress. I've gained four pounds, and I'm blaming it all on Vaughan's escapade."

Jenna laughed. "You love your sweets. It isn't *all* his fault."

"True enough." Carla looked at her watch and yelped. "Gotta go, or I'll be late for work. See you later." Carla pulled her jacket on, grabbed her umbrella, and raced out of the coffee shop.

Watching a gust of wind almost blow Carla's umbrella inside out made Jenna grin at her ditzy friend. Carla had a heart of gold, but her ADHD often got the best of her, sending her in four directions at once. Jenna left the table and stood in line to buy cinnamon buns with cream cheese icing for her dad, then headed home for a lazy day.

Jenna stuffed a chicken that morning, and it was ready to go in the oven when she returned—good old-fashioned comfort food for a stormy winter's day. Drew was joining them, and they'd probably play a few games of crib or chip rummy with her dad before going to his apartment. Anticipation made Jenna's pulse quicken.

HOLDING DREW'S HAND TIGHTLY, they walked down the hospital corridor to Vaughan's room. They peeked in and saw him dressed and sitting in a wheelchair, ready to be escorted out.

"There you are," Vaughan grumbled as he looked at his watch. "It feels like forever when you're waiting for a r-ride. I h-hate depending on other people for help."

"Better get used to it, buddy," Drew said as he tapped his shoulder. "We have to wait for your doctor to sign you out anyway. How are your pain levels? Do you think you're ready to come home?"

Vaughan nodded toward the bedside table, where a white bag was stapled shut. "As long as I have my m-meds and home cooking, I'll be fine."

"You won't miss hospital food or the cute nurses fussing over you?" Jenna teased.

"Cute numbers..." Vaughan growled. He pounded the armrest on the wheelchair. "I hate when the wrong word comes out of my mouth." Vaughan took a couple of deep breaths and started over. "Cute...*nurses* around here are older than I am, so, no. I won't miss them."

"Your speech is better now that the brain swelling has subsided. Your doctor said you probably wouldn't be bothered with aphasia in another month or two. Be patient. Baby steps will get you back to normal." Drew wheeled Vaughan to an isolated sitting area down the hall while waiting for the discharge papers.

"I don't have to think of the words before I say them as often now, so I hope you're right. I feel like the b-brain fog's lifting." Vaughan looked around to knock on wood, then shrugged—no wooden surfaces in a hospital.

"Great news." Jenna sat across from him and leaned forward, her forearms on her knees and hands clasped. "We won't have any privacy at home, so this is a good time to go over a few things. How much do you remember about your trip to the casino? Be honest, Vaughan."

"Jeeze, do we need to do this now? My headache is starting to throb."

"Yes, we do—unless you want your parents to listen to the details. I think I've been more than patient, and I need to know what we have to do next to resolve the money issue with Murray. He's very unhappy with me these days, and I want to pay him back as soon as possible before he decides to cause more problems for me. I want him out of my life completely."

"I know. I've thanked y-you several times for your help, and so have my parents." Vaughan looked at Jenna and scowled. "If it weren't for *your* package delivery, I wouldn't be sitting here."

Drew heard the hissed intake from Jenna and stepped in. "Back off, buddy. Jenna told you not to open the package, that it was girly stuff." Drew kept his voice calm and low. "But you were nosy and just had to see what was there. So, what'd you do next?"

"What do you think? I went home and counted it, then picked up my—" Vaughan stumbled, "You know—that thing."

Jenna exchanged a glance with Drew and shrugged. "What kind of thing? Suitcase?"

"No, no. The thing that you need when you t-travel." Vaughan's face blushed as he tried to explain. Finally, he used his hands to portray turning a page in a book.

"Passport?" Drew suggested. "Try speaking slower,

Vaughan. We aren't in a hurry. And why would you need a passport?"

"Yeah, passport," Vaughan grumbled, then calmed down. "I planned on hitting the new Lionsgate Casino and trying my luck there. Usually, new casinos pay out more often to attract customers. Then I was going to head to B-b-Bellingham and fly to Reno." He threw his hands up in self-defense. "I was excited. I've been to Seattle for ballgames but nowhere else. So, when I saw a travel agency near the casino, I b-booked a flight from the Bellingham airport to Re-reno." Vaughan shook his head, closed his eyes, and breathed deeply several times.

"How did you get through customs with all that cash?" Jenna questioned.

"I didn't. I stopped in Port Alberni and rented a --" Vaughan's eyes glittered with frustration as he rolled his hand forward for more suggestions until she hit the right word.

"Safety deposit box?" Jenna guessed.

"Yes, safety deposit box. It would be all over in this small town if I did that here. I added a few thousand to my account and headed out."

Jenna blew out a relieved sigh as Vaughan allayed her worst fears. "How much did you leave in there?"

Vaughan's eyes darted around the room before his shoulders dropped. "Pretty well m-most of it." The growing panic made him stutter again, so he closed his eyes and clenched his fists, breathing deeply. "I knew I couldn't bring more than ten thousand cash over the border, so I kept nine thousand and left the rest there. If I blew the money on Texas Hold'em, it was time to c-come home. But I'm pretty good at po-poker, and I was hoping —" Vaughan's voice trailed off as his eyes darted around the hallway. "I didn't even make it across the damned border."

"Thank God," Jenna's eyes teared as she realized how lucky he was. Jenna's fingers trembled as she put them across her mouth to stop her from crying. Her chest heaved as she struggled to contain her relief.

Confessing the truth weakened an already emotional Vaughan. His eyes watered as they flicked from Drew to Jenna and back. "I'm sorry, Jenna. I didn't mean to hurt you." Vaughan sniffled, then cleared his throat. "I planned on bo-borrowing ten thousand and taking a chance." Vaughan wiped a tear streaming down his cheek and used another tissue Jenna passed him to wipe his nose. "I might've got l-lucky and made enough to buy into the Black Fin. It c-could've happened."

Vaughan spread his hands before him, defending his actions. He paused for a moment, "Then I'd pay you back. I was destined...not destined." Vaughan groaned and took a deep breath. "I was *desperate*. I wanted a chance to be some-body." Vaughan's speech began to falter under stress. "I-I-I'm really sorry."

"So, there's about forty thousand in the bank deposit box?" Drew asked. "Nobody else knew about your stash? Nobody else had access? Where were your bank cards?"

"I only use a debit card. I put it in the safe at the hotel and asked them not to give it to me until I checked out. I promised myself I wouldn't use my debit cards to gamble. N-nope. I wasn't going to touch that, honest."

"Then that must be what the RCMP sent your parents in the envelope. So, you got a nice room at the Renaissance?" Drew prodded.

Vaughan's eyebrows shot up, then crashed as he realized the RCMP would've checked his activities and reported to his family. "Yeah. Go big or go home, right?" Vaughan's gaze dropped down to the shiny hospital linoleum floor.

"Meet anyone along the way?" Jenna's voice wasn't soft anymore. It was harsh and judgemental.

"Maybe," Vaughan raised his eyes slowly. "I don't remember much. A blonde was sitting beside me at the poker table, learning to play. She was with a friend. When I moved over to the slots, the girls followed. I was drinking, playing those...*things*, flirting a little." Vaughan dropped his head into his hands and rubbed his forehead. "Look, can we talk about this again later? My brand...brand," Vaughan shook his head and took another deep breath. "My *brain*'s turned to mush, and my headache's killing me."

Jenna leaned over and placed her hand on Vaughan's shoulder, rubbing it in circles. "Sure. You made a stupid decision, but at least you were smart enough to leave the bulk in a safety deposit box. It could've been so much worse."

Drew agreed. "Alright, buddy. We'll talk again in a few days. The more you can tell us, the more we can tell the police in Maple Ridge. Maybe they can catch the cons who rolled you."

A nurse approached with discharge papers in hand and a puzzled expression. "Mr. Walsh? You don't look so good. Maybe we should put you back to bed. I've got your release papers, but perhaps I should call the doctor to check on you again."

"No, please d-don't. It's only a headache, and I'm due for my meds in half an hour. I'll be fine once I'm home."

"If the paperwork's in order, we'll take him and get him settled at his parents. We'll be sure he takes his painkillers when he arrives and gets bed rest." Jenna wiggled the prescription bag. "May we go now?" Jenna's charm worked, and the nurse walked Vaughan outside under the portico while Drew drove the Dodge van underneath.

Jenna sent Drew a worried glance as they helped Vaughan into the vehicle. Drew assisted in buckling him and then loaded the rented wheelchair in the back. Vaughan's eyes shuttered several times, and Jenna didn't know if it was due to the headache or the exhaustion from their discussion with him.

"Five more minutes, then you'll be home." Jenna crooned as she leaned from the front seat to pat his knee. "Hang in there, buddy." Relieved to see him nod, Jenna turned as Drew climbed into the driver's seat

Drew saw her concern and reached over to squeeze her hand. "He'll be fine after taking his meds and resting." He glanced in the rearview mirror to check on the patient, then put the Dodge in gear and quietly pulled away from the hospital.

A week later, Vaughan's facial bruising faded to yellow, and his confusion cleared as he interacted with family members and friends. He continued his story that he'd taken a spur-of-the-moment long weekend and was mugged. He blamed the blurred details of the trip on the concussion, which could very well be true. Jenna wondered if it could also be a convenient excuse to avoid embarrassment, but for now, everyone was content not to push for the truth.

CHAPTER 16

I n February, when Vaughan recuperated well enough, he and Drew took a day trip to Port Alberni and emptied the safe deposit box—returning $40,000 to Jenna. The RCMP suspected they knew who was responsible for Vaughan's injuries, but there was insufficient proof to bring it to trial. The police department found the name connected to the suite where Vaughan was found, but it was booked with a stolen credit card, so it proved to be a dead end. It was frustrating, but as Vaughan admitted, a valuable lesson learned.

"Thanks, Drew." Vaughan leaned his head back into the headrest and briefly closed his eyes.

"What for?"

"For not lecturing me on this trip. I'm tired of being reminded how stupid I was."

"At least you were smart enough to squirrel most of it away in a safe deposit box." Drew glanced over at his new friend and felt a pang of sympathy. Vaughan paid a steep price for a reckless decision, so it probably wasn't anything he'd soon forget.

"I've arranged a loan through my parents for ten thousand dollars to pay Jenna back."

"Your mom and dad have been very understanding, and I know Jenna appreciates it. They told her the money is a cheap price to pay to have you back. Although, they'll still charge you interest on the loan."

"Of course. I expected that. My parents have always supported Carla and me, but they don't give anything for free, and that's how it should be." Vaughan's voice trembled. His emotional state was still fragile after the beating and consequent injuries. His guilt and shame often brought him close to tears, making him feel even worse.

Vaughan pushed the seat back farther in the car so he could stretch and wiggle his left leg. His doctor applied a new cast last week after the swelling subsided, and the skin was so itchy that it drove him crazy. He took his trusty ruler from the side panel again and inserted it slowly as far as possible, trying to control the need to scratch his leg furiously.

"My doctor says if the next X-ray shows the bone's healing well, he might exchange the cast for a splint. I can't wait."

"You'll still need to be careful. I hope you aren't counting on working before your therapy's finished." Drew turned his left signal on and headed toward Tofino off Highway 4.

"I've got people nagging at me left, right, and center, so I wouldn't have a chance to go back earlier, even if I could." Vaughan smacked his friend lightly on the shoulder. "So, I see that you and Jenna have reconnected. How's it going between the two of you?"

"Great. I'm letting Jenna take the lead," Drew shrugged. "We'll go as slow or as fast as she wants. The ball's in her court. That woman is independent and will fight for what she wants. Kind of hot, actually." Drew smirked. "Make-up sex is almost worth an argument."

"Whoa, I don't want to hear about my little neighbor's sex life, but I'm glad things are going well. What about your work situation? Will you be going back to Haida Gwaii? I can't see Jenna following you there and leaving the lease just when she's figured out all the financing."

"I'll return to *Daajing Giids* for a short time. I've put in for a transfer to Bamfield, but if nothing comes up in a few months, I'm considering going independent. Many grants are available to study the marine environment through universities or government programs. I'd be my own boss and pick the projects I want to work on. It might be the perfect solution for Jenna and me." Drew held up two crossed fingers.

"I hope it pans out for you. I could use a trusty friend." Vaughan smiled. "Do you think you'll buy a home around here?"

"It depends on what Theo plans to do. He's considering giving his tenants notice to leave and moving back into his home after doing a few renovations. I'm not sure what's up his sleeve, but I know Jenna's dad and her aunt, Daryl, and Carla have been throwing a few ideas around." Drew shrugged. "Who knows? I'll keep my apartment until I return to Haida Gwaii. Then Jenna and I'll figure it out once I've decided on my future with the Department of Fisheries."

"That's a lot of things up in the air. I wish you luck."

Drew sighed. "I'll need it. One day, Jenna and I will get engaged. I've got an idea I'd like to surprise her with. If we can get the proper legal work approved, I want to build a small cottage on McKenna Island where we can escape to or work from. Theo's off his crutches now, and his leg and shoulder are healing well. He wants to return to the oyster lease eventually, and it'll be easier for Jenna and me to help him if we have our own place there."

"She'll love that idea. Jenna and Theo have a very close relationship. Not making her choose between you and him is a smart strategy."

Drew agreed. "I know which way the wind blows. Besides, I like Theo. And I must admit that living there might help me access more areas easily if I turn independent. Maybe it'll cut down on travel time. You never know what'll happen."

"Exactly. 'Man plans, and God laughs.' I've been at the end of that stick. I'm not sure what I'll do. My job's waiting for me at the Black Fin, but I've been thinking of doing something different lately. Maybe go back to school."

"Anything in particular you're considering?"

"Something outdoors. I'm kind of done working in the restaurant business, always comparing myself to the elite that frequents our pub. There are so many parks around the island that I thought of something in that field. Management maybe? Or park ranger?" Vaughan waved his hand side to side, considering his options. "I'm going to research the field and see what attracts me. At least I have a plan to work toward now."

"I have only one word of advice. Do what makes you happy. What makes your day when you get up in the morning. That's what drives me."

WHEN JENNA RECEIVED a money order from Mr. and Mrs. Walsh, she put it in her bank account along with the forty thousand cash. She and Drew discussed how to send the money back to Murray. Finally, they contacted Clint, who apologized for his nephew's behavior and agreed to act as the go-between for the money.

Jenna sent the money to Clint by e-transfer. They texted a copy of the transmission to Murray, along with a note advising him no contact was necessary and preferable. Afterward, Drew and Jenna went to the Black Fin, where they met the Walshs and Theo to celebrate the end of a financial and emotional nightmare.

With the new financing and an optimistic attitude, Jenna, Drew, Lee, and her dad shopped for rope, barrels, and seed. Once it was delivered, they hired three experienced oystermen to help them reconfigure and improve the lease. Although Theo was still physically limited in what he could do, his knowledge and guidance were invaluable. Jenna could see her dad's self-confidence building daily, which enhanced the pride of the supportive friends who had created the opportunity.

AN OUTDOOR EASTER picnic at the cottage brought the Walsh, Campbell, and Jenna's families together. There was an energetic festive atmosphere that cheered everyone on to participate. Playing horseshoes brought the competitiveness out, and as Jenna looked around her, she couldn't be happier. Glancing at Drew's father, Bryan, and her dad, Theo, conspiring to win the most matches at horseshoes, warmed her heart as the smiles and jokes bonded the two men.

After losing the last afternoon game to Theo and Bryan, Fred and Drew retreated to the cooler, nursing damaged egos. Drew held an armful of icy Kokanee and offered his mom, Marilyn, and his sister, Anita, a cold brew. He approached Jenna and twisted the top off, the condensation dripping from the bottle. Handing her the beer, he leaned over and kissed her.

"You can't get it any icier than that," Drew joked as he tapped his drink against hers. "A toast?"

"You either like making toasts, or you like having an excuse to drink." Jenna laughed at him. "What are we celebrating this time?"

"Both." Drew leaned over to the picnic table, picked up two knives, and clanged them together. "People? Can you come over here and help me out?"

"What's the matter? Is she giving you a rough time again?" Vaughan hollered over the chatter, causing the family to laugh. "You have to lay the law down, man. Tell your woman who's boss."

"Yeah, right. Like that would ever fly." Theo said amid hoots and laughter.

Drew picked Jenna's hand up and kissed her fingers as the group assembled around them. "I want to thank all of you for welcoming my mom, dad, and the bane of my existence, my sister, Anita, and me into your homes. Jenna's a fortunate lady to have family and friends like you." Drew lifted his beer to them and eyed them individually. "A toast to Jenna, who welcomed me into her world."

Amid answering toasts, Drew leaned over and kissed Jenna tenderly, his eyes moist with emotion. He cleared his throat and turned to face his new family. "I hope you'll all help Jenna with my next request. She has trust issues, as we all know."

Outright laughs of agreement echoed his observation. Drew pulled Jenna in for a hug, then pulled back nervously. "Jenna, there's nothing I want more than your happiness. If my love makes you as ecstatic as you make me, I'd be proud if you'd be my wife. Will you marry me?" When Drew noticed her eyes widen and her lips formed a silent 'oh,' Drew hastened to add. "Not right away, of course, but whenever you're ready."

Bursts of laughter acknowledged that Jenna's family knew of his promise not to push her. "Good save, big brother!" Anita hollered.

Drew's face blushed as he turned to face them. "Give me a break, you guys. Once burnt, twice shy—if you're smart."

Jenna stepped closer to Drew and wrapped her arms around his neck. "Looks like he's learned a little more about me, doesn't it?" she tossed the comment to the group. "Drew Cameron, as long as you don't want to set a date today, I accept your proposal. I've never been happier since you've re-entered my life." Jenna stood on her tiptoes and kissed him long and hard as cheers erupted.

As they separated, Drew pulled a navy blue velvet box from the inside pocket of his jacket. "I'd be proud if you'd wear this as your engagement ring." He opened the lid and presented it to her.

"Wow. That's beautiful, darling. Of course, I'll wear it."

Drew slipped the exquisitely scrolled band encasing an 8mm blush pearl surrounded by tiny sparkling diamonds on her finger. "It seems a bit loose, so we can look at others if you'd prefer."

Jenna looked at the perfect gem set deep in the setting. "No way. This is ideal." Jenna's eyes teared. "Not only beautiful, it also represents our life." Jenna leaned over and gently kissed Drew's lips. Jenna tilted her finger to catch the light reflection, then looked at Drew.

"This ring is stunning and so unique. It fits us. I would've never thought about one like this. I totally love it."

Jenna lifted her hands to his head and pulled him down for a deep kiss. When they broke apart, Jenna quickly turned to the family and showed off her ring.

"Woohoo!" Lee cried out. "It's so beautiful. Congratulations." He hugged his friend tightly, "You've got your knight in shining armor. You'll have a wonderful life together."

"I know. It's early to start planning, but will you be my best man?"

"Of course I will." Lee rocked her from side to side. "I've never been one before, but I'm sure you'll tell me what to do."

"Definitely. I'll ask Carla to be my maid of honor and Ali and Sara to be my bridesmaids. Neil can be an usher, and Drew can ask one of his buddies to be part of it, too."

"Look at you. Engaged five minutes, and you've got the lineup covered already."

"Did I hear my name?" Carla wrapped one arm around Jenna's shoulder and the other around Lee.

"You did. I want my forever girlfriend to be the matron of honor. Do you think you can handle that?"

"Of course, unless you wait so long that I'm in the grave or something." Carla kissed her friend on the cheek. "I'm so excited for you two. If anyone deserves a happily ever after, it's you, Jenna. You've worked so hard and helped anyone who needed it. It's nice to see you shine."

Jenna pulled her best friend aside. "This ring is like a sign to me, Carla. It's so perfect, the size, the color of the pearl. The diamonds surrounding it make the pearl look lit up from within." Jenna lowered her voice and whispered. "The pearl is as perfect as our love for each other."

"Not like that ugly, misshapen pearl that Murray found and gave you?" Carla teased. "That should've been a sign of his character right off the bat."

"I know, right? No wonder my guts were screaming at me to stay away from him."

"Well, you and Drew make a good pair, and I know you'll be wonderful together. Congratulations." Carla pulled away as she saw Theo approaching. "Here comes your dad." Carla left and joined Lee so Jenna and her dad could hug each other.

"Well, sweetheart. Were you surprised? I wasn't sure how you'd handle it when Drew came and talked to me about it."

"You knew?"

"Chivalry isn't dead yet. I like Drew, especially if you're in love with him. He's a good guy."

"Awe, thanks, Dad." Jenna hugged her dad fiercely and kissed him on the cheek. "If we can be as fortunate as you and Mom were, we'll have a great life."

"I've no doubt, Jenna. Your mom's probably looking down, smiling and clapping, pleased with your choice."

"I hope so. I like to think that Mom keeps an eye on me."

"Without a doubt, if it's possible, she would. Like you, she never gave up on anything she wanted to do." Theo kissed his daughter on her forehead and hugged her. "I wish you all the happiness in life for you and Drew."

"Thanks, Dad. Me too." Jenna spied Bryan and Marilyn, slowly approaching. She reached for Drew's hand and embraced each parent, noting their pleasure with their son's engagement.

When Jenna decided to have a June wedding the following year, her dad beamed his approval. As far as he was concerned, it was the crowning event for a year that promised so much for the future. The intimate wedding on the Walsh's beachfront was storybook-perfect, a memory both families would always treasure.

It seemed that rebuilding the oyster lease was filled with research, planning, and unending work. The joy and pride the project gave each of them proved well worth it. The Sorensen name was a popular source of local discussions as Westerlea Cove re-invented itself. Theo and Jenna hosted a celebratory barbecue at the community center for almost a hundred people who'd been instrumental in creating a successful comeback. The Sorensens would never forget the generous outpouring of support the small town of Tofino gave them.

Eighteen months later, the sky was clear and cerulean, and March's light spring breeze was warmer than usual. Jenna slapped on a wide-brimmed hat, applied sunscreen to her bare arms, and checked the barometer. This week, the afternoon sun created temperatures more like those of late June.

Westerlea Cove was the perfect setting to showcase nature's optimism and regeneration. Pollen dusted the outside table and chairs on the deck. It was that time of year when the cedar, fir, and spruce allergens blew across the water. The blossoming pollens often created a beige or pale-yellow skim in protected coves. From February until mid-April, cleaning the outdoor furniture and windows almost daily was common. Jenna could handle the evergreen pollens, but when the cottonwoods spread their seed, Reactin became an everyday necessity.

It wasn't the allergens that made her eyes water again today. The tears appeared almost every day at the oddest times. Always one to control her feelings, Jenna found it frustrating when emotions overwhelmed her. Nostalgia nipped at her heart, threatening a storm of sensitivity. Jenna thought of her mother often, wondering what advice she'd give.

The first trimester of her pregnancy was exhausting until the obstetrician gave up on the bi-weekly injections of iron and ordered an IV drip. Two treatments later, Jenna's energy returned to normal, and she bloomed with the pride and happiness of carrying Drew's child. During this time, Jenna began dreaming of her mother at her side.

How Jenna ached to feel her touch, ask her questions about her own pregnancy, or vent her frustrations. Most of all, she yearned to hear her laughter and the excitement she'd undoubtedly feel for her first granddaughter. Two weeks ago, Drew finished painting the nursery a creamy yellow. Jenna and her Aunt Pat chose pale pink cotton with a pattern of barnyard baby animals. Together, they created a warm quilt to welcome the newest addition to the Sorensen family. Bonding with her aunt felt good, although it was a subtle reminder of her late mother she yearned for.

Last night, her father came over to help assemble the crib. He also brought the refurbished rocking chair Meg had used when Jenna was born. Seeing it nestled into the corner beside the crib, with her mother's mauve afghan draped across the back, intensified the lonely pit inside Jenna. She suspected the pregnancy hormones were partially to blame for her heightened emotions. Still, reasoning didn't alleviate the pain of not having her mother to confide in, to find comfort with.

What she wouldn't give to see her mom again, to see her hold her first grandchild and rock her granddaughter to sleep. Her parents probably assumed they'd share their daughter's pregnancy filled with pride and anticipation.

Jenna dried her eyes for the third time, then blew her nose. Enough. Wishing wasn't going to make her mom appear magically. The best she could hope for would be the continuation of the vibrant dreams that allowed her to feel the touch of her mom's hands on her, the smell of lilacs in the air as her mother sat near her, or to see the dimples her infectious laughter would create. It was like having a personal visit that touched her soul and made her whole again.

Suddenly, Jenna knew what she needed to do. She was confident that she'd be a grandmother one day, that she and Drew would hold their grandchild and giggle like children with joy.

But what if? What if something happened to her, too? Living a long life was no guarantee, no matter how one looked after oneself. She wouldn't ignore this nagging feeling like a few years ago. Jenna had disregarded her instincts while trying to find an easy solution to the financial woes of her family's oyster lease. Thankfully, she finally listened to her gut and tossed away her lusty attraction to the wrong man. A man who thought he had so much to offer her—everything except her self-respect and dignity.

Thank God for her dad and friends who stood alongside her while she got her act together. She mustered the courage to listen to her instincts, accept her mistakes, and stand up for her principles. Jenna hoped to deliver that lesson personally to her precious daughter, but she wouldn't take any chances.

A strong urge to tell her story consumed Jenna. She reached for a yellow-lined pad of paper. She'd compose a rough draft today for her baby girl, purchase some quality stationary, and create a loving letter of hope and encouragement. God forbid something should happen to prevent her from enjoying every step of her daughter's pregnancy. Jenna believed she'd share her story with her daughter when the time was right.

Jenna massaged her growing abdomen. What a true gift love was. Without it, she would've missed the most incredible adventure of all, creating this new life with her soulmate, Drew.

And she'd start journaling right away. Her daughter would never wonder how her parents handled the ups and downs of getting ready for their beloved baby. Jenna would tell her about her problems with anemia. And the heartburn when she ate anything tomato-based.

She'd relate stories of Drew, who was so excited to become a father. And funny stories of his patience and spontaneous distractions when she longed to have her mother beside her. Drew vowed to make her pregnancy as healthy and stress-free as possible, and she'd never forget his thoughtfulness.

Her daughter could read it all for herself and know the commitment and love her parents felt while preparing for their child's birth. And, if she could find a man similar to her father, she'd feel the same way Jenna felt—like she'd won the ultimate lottery.

Jenna scribbled furiously, searching for the nuggets of wisdom that she wished she'd had from her mother. Crumpled pages littered the floor as Jenna scrubbed one idea after another. She didn't want to make the message a rambling, boring statement that her daughter would roll her eyes at. She'd aim for funny, hopeful, and loving.

My darling baby girl,

Your dad and I debated whether to know if you were a boy or a girl, but curiosity got the best of us. It's given us time to search for the perfect name for you. At this point, you'll either be Jessica or Hannah, with Megan as your middle name, after your grandmother—although the order could be reversed.

We're excited to be your parents, watch you grow, and make this world your oyster. When you become a mother, I'm sure I'll be right beside you for every question you have, for every shopping trip to decorate the nursery, or to hold your hand and tell you everything will be fine.

Pregnancy is such an emotional time, and even more so if a parent has passed on. There have been so many times when I wanted to ask my mom how she felt, or how she handled the different stages of pregnancy, or to have her hold me and reassure me that you would be perfect. God willing, you'll never experience that.

You are loved before you were born. My future is brighter because now you're in it. Your dad and I will do everything possible to keep you safe, healthy, and loved. Every generation wants the next one to be even better in every respect. So, in a nutshell, here's my advice: Take your time making decisions, and always trust your instincts. Be courageous in life and love. You won't be sorry.

Love always,
Mom

THE WHINE of a 9hp motor heralded the aluminum boat to the dock. Jenna folded her notes and slipped them into her purse. She'd check with Drew about the content and whether he wanted to add something, then transfer her loving thoughts onto quality stationery. Finding a solution to her emotional worry made Jenna feel confident that her daughter wouldn't ever feel the loneliness she'd gone through. Jenna smiled as she pictured her daughter reading this one day, with or without her mom beside her.

Warm arms wrapped around Jenna's body, and Drew kissed her hair. "How are my girls doing?" Drew's golden-brown eyes searched her face, noting the tired eyes. "You didn't sleep very well last night. I heard you get up."

"Restless legs. Sometimes, I have to get up and walk it out. I'm sorry if I woke you up," Jenna said.

"Never apologize for looking after yourself. Soon, you'll need to cut back on the work here before it's too much for you."

"I've got another couple of months before that happens. I'll take it easy." Jenna massaged her maternal bump. "I'm stronger than you think, but I'm not stupid. Baby comes first." Jenna pressed her left hand to her lower back and stretched backward, easing the pressure.

"I can see a back rub is in the cards when we return home," Drew promised. "And I'm looking after dinner and dishes while you enjoy a hot bath." Drew lifted her chin and gazed into her eyes. "I almost feel guilty about my part in this thing. All I have to do is say yes to whatever you want."

"Don't worry. You can make it up when the baby's born. Midnight feedings will be your area of expertise." Jenna raised her eyebrows, then winked.

"I've watched half a dozen U-tube videos on this. I'm ready." Drew leaned his forehead on Jenna's. "I can't wait to start this next journey with you and our baby."

"Be careful what you wish for. It might be more adventurous than you think, sweetheart. Especially if our daughter takes after me."

～

Thanks for reading *Westerlea Cove*. Keep reading for an excerpt from *8828 Westerly Way* – Book 2 of *The Westwind Trilogy*.

Excerpt from *8828 Westerly Way*, the second novel in *The Westwind Trilogy*…

~

8828 Westerly Way

"Stacy, get a grip. You've checked the perimeter twice already." Kevin's clipped tone reflected his irritation with his aunt's neighbor's endless preoccupation with security. "Let's go!"

Kevin's rippled physique oozed confidence, a trait Stacy tried to emulate. Sucking in a deep breath, Stacy concentrated on slowing her breathing and willing away the anxiety that often overcame her. She tossed her golden-brown hair over her shoulder and glanced down at her developing frame, appreciating the muscle tones in her long legs, now tanned a rich caramel. Her physical form reflected the self-care she'd created, but the uneasy foreboding that haunted her still needed taming. Stacy had come a long way since moving to Gabriola Island and couldn't allow herself to slip back into the state she'd been in.

"Sorry, just one more thing." She sprinted back up the front stairs and jiggled the door handle again. Stacy knew she'd locked it earlier, but old habits were hard to break. She needed to double-check everything, security system or not. Glancing toward Kevin impatiently jogging on the spot, Stacy managed a cheerful grin. "You're right, I'm over-thinking this." She shook her long bangs away from her eyes, glanced at her watch, and noted the time. "We might need to shave off part of the run if we're going to get back in time."

"Oh no, we're not. You'll just have to pick up the pace. The security system I installed for you is top-of-the-line, and you know it. If you don't trust it, then trust me. You're safe. Your house is safe." Kevin inched toward the road as he waited for her, eager to start the run. "No more excuses, Stacy—you need this run even more than I do. Do your stretches, then catch up with me." Kevin scanned her face, probably searching for her tell-tale panic signals that often shadowed her obsessive safety checks.

Stacy nodded, smiled bravely, then waved her hand away to encourage his departure. She arched her back and began a series of quad, hamstring, and calf stretches while watching her friend race out of sight. She gritted her teeth, determination strengthening her resolve. Kevin wouldn't witness any meltdowns today. Stacy took things one day at a time, a technique she'd adopted several months ago. It helped to know from recent experience that one rotten day like yesterday didn't mean she'd lost the war.

Jogging in place, Stacy rolled her shoulders and then shook her hands, loosening the tension in her neck. She pulled her mind away from her home and concentrated on the run ahead. Thank God for Aunt Bea, her elderly neighbor, and her nephew, Kevin, who had become friends she could rely on.

Stacy kept her distance from the attractive young man for several months despite Kevin's warm smile and many offers to lend a hand. Slowly, she'd come to trust him, and he'd gradually coaxed Stacy out of her self-imposed isolation to become part of her new community. Almost ten years younger, Kevin had been patiently relentless in persuading Stacy to start jogging again. A smile tugged at her lips as she remembered his Aunt Bea's attempts to pull the two of them together.

Kevin challenged her, that's for sure. Since she took him up on his offer to be her trainer, he'd encouraged her to incorporate a daily fitness program to build her strength and stamina until she felt confident enough to join a gym.

Stacy admitted that as nervous as she'd been at first, the cross-training gym had done her wonders. Three months later, loud noises no longer startled her, as that was often the background of extreme workouts in the gym. Although she still had a long way to go before regaining her former calm demeanor, Stacy now felt strong and in the best shape of her life as her physical fitness and running schedule progressed.

I've nothing to fear except fear itself.

Life is good. Life is good. *I can handle all it throws at me.* The self-help books she read reinforced her multiple daily mantras for a healthy new lifestyle where worry and fear no longer controlled her. Stacy could hardly wait for the day when apprehension would be nothing but a bad dream.

Patience. Once an automatic trait, her best characteristic became elusive. Stacy craved a return to an everyday life when confidence replaced fear. Each time Stacy conquered an anxious moment, it felt like she'd won a battle and her come-back was imminent, but then she'd have a bad day. A sense of foreboding would seize her, sometimes triggering a panic attack, reminding her that until a body was found, she could never entirely discount the danger that her former husband posed.

Thank God, these events became few and far between, probably from her new physical and mental routines, which toughened her. Stacy gradually seized control of her life as time passed, ready to accept challenges and create new goals. Seldom would the shivers of apprehension stop her from moving forward.

Stall? Yes. Freeze and bring her to her knees? Nope, not anymore.

∼

Visit LynnBoire.com to learn more about *8828 Westerly Way's* release date.

ALL FOR LOVE - EXCERPT

~

CHAPTER 1

Anna Taylor rolled her eyes at the final blessing and glanced at her husband Matt's flushed face. She elbowed Jed to stop his fidgeting, sending him a warning glare to pay attention. At fifteen, he was starting to complain about going to church and missing his weekend practice. Standing beside his father, his youthful attitude seemed incongruous with his height nearing his father's 6'2". On Matt's other side, Lisa leaned towards her father, singing along with him for the closing hymn. Anna knew they'd be expected to stay for coffee and fellowship afterwards, which could lead to half the day being lost.

"Matt, we can't stay this morning," she whispered as they began to file out. "Kari and Ray are coming to celebrate their anniversary. I need to get everything ready."

"Really, Anna? Really?" Matt's eyebrows lifted as his hazel eyes challenged her. "You couldn't have hosted your sister's event yesterday, and let me have my Sunday? You know what these days mean to me. You *know* how important these sessions are. There's not much time left."

The exasperation in Matt's voice made her eyes widen. She was sure she'd mentioned the dinner a few days ago. She looked away, uncomfortable meeting his eyes.

~

Purchase *All for Love* and find out what happens next.

DEAR READER

In this first novel of *The Westwind Trilogy*, I hope you enjoyed discovering the beauty on the wild west coast of Vancouver Island in B.C. Canada. It's hard to describe the area's spectacular diversity, but I hope *Westerlea Cove* has given you a glimpse of nature's majesty in all her seasons.

Traditionally a male-oriented occupation, there is now a smattering of shellfish leases operated by women. The main character in my novel is Jenna, a naïve young woman. She develops an independent and strong character as she searches for the strength to resist temptation and make wise decisions as she rebuilds the oyster lease that has been in her family for decades.

I'd love to read your opinion on your favorite scenes and your thoughts on Jenna and her relationships. Your valuable input helps me become a better writer and motivates me to create more novels for you to enjoy.

I hope to finish *8828 Westerly Way*, the second in *The Westwind Trilogy*, by fall 2024. Please visit www.Lynn Boire.com and sign up for my newsletter or email me at Lynn@LynnBoire.com, and I'll be pleased to respond. Keep an eye out for updates on my website.

Reviews are critical to an author's success. Without them, new authors are relegated to the bottom of the barrel. You can leave reviews wherever you purchased *Westerlea Cove*. And if you've never perused Goodreads or BookBub, where novels are featured and reviewed, you might want to add your voice there.

Many thanks. Cheers,
Lynn Boire

DEDICATION

Without the guidance of alpha and beta readers who troubleshoot my work in progress, I'd be lost. These unpaid volunteers point out problems with character development, plot lines, or dialogue that I miss. Sometimes, skipping over the little things is easy because I'm focused on the larger picture. I appreciate all their tactful support, even if it means I need to re-write or delete a scene completely. Their comments have improved my writing, and I value all of them: Ruth R., Gina M., Dolly C., my family members, and the birthday gang.

ACKNOWLEDGMENTS

A group of almost seventy writers makes up the Vancouver Island Romance Authors. Their workshops, encouragement, and weekly check-ins are inspirational. We help each other whenever possible, and I can always find someone who will listen and offer a different perspective to help me push through writer's block. Special thanks go to Dolly Chenard for her photos and information on oyster leases and regulations she deals with. Many thanks to Jacqui Nelson, who continues to impress me with her knowledge, patience, and ability to guide me in my journey to be the best author I can be.

THE WESTWIND TRILOGY

Westerlea Cove - Book 1

8828 Westerly Way - Book 2

My next novel, *8828 Westerly Way*, takes place on Gabriola Island off the east coast of Vancouver Island. Stacy found an isolated location to rebuild her life after her wealthy husband was lost at sea on the east coast of Canada, leaving behind a trail of cheated investors. Afraid that Rob has faked his death and will fulfill his threats, she's determined to start over with a new identity.

∿

THE SAFE HAVEN SERIES

All for Love

A Safe Haven Cli-Fi Suspense Novel

Obsession. Betrayal. Chaos.

Matt Taylor secretly builds a Safe Haven far from the chaos in Washington State. Will his dream for a secure and sustainable lifestyle be everything he hoped for?

All for Family

A Safe Haven Rediscovery Novel

Reunite. Respect. Restore.

After Anna Taylor honors her professional commitments to her community in Olympia, she finally joins her family in Bella Coola. Together they and five other families tackle the challenges of thriving and surviving in an intentional community.

All for Peace

A Safe Haven Self-Discovery Novel

Secrets. Murder. Insanity.

Matt's cousin, Ellen Peterson, avoids conflict at all costs to maintain her illusion of a peaceful and successful family.

But secrets can kill. Can Ellen live with that?

Finding Hope

Young Jim Taylor realizes that his father's harsh and lonely life as a fur trapper in the 1930s beautiful Canadian North wasn't his destiny. Searching for a new life, he 'rides the rails' and builds the courage and confidence needed to become a man of many skills. But the memory of home and Lucy are calling. Will he find what his heart craves?

Inspired by a true story.

ABOUT THE AUTHOR

I write contemporary domestic suspense that reveals how families who avoid conflict find the confidence to voice their opinions and fulfill their dreams. In my stories, it's all about imperfect people finding unconditional love.

Following a lifelong dream to become a published author wasn't an easy decision. It wasn't until I joined the Vancouver Island Romance Authors group that I began to toss aside the self-doubts that had always assailed me. Their encouragement, recommendations, and support started my tenacious journey to learn the craft of writing. I'm constantly reading and studying material to grow as an author, and I've seldom been happier. I'm excited to be on the brink of a new career and hope you'll enjoy my novels.

I live in a seaside town on Vancouver Island in British Columbia, Canada. I use my deep appreciation of every part of my island home for the background in my stories. I feel a spiritual connection whenever I'm near a body of water. Nature puts everything in perspective, and all my doubts and worries float away. Even if a storm's strength frightens me, it also reminds me that—no matter what—all things pass. I'm blessed with many friends and family, including my husband, two grown children, a grandson, a step-daughter and her family.

LynnBoire.com

goodreads.com/author/show/20765007.Lynn_Boire
bookbub.com/authors/lynn-boire
facebook.com/lynnboire